Lorenzo's Legacy

by

John Davies

TONY GOOD FRIEND, EDDIE
NUMERO UNO GYM INSTRUCTOR

John Davies
MARCH 2004

Printed in Victoria, Canada

Note for Librarians: a cataloguing record for this book that includes Dewey Classification and US Library of Congress numbers is available from the National Library of Canada. The complete cataloguing record can be obtained from the National Library's online database at:
www.nlc-bnc.ca/amicus/index-e.html
ISBN 1-1420-2080-8

TRAFFORD

This book was published on-demand in cooperation with Trafford Publishing.
On-demand publishing is a unique process and service of making a book available for retail sale to the public taking advantage of on-demand manufacturing and Internet marketing.
On-demand publishing includes promotions, retail sales, manufacturing, order fulfilment, accounting and collecting royalties on behalf of the author.

Suite 6E, 2333 Government St., Victoria, B.C. V8T 4P4, CANADA
Phone 250-383-6864   Toll-free 1-888-232-4444 (Canada & US)
Fax 250-383-6804   E-mail sales@trafford.com   Web site www.trafford.com
TRAFFORD PUBLISHING IS A DIVISION OF TRAFFORD HOLDINGS LTD.
Trafford Catalogue #04-0004   www.trafford.com/robots/04-0004.html

10   9   8   7   6   5   4   3   2   1

FOREWORD

Lorenzo's Legacy is a work of fiction. Most of the characters, incidents, places and dialogues are products of the author's imagination. Lucky Luciano was a real person, the world's number one mobster. It was true that he was exiled by the US government in 1946. History does not record that this arch-villain ever spawned a son. If he had, this is the legacy he might have left his unfortunate offspring.

DEDICATION

Dedicated to the bravest girl I have ever known, my beloved wife Rosa, who spent many lonely hours while I burned the midnight oil at my computer. Also to avid reader and good friend, Beryl French, who pored over every word and without whose criticism, and some praise, this book may never have been finished.

ABOUT THE AUTHOR

John Davies spent 35 years of his life travelling to many parts of the world as a sportswriter with two of England's top newspapers, the *Daily Express* and the *Daily Mail.*

As an international freelance journalist since 1987, he spent many years researching the evil machinations of the Mafia.

The novel *Lorenzo's Legacy* is the latest addition to his portfolio, which includes the football orientated novel *Golden Studs* and a coffee-table 100-year history of soccer entitled *Moonstruck Parrots* which includes many personal anecdotes of his long career as a sports writer.

He served in the RAF during the Second World War.

CONTENTS

CHAPTER 1

Gina Berni, hazel eyes sunken deep into the bone structure of her skull, gazed wistfully at the bloodied and sagging figure on the crucifix fixed to the wall of a terminal ward in a Naples hospital.

Even in her semi-sedated haze she knew her time was near and marked the grim realization by reciting an Hail Mary...not once, three times, she got as far as ... blessed are thou amongst women and blessed is the fruit of thy womb Jesus...but could not remember the rest of that poignant prayer.

The nursing nuns fluttered across the room and along the adjoining corridors like white moths around a guttering candle. A senior sister, the linen of her snowy habit starched a little stiffer as if to denote her superiority, accompanied a doctor on his rounds, stopping at every one of the 30 beds in the ward.

Each temperature and blood pressure reading on the charts hooked at the foot of the beds was carefully scrutinized. Every patient was quizzed about how they felt, about their aches and pains and the regularity of their bodily functions.

'I would like to know the truth,' pleaded Gina. 'How much longer have I got? I need to put my affairs in order before I die.'

Doctor Rafael Frincatti considered the urgency with which the question was thrust at him by this syphilis and heroin-ravaged patient who looked, at least, two decades older than the 20 years recorded on her chart.

'Signora Berni, only God can answer, with accuracy, the question you have put to me,' said the medical man

1

compassionately. 'As I am certainly not God, I can only guess the end will come for you inside a week. The good sisters will try to make you as comfortable and free of pain as possible in the time you have left.

You say you have personal matters to attend to - I will send one of the hospital social workers to see you in the hope they can help you to clear up your affairs. I would suggest also that you make arrangements to see the priest so that you can receive the last rites.'

Later that day one of the hospital's staff of social workers was ushered to Gina Berni's bedside.

'Signore! Can you arrange for my three-year-old son Lorenzo to be brought here to see me?' the dying woman pleaded.
'He is at the Orphanage for Boys which is run by the Sisters of Santa Maria. The doctors say my time is now short and I would like to see my little lad before I die.'

The next morning a little boy, neat and clean in his newly pressed blue school smock, was brought to her bedside holding the hand of a kindly nun who, discreetly, left them alone for a while.

The sad and final assignation between mother and child lasted less than quarter of an hour.

A few minutes after Gina tearfully watched the little lad leave with his nun-tutor the hospital chaplain arrived and began to intone the last rites.
She died peacefully that night.

Her final words were simply: '...Holy Mary, Mother of God pray for us sinners now and at the hour of our death...'

CHAPTER 2

Lucky Luciano, the world's richest and most notorious gangster and the boss of the evil and deadly Unione Siciliano, was unceremoniously booted out of the USA after World War II.

He had served nine years of a 30-50 year stretch in a State Penitentary when the Parole Board and the Governor of New York, Thomas Dewey, commuted the sentence and ordered Charley Lucky, as he was known in the underworld, to be returned to his native Italy and exiled from the USA forever.

In fact Luciano, the godfather of organised crime in the USA, felt more American than Italian, having spent 39 of his 48 years Stateside since his parents had emigrated from the 'old country' in 1907.

Yet in all that time, having climbed from a street urchin on the East Side of New York to the status of multi-millionaire from the proceeds of crime, he had never applied for USA citizenship as thousands of his fellow Italians have done over the past two centuries.
        'I just could not be bothered to sit down and fill in forms with those fuckin' government creeps,' he growled.

Nevertheless he agreed when approached by the US Navy to help curb terrorism and sabotage by Nazi supporters on the New York waterfront during the Second World War.

It was reckoned that, from his prison cell, Lucky's influence amongst the hoodlums who controlled the waterfront trade unions saved hundreds of American servicemen's lives as they crossed the Atlantic and millions of tons of military equipment so sorely needed by the Allied forces in Europe.

His efforts also cut off the supply of information to the bloodthirsty German U Boat packs patrolling the Atlantic run with their deadly torpedo's primed.

Lucky had progressed through the ranks of the American underworld from an apprenticeship in petty crime to rum-running and bootlegging through the Prohibition years to the more sinister and lucrative rackets of protection, prostitution, gambling, drugs and murder.

But in the late 1930's the various tough gun-toting law enforcement agencies began to find ways to attack the violent gang gorillas whose evil activities were bleeding the American nation dry.

In Chicago the notorious Al Capone had been given a mind-boggling prison sentence for defrauding the Inland Revenue Department, while in 1936, the then District Attorney Thomas Dewey nailed Lucky Luciano on a lengthy list of vice and whorehouse keeping offences. The determined Dewey had persuaded numerous prostitutes, brothel madams and pimps to give evidence against Luciano.

If the 'fuckin' cops' - as Lucky venomously called all law enforcement officers - were not exactly victorious in the war against organised crime they certainly won a few battles.

Unlike Capone who deteriorated behind bars and eventually died of venereal disease, Lucky Luciano kept his grip on the rackets throughout his nine long years in the cells of the high security Dannemora and Great Meadow gaols.

As he worked in the steamy prison laundry Lucky remained 'capo di capis' of the Unione Siciliano and, after his release and exile, became chief of the invidious Crime International which controlled organised drug trafficking across the globe.

If there was any doubt that Luciano was the numero uno drugs trafficker in the world they were dispelled by Garland Williams, the chief of the US Narcotics Bureau.

'Less than two years after Lucky Luciano was expelled the first massive shipment of heroin worth $250,000 was smuggled into the USA,' disclosed Williams.

There was no doubt that Luciano was the main purveyor of the slow death of drug addiction to the New World.

CHAPTER 3

Lucky Luciano, once the USA's Public Enemy Number One and now in exile still the world's most dangerous crook, looked out of the window of the green 1938 Oldsmobile, New Jersey registered, sedan and watched the shapely swing of a young girl's buttocks bobbing along a Naples sidewalk.

'Geez, Tony! That sure is a smart lookin' chick,' the gangster snapped at his driver, indicating that he would take over the wheel himself. 'Follow her, don't frighten her. Come and tell me what you find out.'

The driver Tony Scarpone, stepped out of the big car and discreetly followed the girl, who by now was some 50 yards past on the sidewalk.

'She is the only daughter of Umberto Berni who keeps a small bakery near Central Station,' reported Scarpone, whose elder brother had died in Sing Sing's electric chair for a gangland ice-pick killing while working for Luciano. 'She is helpful to her father and has no known boyfriends although many of the young lads in the neighbourhood have the hots for her.'

Lucky was pleased with what he had been told and playfully slapped Scarpone across the face.

'You are a good boy Tony and always do what you are told - just like your brother. Now take the Oldsmobile, give Signor Umberto Berni a box of my Monte Cristo cigars and ask if he would allow his daughter to dine with me at the Zi Teresa Ristorante tomorrow evening. If he agrees then, with the greatest respect, ask the girl if she would like to be my guest. Tell them I will send the car for her at eight.'

Although women had played a large part of Lucky's three decades as a gangland gorilla he had always ensured that his romantic liaisons did not endanger or weaken his security.

'I never allow a broad to learn enough about my business that she could sing against me in a witness box. Fuck 'em and leave 'em that's what I say,' Lucky once told fellow mobster Bugsy Siegel.

Yet in exile an affair with curvaceous Italian showgirl Igea Lissoni lasted six months. But as good living, under his patronage, began to add puffiness to Igea's figure and features he started to play the field again to satisfy his voracious sexual appetite.

Nevertheless Lucky's ego was jolted when Igea stormed off after she found him romping with a mulatto girl from a Naples brothel in the bed they had so often shared in his plush suite at the Turistico Hotel

Luciano was unrepentant.

'If that Lissoni broad thinks she owns me she's makin' a big fuckin' mistake, ' he snarled, seething with indignation that the former show girl had rejected him after the thousands of dollars he had spent on jewelry, perfumes, furs and dresses for her to act the part as his mistress.

Not a vestige of remorse that his own infidelity had caused Igea to decamp!

* * *

Tony Scarpone reported back after his errand to the little bakery and pasterilia situated in a cobbled alleyway near the Naples' teeming Central Station.

8

'Signor Umberto Berni thanks you for the cigars and says he would be proud for you to take his daughter to dinner, boss,' said the gangster chief's chauffeur, smiling in the knowledge of a mission successfully completed. 'Furthermore the Signorina Gina says that she is flattered by your invitation.'

*   *   *

Ristorante Zia Teresa was a haunt of the rich and famous, situated in the Santa Lucian district of Napoli's famous waterfront.

Elegantly appointed, the genuine leather menus with gold blocked lettering and silk-corded tassels boasted 20 different varieties of pasta dishes, of every shape, colour with accompanying sauces.

The lobsters were giants of the crustacean world, the prawns the plumpest, the veal escallope the tenderest and most succulent in the whole of Italy.

*   *   *

Luciano was sat at the table always reserved for him by Zia Teresa's Head Waiter when the lovely 16-year-old Gina Berni entered the restaurant escorted by Tony Scarpone who, as instructed by his boss, had collected the girl in the Oldsmobile.

She was dressed simply in a pale blue shift dress that clung to her slender figure. A tiny crucifix hung on a slim gold chain circling around the olive coloured neck and accentuated the budding cleavage below.

'It is lovely to see you,' said Lucky, stunned by the simplicity of her outfit and her youthful beauty. 'You look wonderful. Now what would you like to drink?'

She asked simply for a glass of white wine, leaving it to him to choose.

He snapped his finger to summon the wine waiter and ordered a bottle of vintage Est, Est, Est.

Within minutes the bottle was placed beside her nestling in a frosted silver bucket of crushed ice. 'It's lovely,' she trilled as she sipped the taster poured by the wine waiter for her approval. 'It's so smooth. I have never drunk wine like it before.'

Lucky smiled at her complimentary remarks and said: 'there is a legend about that particular wine. The story goes that a Cardinal from Rome travelling all over Italy on Church business was also a wine enthusiast. He hoped that as he travelled round Italy he would find the perfect wine. One day after visiting a small village church he stopped at the nearby tavern and was offered the local white wine. After tasting it he sighed with contentment that his quest was over and holding up his glass he said: Est, Est, Est - It is, It is, It is!
    ' That is what that particular wine has been called ever since!'

CHAPTER 4

Rough diamond that he certainly was, with scant respect for the feminine gender, the most powerful drug trafficker and vice pedlar in the world was cunningly prepared to be patient with the youthful Gina Berni.

Dealing with a teenage virgin would be much different than the steamy relationship with his mistress, Igea Lissoni, who had a mind-boggling repertoire of tricks and deviations in bed.

The first assignation with the young and inexperienced Italian girl went well and there was little doubt that Gina thoroughly enjoyed Luciano's choice of his favourite spaghetti, green salad with a garlic dressing and lobster thermidor.

At the end of the evening Lucky thanked her for her company, kissed her on the cheek, and instructed Tony Scarpone to take her home in the Oldsmobile and then come back to the Ristorante Zia Teresa to collect him.

'Gina, I have enjoyed our evening together very much,' Lucky said as he bade her farewell at the table. 'Perhaps you will honour me by dining with me again in two days time?'

Gina blushed, smiled and thanked him for a lovely dinner and said how much she would look forward to seeing him again so soon.   >

On their second date Lucky, carefully, stepped slightly up a gear and became a little more passionate.

He gave Tony Scarpone the night off and collected her, but before taking her home after dinner at Zia Teresa's he drove her to the Turistico Hotel and ordered coffee in his suite.

This time he kissed her fully on the lips but stopped short of inviting her to his bed in case he frightened her.

But Lucky, wise in the ways of women, could sense by the way she responded to his kiss that he would not have long to wait until he possessed her fully!

Meanwhile he assuaged the throbbing in his groin, since his mistress Igea's decampment, by sending a message to the notorious Signora Tara, the hairy madam of a Naples' brothel, which he owned! At half an hour's notice Tara would dispatch a girl, of any size or colour that took his fancy, to the Hotel Turistico.

But there was little doubt that he still yearned for the lusty work-outs he used to enjoy so much with the sexy Igea. What was worse she had bruised his massive ego.

*   *   *

After five dates with Gina the lustful Lucky was ready to spring the trap he had so carefully and patiently laid.

Calling to collect Gina one evening he presented her father Umberto with a bottle of Napoleon brandy.

'I am planning to go to Sicily to see my family in the town of Lecara Friddi where I was born,' Luciano told the baker. 'I will take the car on the ferry from Naples to Catania and get Tony Scarpone to drive us up country from there. I wonder if you would allow Gina to accompany me? We would be away about five days.'

The 48-year-old hard working baker, impressed that such an important and wealthy man should want to squire his daughter, readily agreed to the plan. In poverty-stricken Southern Italy in those immediate post-war years the lines between crime and respectability were blurred. Neither did the three decades gap between Lucky Luciano and Gina seem to matter to Umberto Berni who was already drooling about how the prospect of a marriage to such a powerful man would work to his advantage.

Umberto's dream had always been that one day he would make enough money from his tiny bakery to retire to a small holding in the country with a few chickens and geese and be able to go out each day with his old and favourite shot gun shooting rabbits and birds. Perhaps Signore Luciano would make that dream come true.

They sailed on the early morning ferry from Napoli. Standing at the rail of their private cabin they watched the sun rise on the Mediterranean horizon. Gina, hair wafting in the gentle sea breeze, dressed eye-fully tasteful in a grey silk outfit he had bought for her at the most expensive gown shop in Naples.

Lucky, his dark wavy hair contrasting with his white linen suit attracted the admiring eyes of many of the women passengers. Even at this hour, after an early morning shave, his jowls showed dark stubble, making him even more handsome despite the scarred chin and drooping left eyelid.

As for the male passengers aboard, most of whom, were aware that he was the notorious mobster Lucky Luciano, there was an air of respect for his power, wealth and formidable reputation.

Gina, despite her lack of experience, noticed that Lucky's embraces with his wandering hand, and his kisses and flickering tongue, were getting more and more passionate.

13

Once committed to accompany him to Sicily, the land of his birth, she knew that soon he would bed her and take her virginity. She was naive enough, however, to believe that if she could tempt him to the altar that he would be a tremendous catch for a working class Italian girl.

Better to be the bride of a gangster, she mused, than working behind the bakery counter or in one of Naples' factory sweat shops for a miserly few thousand lire.

Tony Scarpone drove them from the ferry terminal at Catania to an elegant five-bed room villa on the outskirts of Palermo. It had been loaned by Guiseppe Pirigo, a local Unione Siciliano chieftan heavily involved in Lucky's narcotic ring.

They dined that evening at a farmhouse a few miles west of Palermo in the company of three Unione Siciliano hoodlums from the local bandit-infested hills and their women. There was much talk, after an excellent meal of roast suckling pig and local wine, amongst the men about drug trafficking, cigarette smuggling, prostitution and the kidnapping of wealthy tourists from the USA and Europe for ransom money. Gina was told to join the ladies in an adjoining room for delicious pastry and glasses of chilled sparkling wine.

*   *   *

She knew this was the night as she lay between the black silk sheets waiting for him to appear from the en suite bathroom clad in a dressing gown of brushed scarlet velvet. He pulled his hairy arms from the elegant dressing gown and unceremoniously let it drop to the floor. She gasped with shock as she saw the enormity of his proud manhood.

'God pity me,' she said irreverently. The thought was interrupted as he guided her hands so that the smooth

14

fingers coolly encircled his enormous baton! He coaxed her hand into a rythmic massaging movement and she felt the excitement in her own crotch as she saw what was happening to him.

Groaning with ecstasy he pulled away her flimsy nightdress, lifted her on the bed and sent her wild as his flickering tongue explored her breasts, navel and vagina.

When he entered her she gasped unashamedly as Lucky revelled in orgasm after orgasm throughout the night. By dawn she knew she loved everything about this gorilla of a man, even the drooped right eyelid and scars sustained when he had been beaten up by tough narcotics squad cops in New York.

*   *   *

A fly on the wall in any hairdressing salon or powder room, where elegant women gossip, will gather that the "first time" was nearly always an unpleasant, painful and messy experience. Not for Gina! She was the exception! Lucky Luciano, gangster boss, killer, smuggler, drug pedlar and prostitute-procurer transported this humble working class Italian girl to paradise during their five nights together under the light of a waning Sicilian moon.

The final evening had been particularly wonderful.

Tony Scarpone drove them to a waterside café and then made himself unobtrusive until he brought the Oldsmobile to take them back to the villa three hours later.

They dined on freshly made pasta and a huge platter of mixed grilled fish. He chose a fruity Valpolicella wine, locally grown peaches in brandy followed by coffee and flaming sambuca liquers.

Back at the villa they made love until dawn on a jumbo sized swinging garden seat. His raw passion brought her twice to the peak of orgasm - an experience some women sadly admit, because of the endemic sexual selfishness of the male gender, they have never experienced in a lifetime.

It was the night that Lorenzo Berni was conceived!

In fact, for Gina, the whole of that last day was unforgettable.

They had spent the morning wandering around the town of Lercara Friddi where he was born. He showed her the sulphur mine, now derelict, where his father had worked before immigrating with the family to the USA in 1907.

At the local church, with the help of the priest, he turned up the records to look at the notice of the birth of a son to Rosalia and Antonio on 24 November 1897. The boy was to be called Salvatore Lucania.

It was a name she would never forget. A name that had, as her lover progressed up the sordid and violent ranks of the underworld, changed to Charley Lucky and then to the notorious tag of Lucky Luciano.

Life seemed dull after they returned to Naples although Lucky still occasionally asked her out to dinner or to visit him at his suite in the Turistico Hotel.

But life took a new and bitter turn for Gina when she missed her period and, after seeing the doctor, discovered with alarm that she was pregnant.

CHAPTER 5

Umberto Berni drove his tatty baker's van, with it's rusting bodywork and peeling trade sign, straight up to the imposing marble work at the front entrance of the Hotel Turistico, much to the disgust of the six-foot four inch, blue uniformed, door porter.

'You can't park that heap of shit here,' barked the former Caribinieri sergeant the ornate gilt tassels on his right epaulette shaking with the impetus of his indignant rage.

Umberto was taken aback by the outburst.

'But,' stammered the quaking baker. 'I have come to see Signore Luciano.'

The porter's tone softened slightly at the name Luciano and ordered: 'Well leave your van in the yard at the back of the hotel, which the tradesmen use.'

Umberto did as he was told and, his flour-dusted cap in hand, reported to the hotel reception desk and, nervously giving his name, asked if he could see Signor Luciano. The desk clerk, looking down his nose at the little man in his striped baker's trousers and apron, almost reluctantly, put a call through to Luciano's suite.

Tony Scarpone answered the call from the desk clerk and, after a few seconds conversation with his boss, issued the instruction over the phone: 'Please send Signore Berni up to the suite.'

*   *   *

17

'Signore Luciano,' faltered the trembling baker, twisting and untwisting his dusty cap in the throes of his nervous agony. 'I don't know how to tell you this. It is embarassing! But my little daughter Gina is pregnant as a result of the recent trip to Sicily with you.

'There is no doubt, it has been confirmed by a doctor at the clinic. I know you would wish to be informed of this as soon as possible.'

Lucky contemplatively scratched the old knife scar on his cheek, as he was prone to do when faced with a problem. The silence seemed endless to the nervous Berni as the gangster boss studiously pierced the end and lit a jumbo-sized Monte Cristo cigar before he signalled to Tony Scarpone to pour the baker a glass of wine.

'You were quite correct to come to me at once with this news,' said Luciano. 'I will see you get enough money to send the girl to a clinic where the unborn child can be aborted! My assistant, Tony Scarpone, will give you five thousand US dollars - which will be enough to settle this matter.'

*   *   *

Umberto Berni was taken aback by Luciano's curt and dismissive dissertation. Although $5,000 US was a lot of money to a back street Naples baker he summoned up enough courage to say: 'But Signore Luciano we are a good Catholic family and, as you know, the Church of Rome totally forbids abortion.

'I know Signore Luciano that you like my Gina very much - she is young, beautiful and was an innocent girl of barely 16 years of age when she met you. I am sure you are a man of honour and would want to do the right thing by her! I would approve a marriage which would not only make an honest woman of her but would give the baby a father and a name.'

There was another, almost agonizing, silence. A white streak appeared along the scar line on Luciano's cheek.

'Signor Berni - let me make it quite clear I have no intention of marrying your daughter, or any other woman if it comes to that. Now I have made you a generous offer - so collect your money from Tony Scarpone and that is the end of this matter as far as I am concerned,' he grunted dismissally.

The crestfallen and humiliated Berni left the hotel head bowed clutching the bundle of $100 bills that Luciano's assistant had thrust into his hand.

'We will have to watch him,' Lucky told Scarpone. 'The little runt might cause trouble. If he does we will have to take care of him.'

CHAPTER 6

Lucky Luciano was much too busy as the world boss of the sinister Unione Siciliano to spare a thought for the young girl whose life he had ruined.

The master of cover-up left no trail for the law enforcement agencies, both sides of the Atlantic, to indict him on the multifarious enterprises he conducted in drug trafficking, prostitution, gambling and smuggling, from his plush suite at the Turistico Hotel, Naples.

Some of the minions working in the rackets were caught, apprehended, charged and convicted by the FBI, USA Narcotics Bureau and the Italian Caribinieri but all were, at least, twice removed middle men.   Not one witness could, or dared to, point the finger in a witness chair directly at Luciano.

A 290-ton cargo ship registered in Holland, incongruously called the Rosegarten, docked in Naples after sailing from New York.   A careless Neapolitan docker let a crate fall from his forklift truck and the smashed wood revealed a one-armed-bandit gambling machine.   It was one of a consignment of 100 such 'bandits' marked on the crates as MACHINE TOOLS-MADE IN DETROIT.   It was the third shipment of such slot machines to arrive in the port of Naples that month.   The name 'Charles Luciano' was not on the manifest but Lucky was the importer and the promoter who coined 20 per cent of the lire that would pour through the hungry slots in bars, bistros, clubs and restaurants throughout the length and breadth of Italy and Sicily.

When taken down to police headquarters in Naples the indignant Lucky, his lawyer present throughout the meeting, growled: 'I don't know anything about any one-

armed bandits.   What do you think I am some fuckin'
small-time slot-machine hustler?   I don't know who
shipped them 'bandits' from the States and I don't fuckin'
care who owns 'em.'

A few minutes later he walked down the steps of the
Central Police station, his lawyer, Gaetano Mattinetti,
alongside him. He stopped to tell waiting journalists: 'Look
fellas I need dough badly but I ain't in any slot machine
racket!'

Then, grinning broadly, he paused dramatically to light his
cigar before stepping into the Oldsmobile where Tony
Scarpone was waiting at the wheel.

Once more the indefatigable Lucky Luciano had made a
monkey out of the law! The one-armed bandit industry in
Italy alone was a nice little earner for Lucky, grossing him
a steady $750,000 a year with further pay days as the
hungry slot machines found their way into France, Spain,
Portugal and into the clubs and pubs of England.

*   *   *

Law enforcement officers throughout the globe knew but
could not prove that Luciano was the biggest brothel
keeper and prostitute procurer in the world!

He owned the action of bordellos in New York, Chicago,
Detroit, Washington and Montreal. He was the sole owner
of Madam Tara's bawdy house in Naples and had
controlling percentage in Rome's notorious Orchidea Rosa
 and Turin's Sexy Pappagallo - Pink Orchid and Sexy
Parrot.

It was a business that cost him nine years of freedom and
could have kept him behind the bars of Danemorra for 40
years more had the US Government not decided to
commute his sentence and exile him for life.

As Madam Tara, brushing the whisper of a moustache that grew grotesquely on her upper lip, would often comment, Luciano was not averse to sampling the wares, of every colour and race, on offer in his own whore houses.

Yet he never let an insatiable sex-urge lure him into the same hell as his notorious fellow mobster, Al Capone, who died of syphilis on being released from Sing Sing after defrauding the US Inland Revenue.

*   *   *

Lucky returned on a business trip to Rome one day to find his former mistress, ex-show girl, Igea Lissoni sitting waiting for him in the lounge of the Turistico Hotel, Naples.

His brooding eyes, ever alert for a lurking enemy or waiting friend, spotted her immediately and he nodded to Tony Scarpone, who was carrying his leather valise to bring her up to his suite.

Scarpone discreetly left them together and went to his own small room in another part of the hotel.

'What the fuck do you want bitch?' Luciano yelled, sending her reeling across the room with a vicious backhanded swipe across her cheek. Igea rose, still dazed from the spiteful blow, which had already raised a large weal across the smooth olive skin of her cheek.

'I am sorry darling,' she sobbed. 'I was wrong to leave but I could not bear the sight of that coloured girl in our bed! But I have missed you so much.'

Lucky felt the throbbing in his groin as he recalled the erotic sessions they had shared in the past and the variety of tricks she had used in bed to rouse him.

23

He grabbed her round her waist. Half-pulling and half carrying her he dragged her into the next room and flung her on the bed. They stayed there for nearly 12 hours in a lustful orgy which embraced unbridled sex in almost every position and method that man and woman had ever thought of since Adam and Eve first discovered the pleasures of the flesh.

By the time room service delivered their breakfast of smoked salmon and scrambled quails' eggs, accompanied by a bottle of Dom Perignon champagne on ice, Igea was once again established as Lucky's mistress - despite the ripening bruise that tracked from her left ear to upper lip.

CHAPTER 7

Umberto Berni was determined to protect his family's reputation of being devout Catholics and hid his daughter's pregnancy until the fifth month when it was beginning to look obvious.

He then closed his baker's shop for a day and took Gina by bus to his sister's small farm near Lorica at the foot of the Butte Donato Mountain. There, it was arranged, she would give birth with the help of his sister, who had produced six children herself, and the village midwife.

Questions about the father were fended in concert by Umberto and Gina claiming that it was a boy from the same district in Naples who had now immigrated to the USA with his family and could not be traced. Not one whisper of the name Lucky Luciano was uttered.

All went well. Gina was a healthy young girl in her 17th year and appeared to bloom and flourish under the strains of pregnancy. At times she mooned for Lucky's lovemaking for she had thought at the time she was hopelessly in love with the mobster. But she was a sensible girl, brought up in a hard neighbourhood of Naples, and conceded that like a lot of innocent girls she had been duped, and likely would never see the lecherous Luciano again.

The birth went well! A bonny boy that scaled at 3.8 kilograms.

'As fat as an Easter Goose,' laughed midwife Anna Donatti as she slapped the baby's backside inducing the first lusty yell from those young lungs.

'A fine looking lad,' mused Umberto Berni's sister. 'But what is to become of him with his father flown to America?'

Gina cradled her baby son in her arms for the first time and, noting the thin thatch of black hair, sadly contemplated: 'Just like Lucky! My little Lorenzo is just like his father the famous Lucky Luciano.'

CHAPTER 8

Luciano had the one-armed bandit racket in Italy sewn up tight within three months.

There were small pockets of resistance from petty local crooks in various parts of the country that had to be squashed. In Rome a group of freelance hoods had imported 50 slot machines, made in France, and spread them round the clubs, bars and bistros throughout the capital.

Unione Siciliano were not having that, and their capo-di-capos, Lucky Luciano, spat out his instructions to his lieutenants.

'Make them an offer and if they don't fall in line wipe the fuckers out,' rapped the most dangerous mobster in the world.

So the word went out to the would-be Roman Emperor's from the dreaded Unione Siciliano: 'Pay us $10,000 US and we will cut you in for one point of the action when we move in with our American-made one-armed bandits!'

The chief of the Roman gang, a Spaniard with many convictions for smuggling, sent back the terse message to Unione Siciliano saying: 'Testicolos! Balls to you.'

The Roman leader, Pietro Cavalle, was an egoist. He could be seen most evenings, wearing his white fedora, strolling down the Via Veneto with his pet leopard cub on a lead.

But he was horrified one morning when he came downstairs to find the leopard cub with its throat cut, its severed testicles in a bag, and a crudely printed note saying: 'Balls to you too.'

Within minutes he received a phone call to tell him the warehouse, where his stock of one-armed bandits were stored, had been blown to bits by a shrewdly placed parcel of explosive. What was worse, two of his hoodlums had been killed and a third, with both legs blown off, had been taken to the infirmary, where he would die 48 hours later.

The shell-shocked Signore Cavalle immediately put in a call and instructed his bank to wire $10,000 to a bank account in Naples used by the sinister Unione Siciliano.

The detective division of the Caribinieri strongly suspected Luciano of being behind the outrage. But Lucky, a genius of the cover-up, had flown to his homeland of Sicily four days earlier where he made a high profile visit staying in a top Palermo hotel. Within days Unione Siciliano had shipped in 100 of their own USA made slot machines, and ordered the remainder of Cavalle's decimated mob break up the French-made one-armed bandits.

There was even an hilarious rumour amongst Lucky's mobsters that several of the lire guzzling 'bandits' had found their way into the Vatican where certain priests and monks assuaged the pangs of chastity with a flutter on the machines. No spokesman from the Eternal City ever denied the rumour and Il Papa certainly never mentioned it in his traditional Sunday address to the throngs in St Peter's Square.

The petty hoods who ran crime in Milan, having heard what happened to their cousins in Rome, paid the dreaded Unione Siciliano demand for a $10,000 protection fee. In return Lucky's lieutenants handed the Milanese brigands the task of collecting the one-armed bandit takings from the innkeepers, bar owners and club managers when the Unione's own machines were installed in a matter of days. There was more serious resistance from the Turin capo, Eduardo Bertorelli, when he received the ultimatum from Luciano via Unione Siciliano. Lucky was in no mood for silly games and he whispered a curt instruction down the phone to a henchman who in turn passed the word to a seasoned gunman: 'Fix him and leave a message for anyone else who refuses to tango.'

Bertorelli was found outside the Juventus Soccer stadium with a bullet hole in the centre of his forehead and a copper coin placed over each eyelid - a Unione Siciliano trademark! All resistance in the city, where thousands troop to work in the mammoth Fiat car factory every morning and spend big earnings in Turin's pleasure palaces, ended forthwith.

Without further ado Lucky Luciano hd imperiously added the title 'King of the One-Armed Bandits' to his curiculum vitae of evil.

CHAPTER 9

Baby Lorenzo progressed, like any healthy child putting on weight steadily, thriving on Gina's loving care and breast-feeding, until he was two months old.

Umberto Berni knew the time had come for decisions to be made. Already inroads had been made into the $5,000 that Lucky Luciano had passed over as if it was blood money to abort the child.

As he watched the little boy gurgling, kicking, smiling and, sometimes, yelling in his cot Umberto Berni's mind began to fester with anger at the gangster chief's curt dismissal of his 16-year-old daughter and her unborn child.

Looking through family documents Umberto came across Gina's birth certificate, which had been carefully tied up with pink ribbon by his late wife.

He noted, to his surprise, that Gina had not actually reached her 16th birthday while she had been away in Sicily with Lucky Luciano. Although it was true that he had given the gangster chief permission to take his daughter away nevertheless Luciano had breached Italian law by seducing a child under the age of consent.

If he could make out a complaint before a magistrate and convince the mobster that he would prosecute him then maybe he could force Luciano into marrying his daughter, giving the child a father to support him, and provide himself as the grandfather with the cash to retire to the country.

To have been brought up without the love of a mother was a sad enough start, but to be landed with an unwanted child at such a tender age herself was a cruel cross for any girl to bear.

*   *   *

Magistrate Luigi Donatti listened to the little baker's complaint while occasionally jotting down a note or two on the yellow pad on his desk.

'Signore Berni, this is a very serious matter you have brought to my attention,' said the magistrate. 'Particularly as Signore Luciano is such a rich and powerful man. I would like you to return here to my office in two days time when I will have the legal papers drawn up indicting Charles Luciano with this serious offence.'

Umberto Berni left the magistrate's office in good spirits, confident in his heart that he was about to get justice for his daughter, baby grandson and himself.

From the upstairs window of his office Luigi Donatti watched the baker stride purposefully towards the little three-wheeler van he had parked below. As the tatty vehicle rocked off towards the Central Station area the magistrate picked up the telephone and rang the Turistico Hotel.

When he was put through to the extension he had requested his opening gambit was: 'Signore Luciano, I have something important to tell you.....'

Palermo-born Donatti, who had been on the Unione Siciliano pay roll for several years knew that he would be well rewarded for the information he had just imparted.'

CHAPTER 10

For the hard-working Neapolitans, who lived near Central Station, preparing for another week of toil in factory, shop, market or dockside there were no breakfast croissants or rolls on this cold and drizzly Monday morning.

Berni's Bakery was closed. A police cordon surrounded the little shop with the mouth-watering smell of baking bread still lingering through the slanting velux windows.

Umberto Berni was dead. A gaping hole as big as the Grand Canyon at the back of his cranium, the spout of his shotgun, like a jumbo-sized cigar, encircled by his pouting lips. His, nicotine stained, index finger wrapped round the trigger so tightly that an ambulance man feared he might have to break it to release it from the icy stiffness of rigor mortis.

There was no other theory than 'suicide' in the minds of the police inspector and his sergeant. A theory confirmed when Magistrate-Coroner Luigi Donatti arrived at the death scene. There would be no lengthy and expensive investigation into the violent demise of Umberto Berni. The case was closed-cause of death 'suicide'. Besides, who would want to kill a humble baker?

*   *   *

On receiving the clandestine telephone tip-off from Magistrate Donatti, the master of evil planning, Lucky Luciano knew he must act quickly and decisively.

'The fuckin' Italian cops are itchin' to pin something on me,' Lucky told his henchman Tony Scarpone. 'The fuckin' little bread maker could be just the thing the cops are looking for, to put me in the pen. We have to fix this little runt Berni for fuckin' good. But what we do must look good. It must not look like a mob job. It must be carefully done to look like an accident or somethin' like that. We will have to bring in a visiting ' fireman' to do a specialist job like that.

       'I shall arrange to be in Rome when it happens so I have a cast iron alibi. Too many signs point in my direction.'

*   *   *

The hit-man, given the contract to dispatch unfortunate Umberto Berni to the bakery in the skies, was a Basque who normally used his Biretta on behalf of ETA's separatist movement. Wanted on both sides of the Spanish-French border for various outrages, including 12 assassinations, Paco Toba was hired out by ETA in a return arrangement, set up by Luciano, for a shipment of 25 ex-British Army Bren guns and half a ton of plastic explosive, plus an assorted supply of detonators and ammunition, to be delivered to the separatist movement's secret hideout near Pamplona.

Toba, a vicious hoodlum born in Bilbao, slipped across the French border in a hired BMW and motored through to the North of Italy. Having handed the car over to the Avis agent in Rome he caught the express train to Naples ordering and enjoying the most expensive meal and wine the dining car could provide.

Half an hour out from Naples' teeming Central Station he donned black track trousers, a black polo neck jersey and black trainers.

Almost totally inconspicuous Toba waited, in a doorway across the street from the tiny bakery, until Umberto Berni arrived at 11pm to start his night's work producing loaves, rolls, croissants and a variety of fancy pastries.

Within minutes it was all over.   Toba tiptoed into the bakery, positioning himself silently behind the baker's back, and slipping the chloroformed gauze over the unsuspecting baker's face. He pushed the two-bore muzzle into the semi-comatose baker's mouth, closed Berni's finger round the trigger and squeezed.

The report of the shotgun, mixed in with the roar of the three baking ovens that were working full blast, was hardly discernible in the damp and cold night.   The mess was horrific.   Umberto Berni's blood forming gory dough as it spread across the surplus flour strewn over the floor and baking table.

Toba sped quickly away from the bakery, through the back streets of Naples, to where the MV Titania was being readied to sail at midnight on a seven night 'Italian Highlights' luxury cruise.

Luciano had arranged and paid for a splendid outside cabin for him to use as the vessel headed for Rome, Livorno, Cannes and Barcelona where he would catch the plane to Bilbao with a minimum of fuss from immigration officials.

It was a brilliant escape route devised by the cautiously astute Lucky.

CHAPTER 11

Lucky Luciano, the greatest architect in the world of organised crime and a master of detail, strangely never bothered to ensure that his former lover Gina Berni had aborted the child they had conceived beneath the Sicilian stars.

As far as Lucky was concerned the $5,000 he had given to the ill-fated Umberto Berni put an end to the matter. He was not bothered one way or another whether the Berni broad had produced a brat, or not.

He had bought his way out of the matter and did not want, or expect, to hear any more about it.

*   *   *

Life, however, was not that simple for 16-year-old Gina Berni after the sudden death of her father. When Umberto Berni's, rather muddled, affairs were finally settled up there was little money left to look after herself let alone a six month old child. There was the settlement of the outstanding mortgage on the bakery and shop, a hefty unpaid bill to the flour mill, and the balance of the cost of a new baking oven her father had bought six months before he died.

The whole financial mess was exacerbated by the reluctance of more than a dozen restauranteurs, café owners, bistro bosses and club chiefs to pay into Umberto's estate the money they owed for bread and confectionery ordered and then delivered in his quaint three-wheeler van.

Her aunt, Umberto's sister, could not help her financially as she was a war widow dependent on a small war pension.

Gina was heartbroken in the realisation she could not keep little Lorenzo! Desperately she sought the help of the local priest. A kindly old man he arranged for the child to be taken into care at the kindergarten-orphanage run by the Sisters of Santa Maria. There he would stay until he was transferred at five years of age to the Orphanage for Boys organised by the Franciscan Brothers! It solved one major problem but still left Gina with the enormous worry of housing, feeding and clothing herself! Work was not easy to find in post World War II, poverty stricken, Italy, despite the enormous amount of aid poured into the country by the USA.

Young girls were often driven into the cheap end of prostitution while young boys scavenged the streets stealing from the fruit stalls, breaking into cars and running messages for drug pushers and pimps. A route that Lucky had followed himself as a nine-year-old urchin in the teeming lower East Side of New York, after his parents emigrated from Sicily to the USA in 1907.

She had reached her lowest ebb, without stooping yet to sell her body. She was sleeping in shop doorways and derelict sites, covered in old newspapers, when she steeled herself to the humiliation of asking the man who had seduced her, Lucky Luciano, for help.

The pompous desk clerk at the Turistico Hotel looked down his nose, through pre-war pince -nez spectacles, at the skeletal, under-nourished, waif that stood before him asking for Signore Luciano. Her clothes were threadbare, her shoes packed with cardboard in a futile hope that it would keep the damp out. She had not eaten a proper meal for five days just a watery cup of soup and a crust of bread each evening from the shelter for the homeless supervised by the charitable nuns. Although she was still in her teens, death was facing the unfortunate Gina.

The desk clerk hesitated, pondering if he should send the wretch back to the inhospitable streets, before putting the call through to Luciano's sumptuous suite.

*   *   *

If she was looking for sympathy from her former lover - she certainly did not receive it! Help, however, she did get - of a sort! She did not mention the baby to Lucky and he callously did not ask whether she had the child or an abortion.

'I need work,' she pleaded pitifully. 'I haven't eaten for days and I have been kicked out of my room because I can't pay the rent. I need work now - just to keep going. I'll scrub floors, wash clothes, iron shirts or clean dishes - anything! Please help me - you are the only one I can turn to.'

Lucky scowled at her without pity.

'I don't fuckin' know why you have come crawlin' to me,' he leered. 'I gave your father five thousand bucks to take care of you. I suppose he pissed it all away. I gave you a good time - what more do you fuckin' want?
'You need work? I'll fix you up with a job, then I don't fuckin' well want to hear no more from you.'

*   *   *

Unaware, and almost uncaring because of desperation, Gina waited in an adjoining room to hear what Lucky would do for her.

Luciano meanwhile put through a call to Signora Tara, the notorious madam of the biggest brothel in Naples. A

39

whorehouse in which, with several others, he held a controlling interest.

'I am sending Tony Scarpone over in the car with a new girl,' Lucky rapped out instructions to Madam Tara who was noted all over Naples for the unshaven black moustache on her upper lip.

'Her name is Gina - Gina Berni. Make sure she gets the rough trade. I want her hooked on 'H' as soon as possible. I'll send over a 1/4 K of the white stuff with Tony - make fuckin' sure the girl gets it and no one else - you hear me Tara?' There was a menace in Lucky's voice that could not be misunderstood.

It took only weeks to transform Gina Berni into a dependent, runny-nosed, dribbling, heroin addict. Meanwhile, with the occasional painful lash from the cruel leather quirt Madam Tara used to discipline the girls in her stable, Gina serviced the perverted sexual demands of a non-stop queue of rough, tough, unshaven, heavily tattooed and smelly Napoli dockers, stokers, seamen and sewage workers everyday.

In three years she was an incurable junkie ravaged by veneral disease and rushed to the infirmary to die like an unwanted stray cat. Inside 40 months vicious Lucky Luciano had orchestrated the horrific deaths of both father and daughter.

Even so that was not the last dealings the ruthless mobster chief would have with the ill-fated Berni family line. First in a charity kindergarten, then in a strict and Spartan orphanage, he was unaware that his biological offspring was being prepared for life. It was to come as an unpleasant shock to Lucky Luciano, 16 years later, that at birth Gina had registered their baby's name as Lorenzo Salvatore Lucania Berni.

Indelibly his unwanted son carried the name he had himself been given at birth in the Sicilian sulphur mining town of Lercara Friddi in 1897.   Lucky was never to play the part of the proud father but more the savage tiger who devours its own cub.

CHAPTER 12

Lucky Luciano stood on the almost deserted balcony of the Certosa di San Martino, once a Carthusian Monastry and now housing the National Museum, just like a rubbernecking tourist enjoying the splendid view across the City and Bay of Naples.

However Luciano and the swarthy, knife-scarred, man standing beside him on the sun-trapped balcony, Nicolo Gentile, were not interested in the breathtaking vista across the broad, blue sweep of the Mediterranean.

They were discussing plans for the launch of the biggest international drug scam in the history of organised crime. A caper that would pour billions of dollars into the swollen coffers of the sinister Unione Siciliano.

Gentile addressed Luciano on equal terms, acknowledging their joint status in the inner circle of Unione on both sides of the Atlantic.   Their respective bodyguards, the 266 pound heavyweight Joe Vialli and Lucky's ever-faithful Tony Scarpone, standing discreetly out of earshot a few metres away.   They both kept their right hands in suspiciously bulging jacket pockets-and it was certainly not a banana that each was gripping so intensely.

'No one trusts any other fucker' in the rackets,' philosophised Lucky succinctly.

Gentile and Luciano were activating an evil scheme that was to put a shipment of heroin worth $250,000 into the USA - the country that had branded them both as Public Enemies.

Lucky had been given a 30-50 year stretch in the penitentiary for crimes connected with organised prostitution, and was then released and exiled after nine years behind bars.   Nicolo had skipped a $15,000 bail in the USA where he linked up with Luciano to channel 'H', better known as the horrific white killing powder heroin, across the Atlantic.

Between them they would be responsible for the terrible deaths of thousands of unfortunate American junkies in the next two decades. USA Narcotics Bureau officials were to rue the day that Luciano had been released and exiled and Gentile allowed to escape to Italy.

Nicolo Gentile had been a leading light in Unione Siciliano with Lucky Luciano, but in 1937 he fell foul of the narcotic squad cops who were overjoyed that a thorough search of his apartment unearthed two address books listing nearly every drug trafficker, coast to coast, in the USA.

These two big-shot hoods set up the infamous Strada Bianco - the White Road - a vital supply route from the blood red poppy fields of the Near and Far East to the pathetic hulks cringing in the gutters, cardboard cities, casualty wards and morgues of America.

*   *   *

Lucky Luciano was the master planner who painstakingly never left any leads that connected him with the massive worldwide drugs racket. A genius of the cover-up who was always miles away from the scene when the crime he had schemed was perpetrated.

It was Lucky who brilliantly mapped out the logistics of getting the drugs across the USA's many borders by land, sea and air. He decided that to keep the drugs flowing into America in sufficient quantity Unione Siciliano would need at least 25 human 'mules' a week carrying the stuff in various ways across the Atlantic Ocean each week.

'Some will get caught by the fuckin' cops!' Luciano told Gentile. 'That is why we must be sure our names are kept in the clear. We must arrange for the fuckin' mules to be recruited and paid by people who don't know either of us! They will be paid well to keep their mouths shut but only after they deliver the stuff safely at the other end.'

*   *   *

Although the narcotic law enforcement agencies in the USA and Italy spread their nets, and took on more officers to deal with the tide of hard drugs flooding into America from Europe via Rome, won a few minor skirmishes overall they were losing the battle against the traffickers.

During the first six months of the sinister shuttle service master minded by Lucky Luciano and supervised by Nico Gentile only six 'mules' were apprehended by the cops and customs officers out of a total of just over 300 such drug smugglers. Of those six 'mules' that were caught not one of them had ever met, talked to or even seen Luciano or Gentile.

They had all been briefed by people far removed from Lucky and Nico. As Luciano had so tersely summed up: 'They are a business loss to be written off against profits! Just like being a tax deduction - that is if we paid fuckin' tax! What's more they can't sing to the cops because they don't fuckin' well know the tune- nuffin.'

Typical of the 'mules' that slipped through the net was Gianluca Bonet. Lucky arranged, through no less than five intermediaries, for this Turin- born petty crook to haul 40 pounds of 99 per cent pure heroin to the Unione Siciliano mob in Chicago.

Luciano had bought this consignment, again through the safety barrier of four intermediaries, in Istanbul for

$23,000! With his usual immaculate skill for organisation he had it transported to Naples on a lorry carrying crates of figs. Only two of the 200 crates were of interest to Lucky who was not particularly a fruit lover! Bonet was put on a flight from Rome, which flew directly to Chicago carrying the 'H' in the false bottoms of two specially constructed suitcases.

Bonet was instructed on arrival at Chicago airport to be sure to wheel his luggage to customs position Number 40. Both suitcases were given the vital chalk mark by Customs Officer Joe Bogart, whose 78-year-old father, Dino Bogartti, still lived in the township of Monreale, near Palermo in Sicily! Joe was well rewarded.

In Chicago the Unione Siciliano scientists, in their well-appointed laboratary, began to work on the consignment of pure heroin delivered by the 'mule' Bonet. These mob-employed lab' workers cut and re-cut the 'H' with milk powder and sugar until there were a staggering 70,000 shots of what the hoods called 'horse' to be sold on the streets at two dollars a time. A total haul of $140,000, representing a profit of $117,500 which included a fifty per cent cut of nearly $59,000 for Luciano.

A nice little earner for Lucky which explained why it was estimated that his personal fortune was worth $2 ½ billion. No wonder his discreetly tight-lipped bank manager in Switzerland was delighted with his notorious client.

The allegation from the USA Narcotics Bureau head that: 'Luciano is controlling the drugs traffic from Italy,' was strongly denied by the Italian police whose spokesman retorted: 'If Luciano is the head of a global narcotics ring he is conducting a remarkable remote-control operation.'

A statement that concisely summed up the modus operandi of Lucky Luciano, the maestro of the cover-up.

*   *   *

Of course there were bound to be slip-ups and one day a US Military Police Unit was suspicious of a truck driving through an American-British Control Zone in the Balkans. It was hauling a heavy load of timber from a nearby logging camp. One of the white-helmeted military cops picked up an axe split one of the logs and found a wedge of crude opium secreted there.

Further examination revealed the truck was carrying an astonishing 900 pounds of raw opium.

The episode cost Luciano's operation $40,000 but it was a drop in the ocean to the big-shot who a few days later gave one hundred grand to restore an ancient church in his native Sicily.

'Say a prayer for me, Father,' requested Lucky as he graciously handed over the cheque for $100,000 to a delighted parish priest.

Prayers do not come much dearer than that anywhere in the world.

Chapter 13

Little Lorenzo Berni made good progress in the kindergarten under the tutelage of the Sisters of Santa Maria. The kindly nuns considered him to be a lovely boy who learned quickly.

However lots of the nicer aspects of being brought up by your own parents, or in Lorenzo's case his mother, were lost in the institutional system. The nuns were kind and gentle but there was no one to personally comfort a little child when he awakencd in the kindergarten dormitory afraid of the dark in the middle of the night.

Despite the kindness of the Sisters, nothing could replace the soft arms of a loving mother! It was against the disciplines and restraints of their Order for the Sisters to cuddle, become too attached, or to cuddle a little child in torment.

A gentle tap on the shoulder and a whispered - 'Don't cry - everything will be all right. Jesus will look after you,' - could not replace the fervour of a biological maternal instinct! Like many orphans before and after him little Lorenzo had to cry alone at times!

So at five years of age, when he was transferred to the Orphanage for Boys, Lorenzo had already developed the toughness of a lad twice his age.

It was the toughness he would need under the strict Orphanage regime organised by the hardworking Franciscan monks with their roughly woven brown cowls and hands calloused by toil in field, garden, kitchen, foundry or woodworking shop!

Lorenzo could vaguely recall being taken, at the age of three, to see his dying mother in the terminal ward of a

Naples hospital.   She had whispered to him:'My little 'Renzo, your father is a rich and famous man. When you are old enough claim your rights and legacy from him! Always remember 'Renzo your mother loved you with all her heart!'

Each lad at the Orphanage for Boys had been allocated their own locker beside their bed.   All the Franciscan Brothers demanded was that the lockers were kept clean and tidy.   The privacy of the personal possessions in the lockers was sacrosanct.   Lorenzo's locker contained an oil skin packet with a label entreating him not to open the letter inside until his tenth birthday.

Basically the education dispensed by the Franciscan monks was quite adequate to equip the boys for life in the harsh world outside when they left institutional life at 14 years of age. Although the Orphanage was well run and the discipline strict, there were disturbing rumours about some of the Brothers around the time Lorenzo was nearing his tenth birthday.   A couple of the monks, finding the restraints placed on them by the vows of chastity they had sworn, were found guilty of sexually assaulting some of the younger boys.

The issue was treated as an internal matter by Vatican spokesmen when the Italian press learned of the scandal but two Brothers were banished to an enclosed monastery for a year of retreat, prayer and penitence.

Lorenzo was the target of such a sexual assault when Brother Josef crept up behind him in the Orphanage wash room one day.   The agitated monk had lifted his brown habit and tucked the skirt into the leather waist belt.

When Brother Josef put his arm affectionately round Lorenzo, displaying his proudly erect private member, the alarmed boy swivelled and violently head-butted the portly friar in his ample midriff and escaped.

It had taken all the ruthless courage he had inherited from his gang-boss father as he ran to the Orphanage office and reported to the Brother Benedict, the Head, what had happened

A few hours later the weeping errant Brother Josef was hustled into a fast car and taken to an enclosed monastery 40 miles from Naples. The same fate awaited another errant monk after a similar incident three months later. The Head of the Orphanage, Brother Benedict, counselled Lorenzo after the disturbing incident with Brother Josef.

'Remember we should never judge others when they make a mistake,' explained Brother Benedict. 'The Lord tells us to forgive those who sin against us!

'We all face temptation in our life. It is the way we resist such temptations and repent if we do succumb by which God will forgive us. Jesus will always give us absolution, through the confessional, if we show we are truly sorry for our sins.

'Now go to the Orphanage chapel lad and say five Our Fathers and Five Hail Mary's for Brother Josef, who tried to wrong you!'

Lorenzo defiantly wheeled past the Chapel without entering and muttered an invective word he had only recently learned from older boys in the schoolyard: 'Fuck Brother Josef!' he muttered sending a globule of spit into the gravel path he was walking on!

*   *   *

During his last four years at the Orphanage Lorenzo was moved into the metal workshop. He was taught the trade of blacksmith, welding, soldering and how to use an acetylene cutter. His biceps developed into man-size muscles as he sweated for hours at forge or anvil. He learned how to make wrought iron railings, gates and

51

arches that were sold in the hardware shops and builders merchant stores in Naples and the South of Italy.

On his tenth birthday Lorenzo opened the oilskin wrapped package in his locker! He unfolded the letter it enclosed and read on: 'my dearest Renzo-you will be a big boy by now,' wrote his dead mother.

'In another four years you will be sent out from the Orphanage by the monks to make your own way in the world. I am writing to inform you that your father is the famous Lucky Luciano, whose name, I made sure, was embodied in your own when you were born.

'You are entitled to a legacy from your rich and powerful father. Remember although people call him a gangster and a crook that your mother once loved him. Despite his reputation I am sure Lucky will not let you down!

'From your ever-loving mother-Gina Berni.'

CHAPTER 14

Lucky Luciano's portfolio of rackets in Italy and Europe was nearly matching the power he held over organised crime in the USA.

Luciano was adding to that portfolio of evil day by day. Already in control of the supply of American-manufactured gaming slot machines to most of Europe and the huge cut from the bars, clubs, hotels and restaurants which installed the one-armed bandits, Lucky was also the big-shot supplier of hard drugs arriving in the USA from Europe via Italy.

It was estimated that Luciano's setting up of the Strada Bianco - the White Road - the supply route of heroin and opium between Rome and New York was responsible for the death of more Americans than the two World Wars.

Next in line for the take-over of a racket was Lucky's old trade of brothel keeping, for which he had pulled a 30-50 year gaol sentence and his eventual exile from the USA to his native Italy.

Lucky already had a foot in the door of the invidious vice business with his controlling interest in Madam Tara's notorious Naples bordello. Now his aim was to bring all prostitution in Italy within the grasp of Unione Siciliano's greedy talons.

To maintain his grip as capo-di-capos of the sinister Unione Siciliano Luciano always had to show brutal strength when he met dissent in the ranks of the hoodlums who were on his payroll. It was the only way, treachery meant death.

Such a breach of Unione Siciliano's code was brought to his attention by chance when he was on a drug buying expedition to Trieste one day. A big scale Yugoslavian poppy grower and opium supplier casually asked Lucky if Signore Nicolo Gentile had been satisfied with the batch of opium that he had supplied the previous month.

Luciano was non-committal for he knew no such batch of opium had gone through Unione Siciliano's books. It could only mean that his first lieutenant in the shipment of drugs from Italy to the USA was moonlighting, freelancing, pocketing cash that should have been going into the Unione's coffers.

*   *   *

Lucky had suspected for some time that Gentile was getting over ambitious and was envying his own position as capo-di-capos of the Unione. Lucky knew from experience that such envy would have to be squashed like a cockroach underfoot. If he was to retain his reputation as The Boss amongst the mob, both sides of the Atlantic, he must take positive action against ambitious Nicolo Gentile that would reverberate throughout gangland in Italy and the USA.

Gentile's deceit and disloyalty in siphoning off a slice of the opium trade for himself and robbing Unione Siciliano, in which he was a sworn blood brother, could only be punished in one way. The solution would be bloody and painful.

Lucky Luciano, a genius in the cover-up, first of all ensured that he had a cast-iron alibi by checking in to a high profile hotel in Rome on the night, back in Naples, when Gentile met the inevitable fate handed to traitors by the Mafia and by their equally vicious successors Unione Siciliano.

But Luciano was just as guilty of murdering Nicolo Gentile that night as Joseph LoCurto the man chosen for the dreadful deed.   Once again Lucky had covered-up brilliantly.   He had never met LoCurto or spoken to the assassin over the telephone. All negotiations, all financial arrangements for the job were completed through several intermediaries with no link or trace to lead the police back to Luciano.

Gentile suffered the most horrific death at the gnarled hands of Corsican LoCurto acknowledged as the most skilled artiste across Europe in the use of the deadly garrotte! While the ill-fated Gentile was left unguarded for a moment when his body guard went to fetch the car LoCurto stepped up behind him, slipped the knotted leather thong round the victim's neck, twisted the garrotte and thrust his knee into the doomed man's back and pulled and pulled.......

Gentile struggled for less than 90 seconds, his body sagged, eyes bulging and leaking blood, mouth frothing, tongue lolling as his agonising demise arrived inside four minutes.

Gentile's body was found on the steps of Naples noted San Carlo Opera House, the most apt place for singers and traitors according to the warped humour of the hoodlum world!   In accordance with the Unione Siciliano code a copper coin was placed over each bulging eyelid.

The detective division of the Caribierni suspected Lucky Luciano of orchestrating this mob killing from the outset, but what proof could possibly be pinned on a man miles away in Rome at the time of the murder?

Luciano arrived back in Naples the following day, was detained four hours, enduring pointless questioning and then released.

Lucky Luciano was free to start setting up organised prostitution throughout Italy just as he had done in the USA.

CHAPTER 15

Lucky Luciano had learned the business of organised prostitution at its grass roots level in the USA.

However he had paid a heavy price for his interest in the bawdy house rackets when New York's dynamic District Attorney, Thomas Dewey, successfully crafted a prosecution against him which led to a sentence of 30-50 years incarceration in the State Penitentary, later commuted to exile from the USA to his native Italy, after nine years behind bars.

In the 1920's most of the big mob bosses scornfully considered that the prostitution rackets were for minor punks and would not bring in the big cash bonanza they were enjoying from rum-running, illicit hooch distilling, drugs, protection and gang killings.

Luciano, head of the Unione Siciliano, the sinister successor to the murderous Mafia, however visualised the world of whores, pimps and brothels as a potential big earner for his mob.

Although, in exile, he realised that Italy was an entirely different country in which to organise prostitution, he used similar tactics to those that had brought the bordellos of New York and other American cities under the corrupt control of Unione Siciliano.

One of his first ploys in exile was to grab control of Madam Tara's notorious brothel in Naples known by almost every seaman whose ship steamed across the Mediterranean. Most of the women employed by the hirsute Tara were from poverty stricken Napoli families. Most of their clients were horny-handed sailors, dockers, bloodstained abattoir workers and labourers in sweaty dungarees.

Lucky knew that the high-class bordellos he had in mind needed a non-stop flow of girls from various part of the world, of different nationalities and colouring! To keep the high rollers, he wanted to attract as clients, the girls would be switched from brothel to brothel providing a change of what was on offer from day to day and week to week.

To do this he used the system he had devised in the USA by setting up five or six prostitute 'bookers' on the Unione Siciliano payroll. The function of these 'agente prostituras' was to procure, enroll-by brute force if necessary-new talent for the brothels from Italy, France, Spain, North Africa and even the odd show girl from England, down on her luck and stranded in Europe! Each of these agente prostituras had a 'stable' of girls who were regularly switched from bordello to bordello so that the clients were regaled with different faces, figures and sexual deviations.

Lucky Luciano built an Italian empire of evil for Unione Siciliano as powerful, ruthless and rich as the rackets he still controlled from long distance in the USA.

To the mobsters, hoodlums and punks who did the Unione's nefarious work on both sides of the Atlantic he was simply 'The Boss' - the undisputed capo di capos of omnipotent Crime International.

CHAPTER 16

Lorenzo reached his 13th birthday without any celebration or fuss at the orphanage!

In fact he had not even realized that he had reached his teens until Brother Matthew, the Franciscan monk who acted as the orphanage bursar, called him into the office for a talk.

'Now you are 13, like other boys when they have only one year left to stay at the orphanage, you will be sent out into the city to work in order to prepare you for real life,' said the kindly Franciscan. 'You will continue to live here at the orphanage until you are 14 and return every night and weekends to sleep and eat. Any wages you earn will go into the orphanage coffers to pay for your keep but we will give you a small amount of pocket money each week to spend how you wish!

'You have done well here at the orphanage in the past eight years and have worked hard in the last 12 months when you have been in the blacksmith and metalwork shop. That should stand you in good stead when we try to find you a job in that line of business!'

So at 13 years of age, with the hair on his face still unshaven and downy, Lorenzo was sent out into the world for what would have been called in the 21st Century "work experience".

*   *   *

Paulo Tite was a strong man, weighing in at a massive 140 kilos, who had spent the first 30 years of his turbulent life on the wrong side of the law. Having been taught the rudiments of metal work during a five year spell in jail he decided to set himself up as a blacksmith in Naples, on the ill-gotten gains of a burglary, for which he went undetected!

After ten years the smithy brought him a hard gained living, bolstered occasionally by a little burglary or safe breaking!

Never a man to look a gift horse in the mouth Paulo jumped at the chance when the Franciscan Orphanage offered him a cheap assistant in the shape of 13 year old Lorenzo Berni - a boy already conversant with metal work and the way a smithy work shop functions.

It was never going to be easy for Lorenzo under the tutelage of such a brutal man. The kind of sadistic employer that a couple of centuries earlier would have prompted humanitarian Charles Dickens to reach for quill and inkpot!

On his first day at work Lorenzo, not conversant with all the tools in the smithy, lost his grip using a pair of heavy pliers and inadvertently allowed a glowing hot rivet to fall almost on his new boss's boot! He received a vicious kick up the backside for his clumsiness and a warning yell from the irate Tite: 'That will teach you to be more careful you little bastardo!'

*   *   *

Blacksmith Paulo Tite however quickly appreciated that Lorenzo had been taught skills in the orphanage workshop that would be useful to his business both legal and unlawful! The kid was brilliant at welding and using an acetylene cutter.

One morning after Tite had been out during the night burgling an office, he showed Lorenzo a small safe and asked him to cut it open with his acetylene torch. It took the boy nearly two hours to burn his way through and when the safe was finally opened the burly blacksmith was delighted that it contained a sizeable bundle of fairly high denomination lire notes.

He tossed Lorenzo a few coins from his pocket to show how pleased he was, adding the coarse reminder: 'Make sure you keep your fucking mouth shut or I'll burn yer bloody eyes out!'

Albeit unwittingly Lorenzo Berni had committed his first crime!

*   *   *

Lorenzo's skills with an acetylene torch were summoned into use by the torpid Tite on several occasions after his illicit overnight pillaging pilgrimages, particularly when a small safe was included in the pilfered haul! One morning, when he was nearing his 14th birthday, Lorenzo, on arriving for work was called into Paulo Tite's grubby cubbyhole office.

'I've got a job outside for you today 'Renzo,' said the insidious blacksmith. 'It's for Signora Tara, the madam of the bordello near the harbour.
Her wrought iron fencing and gate needs repairing so take your acetylene torch and spend the day putting it right.'

Then, pausing for a moment, the odious Tite leered and added: 'and while you are working amongst all those lovely puttanas I don't want you dipping your wick and sampling the goods. Just go behind the fucking bushes and practise your mastubazione skills!'

So Lorenzo Berni went wobbling off on the smithy's rusting bike with an acetelyne cylinder and tools precariously perched on the rear carrier!

It was an expedition that would eventually steer him in a new direction and add a new purpose to his life!

CHAPTER 17

It is an odd quirk of human nature that harlots, the world over, are frequently emotional caring women giving their hearts and affection to pets and pimps who are often mean violent men addicted to drink and drugs.

Visit the red light district of New York, London, Paris or Rome and you will see the streetwalkers cradling cuddly poodle dogs. Call in the nearby taverns and you will see the pimps grab a purse and help themselves to the banknotes their woman had earned the hard way in some adjacent alleyway half an hour earlier.

These unfortunate women crawl back for more of this vile treatment from men who often beat them up unmercilessly. Many of them have children from an earlier, more civilised, life that went wrong. Every dime, penny, centime or lira they manage to keep away from the greedy talons of their pimp will go towards buying clothes or toys for the little child. Yet in their professional life whores - putas in Spanish, prostitutars in the Italian language - are hard, calculating, predators swooping like vultures to take advantage of mankind's promiscuous urges.

Signora Lisa Tara's days of street walking had ended with her stunning good looks two decades past. At 55 years of age she ran the sleaziest, roughest, most perverted bordello in the teeming seaport of Napoli.

She ran that brothel with a rod of iron! Or more accurately with a knotted leather quirt with which she would viciously crack against the silk covered bottom of one of her girls who failed to please one of the sex-crazed rough-necks who had paid hard-earned lire for their erotic services.

It was thirty long years since Tara had given her heart to any man or beast! In that time her once voluptuous figure had ballooned into a grotesque pear-shaped 120 kilos. Her upper lip was adorned with a black moustache that would have been the pride of Pancho Villa. Her right cheek carried a deep scar that was the result of a razor slash from a former pimp.

Yet unsparingly Tara gave her heart to 13-year-old Lorenzo Berni from the moment he arrived to repair the ferro battuto railings and gate that encircled the brothel grounds. It was not love at first sight in a sexual sense but a deeper even more passionate maternal affection that prompted her to help the unfortunate boy whom life had already short-changed.

Having watched him toil for hours with his oxyacetylene burner she invited him to her private sitting room for a cup of coffee and sweet tortas.

After he had washed his face and hands in her pink and scented bathroom they sat down to talk. She listened, with interest, as he answered her questions!

He had been in the orphanage for eight years, he explained, and before that in the kindergarten run by the nuns, where his mother had left him as a baby.

When he told her his name was Lorenzo Berni it sounded a klaxon warning in her memory bank.
          'Berni?' she quizzed. 'What was your mother's first name?'
She had a feeling of foreboding about what his answer would be.
          'My mother's name was Gina Berni but I can only remember meeting her once. That was when one of the nuns took me to the hospital to see her on the day that she died.'

64

Tara reflected on what Lorenzo had told her: 'Gina Berni - God forgive me for what that bastardo Luciano made me to do to that poor girl. So this boy is her son? Well I like the lad and I'll try to make it up to the lad for what his mother suffered here.'

*   *   *

When Lorenzo returned to the brothel the following day to finish repairing the ferro battuto railings Tara invited him again to her quarters for biscottos ed limonata after he had finished his work. Tara and Lorenzo were enjoying the talk and refreshments when Lucky Luciano knocked on the door and entered as he was prone to do from time to time when he visited for a business discussion with the Madam who ran the brothel he owned.

Neither Lucky nor Lorenzo realized this was a first meeting between father and unwanted son. Tara explained that Lorenzo was the workman who had been welding the broken railings outside the brothel. Although he was employed by Paulo Tite the blacksmith, she explained, Lorenzo was still an inmate at the Franciscan Orphanage for Boys.

Luciano nodded towards Lorenzo and told Tara that he would call in for a talk the following morning - which was in fact the day in every month that she handed over the brothel takings to the mobster.

Before Lorenzo left to go back to Tite's blacksmith's workshop Tara said that she would like him to visit her on Sunday afternoon when he had a day off from work. She slipped several lire notes into his hand as a mancia in gratitude for the work he had done, with the cautionary advice: 'Spend that money on yourself and don't let that greedy pig Paulo Tite get his grubby hands on it.'

CHAPTER 18

Lorenzo, dressed in a freshly laundered orphanage uniform and scrubbed clean with carbolic soap, rang Tara's private bell when he arrived promptly at three o'clock the next Sunday afternoon as requested by the brothel keeper.

Tara's moustache tickled his cheek when she greeted him with a kiss, her breath exuding a pungent aroma of mussels, garlic and a copious quantity of Valpolicello vino consumed during a massive midday pranzo.

'It's lovely to see you Lorenzo, what kind of week have you had?' she asked as she poured him a glass of cool lemonade from a jug and a large goblet of grappa for herself.

After taking a long swig at the lemonade Lorenzo said: 'Oh OK! I have been working in the smithy all week helping Paulo Tite to make some gates for a special order from the Church of San Francesco d'Assi in Palermo. It is a special order Paulo says because it is to be paid for and donated to the church by Lucky Luciano the man, my mother told me before she died, is my father. Who I have never met! When we have finished making the gates I am to go over to Sicily on the ferry with my tools and help Paulo to fix them! Brother Benedict, the Head has given me permission to go to Sicily with Paulo and be away from the orphanage for two nights.

'Sicily is where my father comes from and I am very excited that I am going there. Perhaps I will meet him while I am over there and get the chance to tell him who I am.

'I have read a lot about him in the Corriere di Napoli, the newspaper Paulo buys every day. They say he is a gangster and murderer but the Caribinieri can never pin anything on him, which shows how clever he is.'

Tara was surprised by Lorenzo's passionate dissertation. But it confirmed what she had suspected, when Luciano had sent Gina Berni to the brothel with the evil instructions on how she should be treated, that Lucky was the boy's father! She felt it was better not to tell him that the man who had interrupted them, when she was with Lorenzo the previous week, was his father. At the moment Lorenzo was enamoured with the name and reputation of Lucky Luciano. The rule in the vias of Napoli was "steal if you can but don't get caught". How would Lorenzo react when told how his father had treated his mother when he sent her into prostitution and malevolently had her transformed into a drug addict, virtually sentencing her to an early death?

Lorenzo deserved to be told the truth some time, but he was yet too young. He had his father's Sicilian blood coursing through his veins and vendetta would probably be intuitive. In which case, at this early stage of his life, it would be man against boy -there could only be one winner.

'Now would not be the right time to tell Lucky Luciano that you are his son,' counselled Tara.

'At the moment you are just an Orphanage kid! Why not wait a few years until you are a man and have achieved something in life that will make your father proud?

'Perhaps now is the time when you should be seriously thinking about what you are going to do when you leave the Orphanage in a few months time.'

Lorenzo thoughtfully considered Tara's advice and said: 'Paulo Tite has offered to keep me on and says he would not pay me much more than he is now. But I would have to keep myself on such low wages that I would have little left for anything else although Paulo said I could sleep in the little store room at the back of the smithy!'

That statement from Lorenzo opened the way for Tara to raise a suggestion that she had been thinking about for the past week, since she had last talked with him.

'Look 'Renzo,' she said. 'Paul Tite is not a very nice man. I know because he is a client here. He is cruel, sadistic and more than once I have had to stop him abusing my girls. He is trying to exploit you. He was lucky to get such a good worker as you on the cheap when the Orphanage let you work at the smithy. Now you are nearing the age when you have to face the world on your own he still wants to employ you on the cheap. Although you will be only 14 when you leave the Orphanage you have learned the skills and developed the strength of a full-grown man.

'I have a suggestion to make. Our portinaio here at the bordello, Carlo Bona is retiring because of old age in four weeks time. I will need to replace him and would keep the job open for you. Your duties would be as a door porter, handyman and to carry messages for me when necessary. You would be supplied with a new uniform and I would pay you the same money as Carlo is getting - a man's wages. Also you would have your own private room and your meals here. You would have every Sunday off, the day when we close the bordello! During the hours the bordello are open you would be the door porter in uniform admitting the clients and showing them to the lounge where they would wait for the girls. You would have to deal with awkward customers, but that should not be a problem because you already have developed the strength of a man and many of our clients are too drunk to cause you much trouble.
'Think about it.'

It certainly gave Lorenzo a lot to contemplate during the next week until he visited the bordello again. But before he left Tara handed him a parcel, neatly tied in brown paper.

'Go on open it.' she urged him.

He undid the string, excited by the fact that it was the first time in his life anyone had given him a present. He pulled away the brown paper and revealed a brown suit with matching shirt, shoes and socks and a neat striped tie to round off the outfit. It was the first 'proper' suit he had ever owned.

'Next time you come to see me wear the suit instead of that drab Orphanage uniform,' she said, adding, 'that's if they will allow you.

Lorenzo smiled, and thanked Tara emotionally: 'It's the best present I have ever had. Brother Benedict, the Head of the Orphanage, allows us to wear our own clothes, if we have any, on our day off on Sunday after we have attended Mass. This will be the first time I have had clothes of my own and I have a private locker to hang them up in. Thanks Tara for such a wonderful gift.'

She watched him through the window depart through the bordello's wrought-iron gate, which he had repaired himself only a week previously, his parcel under his arm. He was whistling merrily as he turned in to the street heading for the Orphanage.

Lorenzo Salvatore Luciana Berni was probably the happiest lad in the teeming city of Naples that Sunday evening.

CHAPTER 19

Lorenzo next saw his father during the first week that he started work for Tara as the bordello's portinaio.

Dressed in his new doorman's double-breasted green uniform jacket, with silver buttons, and matching trousers, Lorenzo looked smart. Although he had only just passed his 14th birthday he was an impressive two metres in height and went to the scales at 76 kilos with biceps and shoulders hardened by hours of toil at his former employer, Paulo Tite's, anvil.

Lucky Luciano strode purposefully into the elegant foyer of Tara's pleasure palace. The freshly lit Monte Cristo cigar in his mouth already aglow. His alert eyes targeted on Lorenzo and his keen memory bank quickly booted up as he said: 'aren't you the kid who used to work for that fat old bastard Paulo Tite? The lad who did the welding and repaired the fence a few months ago?
Well I am Charley Luciano, some people call me Lucky, and I own this joint. So now you are working for me! What's your name son?'

Lorenzo, recalling the advice Tara had given him, was careful not to give his surname and just told Signore Luciano his Christian name.

'Well I'll keep my eye on you kid,' said Lucky slipping a $10 bill into Lorenzo's hand. 'We are always looking out for promising lads in the organisation.'

Lorenzo was the best portinaio that Tara had ever employed. He was polite to her girls and their clients alike. He dealt firmly with any customer who arrived at the reception desk likely to cause trouble through excessive drinking. If necessary, despite his age, he had the strength to eject anyone threatening to be a nuisance. The plain fact was that he was efficient at his job and liked by the girls.

In the 21st Century the thought of a 14-year-old youngster working as a porter-doorman at a brothel will shock and even horrify some people. Yet times and attitudes change. There were 12-year-old boys serving as midshipmen in the Royal Navy at the Battle of Trafalgar while campaigning journalist and author Charles Dickens was forced to go to work at eight years of age to help out when his father was committed to a debtors' prison.

Boys quickly become men in certain circumstances and that is what happened to young Lorenzo.

*   *   *

Although Luciano had been convicted in the USA for his involvement in organised prostitution and was given a 30-50 year sentence in the New York State Penitentary at Dannemora his arch-enemy, New York District Attorney Thomas Dewey, had not proved conclusively that Lucky had personally extorted money from a prostitute or brothel madam or had ever himself procured a girl for any bordello.

Lucky's defence was simple but contradictory.
         'I never fuckin took money from a dame in my life.' he claimed vehemently. 'What did we need to move in on the whores when we were clipping the pimps?'

But the jury just did not believe the man who was reputedly the biggest whoremaster in the USA and he paid the price with nine years behind the bars of the State Pen'. But during his near-decade in jail Lucky was still The Boss as far as the Unione Siciliano mobsters in America and Italy were concerned.

He had very little trouble setting up a vice empire in the old country. His opening gambit, only a few weeks after disembarking from the SS Laura Keene after his exile from the USA to Italy was, to take over the largest and biggest money-spinning, bordello in Naples. Madam Tara's was then owned by a Neapolitan thug with the tongue-twisting name of Gianluca Casireaghi, formerly one of Mussolini's brutal Secret Police who had been trained in the arts of torture and interrogation in Germany by Hitler's sinister SS.

Lucky sent his emissary, Tony Scarpone, round to Madam Tara's with a pithy offer: 'Signore Luciano sends you his compliments and informs you that Unione Siciliano will take over Madam Tara's at the beginning of next week. Generously, Signore Luciano will allow you to keep this week's takings.

'The boss also says that if you want to buy your way back into the business it will cost you $10,000 for a one point share of the profits. Take it or leave it - the organisation does not care one way or the other.'

Casireaghi, who had committed three brutal murders, was not used to being spoken to so bluntly. Instinctively he felt for the stiletto secreted in the soft suede shoulder sheath beneath his left armpit. Scarpone, a born street fighter whose aggressive skills had been honed by a score of bloody gang battles, quickly responded and slid his right hand into his jacket pocket where his Luger pistol nestled.

'Listen punk,' growled Lucky's trusted henchman. 'Make another move for that knife or even twitch your eyelid and I'll blow your fuckin' balls off. I assume that is your answer to Signore Luciano's offer? I'll see you at your funeral, asshole.'

Scarpone backed cautiously out of the room his finger poised on the hair-trigger of the Luger.

*   *   *

Lucky once again showed his mastery of the art of the cover-up when he arranged to be in Palermo on the day Gianluca Casireaghi met his horrific fate.

Lucky, astutely, took Tony Scarpone with him to his home land of Sicily in case his aide had been spotted during the stormy confrontation with the condemned Casireaghi.

Lucky had convened a meeting of Unione Siciliano's leading mobsters at a top Palermo hotel on the very morning that the bomb attached to the underside of Gianluca Casireaghi's Mercedes reduced the former brothel owner to ashes, sending him to a well-plotted cremation. Once again Luciano had crafted the perfect alibi when the police investigated Casireaghi's demise.

The Unione Siciliano's top brass listened intently as Lucky Luciano outlined his plans for the take-over of organised vice throughout Italy.

'We must create a syndicate which will control the brothels in every city and big town in the country-just like we had in the USA,' were the orders of the Unione's world famous capo-di-capos.

'A syndicate as well organised and efficient as the A.P Stores chain in the States. We will take 80 per cent of the profits from each house, the madams will keep five percent and the rest split amongst the girls. Each of the six agentes prostituras I have appointed based in various areas around the country will receive a bonus of $1,000 for each new girl they enlist plus the 10 per cent they will keep from the earnings of every girl in his stable.

'The whores will be switched from bawdyhouse to bawdyhouse and from city to city on a regular basis so that there is always fresh "meat" on offer to the customers.

74

'Anybody unwilling to toe the line will be dealt with firmly and decisively so the message will be loud and clear to everyone. As we did in the States, I will make sure that we enlist magistrates, caribinieri and police of every rank, local prosecutors and even judges on to the organisation pay roll to look after our interest in all activities including, gambling, drugs and the whore houses.

'They will be well rewarded to turn their backs on what goes on at their local brothels - where they will be given free and privileged access to the girls. That will work in our favour because we will have a hold over them with the threat of telling their wives they had consorted with professional whores. It is important that we get pictures when they personally visit the brothels and we will employ photographic experts to set up secret cameras.'

Under Lucky Luciano's orders Madam Tara's had a $50,000 makeover. The builders, decorators and furnishers moved in for a month to complete an amazing face-lift for the bordello. The decor was based on illustrations and sculptures depicting the uninhibited orgies that had been staged by the ancient Romans - history was about to repeat itself.

With the recruitment of younger and better class girls from the agentes prostituturas, that Luciano had organised throughout the country, brothels like Madam Tara's were able to raise their charges and go upmarket. Lucky, as usual, made sure that he personally distanced himself from any day to day control of Madam Tara's or any of the other bordellos in the Syndicate.

Within two years Unione Siciliano were grossing $15 million a year from the brothels, after expenses and pay-offs the organisation finished up with $4 million proft, leaving Lucky, The Boss, with a personal annual hand-out in the region of $1 million - quite a nice region to be in from only one of the rackets he controlled.

Yet spare a thought for the unfortunate girls who had to spend hours on their back to earn $500 a week, yet after deductions due to their agente prostitura and to the brothel management for towels, maid service and meals and drinks personally took only $50 a week home, where, usually, there was a predatory pimp waiting to grab that comparative pittance from her.

As for young Lorenzo Berni he had a toe hold on the bottom rung of one of the most lucrative criminal rackets in Europe and was already being eyed as a possible likely recruit to his father's iniquitous organisation.

CHAPTER 20

There was no doubt that Lucky Luciano remained as "The Boss" of organised crime both sides of the Atlantic.

Even after he was exiled for life from the USA, and unceremoniously booted out to his native Italy in 1945, he continued to draw millions of dollars from the American rackets he had launched, organised and controlled for the powerful Unione Siciliano.

The size of his continuing annuity from criminal activities in the USA was settled at a plush hotel in Havana when, surprisingly, the ageing Lucky appeared again in the Western Hemisphere 16 months after he had been put aboard the SS Laura Keene in New York harbour and despatched into exile.

It was the biggest get together of top criminals ever convened. At that meeting were gang-lords Frank Costello, gambling chief Willie Moretti and the notorious Fischetti Boys, Charlie and Rocco who had taken over Chicago from the ailing Al Capone. New York and New Jersey were represented by Joe Adonis, Albert Anastasia, 'Joe Bananas' Bonnano, Tommy Luchese, Joe Profaci and his protege Guiseppe Maglioco, Augie Pisano, and Mike Miranda. From Buffalo came Steve Maggadino while Chicago was represented by Tony Arcado, Carlos Marcello from New Orleans and Santo Trafficante flew in from Florida.

Also at this important Unione Siciliano soiree were two mobsters, Meyer Lansky and 'Dandy Phil' Kastel, who both carried immense power despite the fact that they were Jewish and not eligible to vote.

'Charley Lucky is the most persecuted man in the world,' the meeting was told by gambling guru Willie

Moretti, who was assassinated nine months later when a group of hoods, ignoring the other diners, walked into a New Jersey restaurant and filled him full of lead.

The meeting, following Frank Costello's proposal, agreed that Lucky, despite his exile from the USA, would still retain his powers as the Unione's 'Boss of Bosses'and arbiter. As it was put in the Sicilian dialect: 'Capo Di Tutti Capi'.

It was the title that Lucky had held ever since he had succeeded the old Mafia godfather, Salvadore Maranzano, who had been blasted to where gangsters go in the after life with his throat cut, six stab wounds and four bullet holes, just to make sure.

Luciano would keep the rackets he had already set up in Italy, black market and currency exchange dealings, smuggling, gambling and whore houses. But the profits from drugs trafficking which he had organised the supply route of cocaine and heroin from Europe to the USA would go into the Unione Siciliano's coffers of which Lucky would receive a ten point share.

The mobsters had a convenient cover-up for their curious Cuban convention. They let it be known that it was merely a party to honour a promising Italian singer by the name of Frank Sinatra who was hitting the 'showbiz' headlines as the resident singer with the renowned Tommy Dorsey band.

As head of Unione Siciliano, Lucky Luciano had sanctioned, that to help launch the young crooner's career, cash should be released from the organisation's funds to sponsor him. There was never any suggestion that the entertainer, known later in his life as 'Ol' Blue Eyes', was ever personally connected with the rackets. Sinatra said he was in Cuba to thank Lucky for his support and obligingly sang one evening for the assembled gang lords.

This conclave of crooks agreed with Meyer Lansky's proposal that Luciano should be sent $250,000 in cash via courier on the first day of March, June, September and December-a million bucks a year- as his share of the USA rackets he personally had set up, which had been run by the organisation since his exile. The money would be laundered in the familiar way through the gambling industry and delivered to Lucky in Italy by a bagman of his choice! The parameters of the prospective qualities of the bagman or courier, in the interest of Unione Siciliano's security, would be (1) a person without a criminal record and with a valid excuse to travel frequently between the USA and Italy, (2) trustworthy (3) a guy physically strong enough to take care of himself as he would not be armed, and, (4) an unassuming personality who would not attract the attention of police and customs officers. LUCKY.... 88
With 250 grand, in large denomination bills, nestling in his case the bagman would carry a cover-up gambling slip from a New York bookmaker proving that he had won the cash in a betting coup.

*   *   *

Lucky thought carefully about whom he could trust as his bagman in such an important errand.

Obviously his chauffeur-bodyguard Tony Scarpone, or any of his other Unione Siciliano hirelings in Italy, would not be suitable because of their police records. If any of these guys were caught on such a mission the cops would assume, quite correctly as it happened, that the cash was crooked.

One morning Lucky was thoughtfully eating his midday breakfast of caviar and scrambled eggs, washed down with a bottle of Dom Perignon, in his suite at the Turistico Hotel in Naples, when he had an inspiration.

He remembered the fresh-faced kid he had met at Madam Tara's - the new portinaio at the bordello - Lorenzo, yes that was the kid's name he recalled. Yeah! He would be just the one to act as bagman. Clean cut, obviously with no police record, quite strong for his age and able to look after himself. The kid would be ideal for such an important task.

CHAPTER 21

One morning after breakfast at the brothel, where he had been given his own tiny room, Lorenzo was summoned to Madam Tara's office.

'Lorenzo, dear, I have just had a phone call from Signore Luciano,' she said looking up from the papers strewn across her desk. 'He wants to talk with you. You are to go round to the Hotel Turistico to see him in his private suite.

'I don't know what it is all about, but it will not do to keep him waiting.'

Tara reached into her desk draw and brought out some lire notes: 'Here's some money so take a taxi and get over to the hotel as soon as possible.'

Lorenzo went back to his room, changed out of his portinaio's uniform into his street clothes and rushed off to do as bid.

*   *   *

'Sit down kid,' said Lucky, noting how much the boy, now 16 years of age, had filled out and grown even more since he had first seen him at Tara's bordello more than 12 months previously. 'Lorenzo - that's your name isn't it ? I've got an important job that I think you could do for me.

'I want you to fly to New York and collect a package of money for me and bring it back safely to Naples. It is vital that no one must learn that the mission you are embarking on has anything to do with me.

'As far as outsiders are concerned you have never met or even heard of Charley Luciano. You will be briefed by my assistant Tony Scarpone before you make the trip and, of course, your travel expenses, hotel bills and spending money will be taken care of.'

Lorenzo was given a bundle of lire notes and told to go the government offices in Naples the following day and apply for a passport.

'That should take about 14 days and then we will set about getting you a visa to visit the USA,' said Lucky. 'When all the formalities are completed we will brief you on where you will be going when you arrive in New York and where you will be staying. I will ring Tara and tell her she will have to do without your services for about two weeks. Let Tara know when your passport comes through and then Tony Scarpone will coach you on what you have to do when you get to America.'

*   *   *

The cover story for Lorenzo's trip devised by Lucky was typically brilliant in its fine detail.

Italian piastrella mosaico were much sought after by builders and decorators working on the big houses, apartments, luxury restaurants and hotels. A bathroom, patio or conservatory floor laid with Italian mosaic tiles was a sign of opulence.

Lucky arranged with a business acquaintance Pietro Mineo, who owned a factory on the outskirts of Naples which manufactured some of the most beautifully designed tiles in Europe, that Lorenzo would travel to the USA as one of his firm's sales representatives.

Lorenzo would spend a couple of days at the Mineo Tile Company learning about the colourfully unique mosaic tiles he was supposed to be selling.

Lucky arranged that Lorenzo would take the sample tiles to Simon Grant the boss of a New Jersey construction company which was in the process of building a new plush gaming casino for Unione Siciliano.

After only a few days in the USA Lorenzo would fly back to Rome carrying not only a signed order for a shipment of mosaic tiles but also Lucky's handsome quarterly pay-off from Unione Siciliano funds of quarter of a million US dollars. As an explanation if, by some unlikely mischance, he was caught carrying such a large amount of money he would also have in his pocket a slip from a New York bookmaker proving that he had won the money on a bet.

*   *   *

Tara was not happy that Luciano had press-ganged her protege into doing a job for the mob. She just hoped it was a one-off request by Lucky and after that was done Lorenzo would be free to return to his work at the bordello.

Tara passionately did not want her beloved 'Renzo to be transformed into one of Lucky Luciano's vicious hoodlums. Her maternal instincts for the lad was as deep and sincere as if was her own son.

*   *   *

It took Lorenzo nearly two weeks to obtain his passport. There were so many detailed formalities to attend to. He asked a photographer, who did work for the brothel, to take a set of passport pictures of him. Next he visited a local magistrate, Luigi Petronello, who was a regular client at Madam Tara's bordello and was on the Unione Siciliano payroll, to certify that he knew Lorenzo and that the pictures were a true likeness.

Lorenzo then went through the long-winded task of getting his birth certificate which detailed the name his mother had given him: Lorenzo Salvatore Lucania Berni. If Lucky happened to get sight of that birth certificate or Lorenzo's full name in his passport it would set the alarm bells ringing and certainly alert the gang chief that the kid was his son.

Five days later Lorenzo proudly collected his new passport and took it with him when he went to see Luciano at the Turistico Hotel the following morning. The next few days were hectic as Lorenzo was briefed and prepared by Lucky's aide, Tony Scarpone, for the forthcoming transatlantic errand.

He was sent to the USA Consulate in Naples where his visitor's visa was stamped in his new passport and Scarpone handed him his return airline tickets from Rome to New York and a letter of authorisation stating that he was a sales representative for the Mineo Tile Company of Naples.

His metal-lined brief case was specifically fitted to carry a selection of sample mosaic tiles that the firm manufactured. There were also special compartments concealed in the case where $250,000 in used and laundered bank bills would be secreted on his return journey.

A few hours before his departure from Naples airport, via Rome, enroute to New York, Lorenzo said goodbye to Tara and, careful to follow Luciano's instructions, avoided telling her what the nature of his trip to the USA was all about. Having worked for the mob herself and knowing how cruel they could be Tara was wise enough not to press him for further information.

'Look   after   yourself   'Renzo,'   she   said affectionately.

'You have been given an honour for one so young to be given a mission of importance. Just appreciate the trust that Signore Luciano has placed in you.'

Tara had been tempted to tell Lorenzo the truth about his mother. How Lucky Luciano had seduced his mother when she was a young girl, placed her in a brothel when he knew she was pregnant and then, evilly ordered that she be turned into a heroin addict thereby sentencing her to an early and horrible death.

But after much soul-searching Tara pulled back from the brink of making what could be a very dangerous disclosure for Lorenzo and herself.

'Not yet,' she muttered to herself as Lorenzo kissed her farewell. 'The time is not yet right for my dear 'Renzo to be told the truth.'

CHAPTER 22

Lorenzo wandered wide-eyed through the Duty Free area at Rome airport oblivious to the cadaverous little man in the grubby trench coat and sweat-stained fedora who followed his every move.

Lucky Luciano was satisfied with the cover-up story that he had devised for the 'mule' who would carry his quarter of a million bucks from New York to Naples. But the gangster chief was not stupid enough to let a 16-year-old boy travel half way round the world to collect a small fortune without protection.

The man delegated by Lucky to be Lorenzo's shadow was one of Unione Siciliano's toughest 'gorillas' by the name of Giovanni Castigla. With a formidable criminal record in Italy, Castigla was the elder brother of Lucky's boyhood buddy, top US mob leader Frank Costello who had changed his surname to con the underworld and the police he was of Irish extraction.

Giovanni was only 5ft 5 inches tall in his smelly socks and went to the scales at a paper-weight 60 kilos! But a diminutive stature and skeletal frame belied the fact that Giovanni was one of Unione Siciliano's most fearsome hit men on the European side of the Atlantic. Frank Costello would often boast: 'There's more fuckin' meat on a brush handle than on my brother Giovanni, yet put a shiv or a pistol in his mitt and he becomes a fuckin' tiger.'

Yet Giovanni Castigla was 'clean' as far as the FBI and the US cops were concerned having never been caught breaking the law in his three previous trips to the States which, nevertheless had resulted in three unsolved New York gangland murders.

'Keep your eye on the kid on the way out to New York,' Luciano growled his instructions. 'While he is in the USA and particularly on his way back.   If anything happens to him I'll pluck out your fuckin' eyes and use them for fuckin' ten pin bowls.

Chapter 23

Every minute of the seven-hour flight from Rome to New York was an experience to Lorenzo Berni.

The elegance and charm of the blue-uniformed air hostesses. The drinks trolley loaded with every type of alcoholic beverage. The neatly arranged meal tray with it's roast chicken dinner, apple pie and and choice of red or white wine in miniature bottles.

The occasional messages from the captain over the Pan American tannoy system informing the passengers of estimated time of arrival, weather fronts ahead and the prevailing weather in New York, where the Spring sun was encouraging an unusually flush display of cherry blossom in Central Park.

He was just finishing his breakfast of scrambled eggs when the Captain came on the tannoy again to point out on the starboard side of the aircraft the Statue of Liberty and Ellis Island.

Despite being raised in an orphanage Lorenzo was a well-read lad who had studied hard. The sight of Ellis Island looming through the clouds below conjured up visions of millions of poor Italian immigrants passing through its doors in the largest migration in history between 1892 and 1924. The Italians were not on their own, there were also Russian, Irish, German and other refugees from southern and eastern Europe.

The wonders of his trip to the New World completely dulled Lorenzo's ability to spot the wee man, in the crumpled brown suit, who had followed him at Rome airport, sitting in the aircraft ten rows behind. Although Lorenzo spoke faltering English, learned partly at the Orphanage school and partly from clients at Madam Tara's bordello, he was pleasantly surprised that the driver of the yellow taxi-cab that took him to his downtown hotel also spoke a mixture of Brooklyn slang and Italian.

'Your first visit to the Big Apple buddy?' queried the cabby using New York's nickname invented by horse racing writer John Fitzgerald in the City's "Morning Telegraph" in 1924. "Waal, Signore, you've got it all here Signorinas, booze, narcotics if go fer that kind of thing and the biggest thieves, crooks and murderers in the USA. Just watch your pocket book while you're here pal! That's my advice there's guys in this town who will slit your gullet for five bucks.'

After settling into his hotel Lorenzo, knowing that he had no commitments until the following day, took the subway to Spring Street on a quest to explore the romantic area of New York known as Little Italy. In the adjacent Mott Street he experienced smells and sights that were reminiscent of his home city of Napoli. Within a few hundred yards of each other he came across such noted restaurants as Il Fornaio's, which specialised at cooking in the style of the old country with emphasis on the baked clams and stuffed artichokes; and La Mela's a noisy eaterie which has no menu yet dishes up the greatest pasta in town on the recommendation of your personal waiter.

In neighbouring Silver Street he called into the world famous Lombardi's Ristorante which is the birthplace of New York pizza pies baked in a coal oven and featuring mozzarella and pecorino imported from the old country.

Lorenzo felt like a real man about town as he lunched at Lombardi's on a mouth watering Margharita pizza and a spaghetti with meat sauce washed down with a small carafe of white Chianti. All around him in this boisterous restaurant there were families speaking, laughing, and

90

quarelling in the Italian language. He felt very much at home.

That evening, after a brief nap in his hotel room, Lorenzo decided to explore the interesting and exciting area between New York's 41st and 53rd streets known as Broadway. His eyes goggled at the neon signs down the Great White Way advertising shows crafted by such entertainment maestros as Cole Porter, George Gershwin and Damon Runyon whose famous show Guys and Dolls was in the middle of a lengthy run that would stretch into years.

Later he dined on pastrami bagels, cheese cake and a frothy glass of beer at Jack Dempsey's bar on Broadway and was thrilled when the former heavyweight boxing champion of the world shook his hand and presented him with a signed photograph.

But always, no matter where he wandered throughout the day, there was a diminutive little figure in a brown suit and tatty trench coat following him and watching his every move.

After making sure that Lorenzo Berni was safely tucked up in bed for the night at the hotel the shadow, Giovanni Castigla took a cab across to Fulton Street to meet his younger brother, notorious gangster Frank Costello, at the Gage and Tollner restaurant. This elegant eating place with its mahogany framed mirrors and original gaslights had been serving seafood and steak to New York's famous and infamous since 1879.

'Hi there little brother!' Giovanni shouted as he spotted Costello at a corner table tackling a two-pound rib steak. An incongruous greeting considering that Frank towered 30 inches above his brother.

91

The Italian born mobster with the adopted Irish name abandoned his aggressive attack on the beef to shake Giovanni's hand: 'So you are nurse maid to Charley Luciano's mule? Well they don't call him fuckin' Lucky for nothing. He was always the man to plan a heist, or work out a cover-up story. The smartest man in the mob in the old Prohibition days.

'Charley deserves every nickel of that quarter of a million bucks for what he has done and is still doing for the mob. But there are guys in the Unione Siciliano who are jealous of Lucky and would like to dethrone him as the Capo di Tutti Capi and what is more they would not pay him a nickel now that he is exiled forever from the USA.

'You had better watch this kid Lucky has chosen to carry his dough back to Naples very, very closely. There are hoods out there who would just love to poke Lucky in the eye and take his money.'

*   *   *

The New Jersey based Grant Construction Company was 75% owned by the mob which came about when the Company's President, Simon Grant, lost $50,000 on roulette, black jack and poker at a Unione Siciliano casino based on the edge of Chinatown on Bayard Street.

Grant struggled to pay off the debt month by month but failed. He was in danger of a pistol-whipping, knifing, knee-capping, or even worse, from the Unione Siciliano thugs but finally settled the bill by handing over 75% of the Company stock to gang-lord Meyer Lansky.

Lansky, one of the young Lucky Luciano's East Side Gang with Frank Costello and Bugsy Siegel, in the Prohibition era, was known as the 'Little Man' amongst the Unione Siciliano mobsters. Despite being Jewish he was the organisation's financial guru and treasurer but the strictly Sicilian membership never granted him voting rights in the

Unione's affairs although he was a full financial partner in the mob.

Simon Grant was not entirely unhappy about losing control of his Company because his 25% slice of the take was amounting to more than his original 100% share because of the business Unione Siciliano had put his way. He had already been the main contractor in the building of the mob's new casinos in the up and coming desert play resort of Las Vegas.

Now the Simon Construction Company was engaged in building another big pleasure palace and casino less than seven miles from the famous wooden boardwalk of New York's vibrant playground at Coney Island. That is where thousands of the elegantly designed mosaic tiles, that young Lorenzo was supposedly peddling, in reality would end up as part of the plush and luxurious decor.

As arranged a gleaming chauffeur driven limousine arrived at Lorenzo's hotel promptly at 9am to take him to the Simon Construction Company's headquarters in New Jersey. Carrying his specially designed case with the sample mosaic tiles, Lorenzo, was ushered into a waiting room and a fresh cup of coffee placed in front of him.

Soon he was called into the room boldly marked 'PRESIDENT', where he was greeted with a warm handshake by Simon Grant, who was accompanied by a little man in a grey pinstripe suit.

'My name is Lansky,' said the wee man rising to his full height of 5ft 4ins. 'Meyer Lansky! I am very good friend of many years standing with your boss Mr Luciano. How is Charley Luciano? Well, I hope. He has sent you on a very important mission, which shows how much Charley Luciano trusts you.'

Lorenzo assured Mr Lansky that Mr Luciano was in the best of health.

'That's good to hear,' said the gangland chief. 'Because as I have said Charley and I go back a long way. We went to school together or rather we more often or not played hookey together.'

Before leaving the Simon Grant Construction Company's offices in the same limousine Lorenzo was handed a typewritten order to the Mineo Tile Company of Naples, Italy, for many thousands of beautiful mosaic tiles to be despatched to the new Unione Siciliano casino at Coney Island. It was a genuine enough order that would end in the substantial shipment of the elegant tiles from the port of Naples to the docks at New York.

Lorenzo was also given an oilskin package containing $250,000 and a betting slip from a New York bookmaker confirming that the money had been won on a horse called Rosie Lee which won at the Belmont track the previous afternoon with the staggering odds of 500 to one.

As the black limo sped Lorenzo back from New Jersey to his downtown New York hotel once again he never noticed the little man in the trench coat following in the yellow cab that he had booked for the day. But the alert Giovanni Gastigla, despite the massive hangover after quaffing a massive amount of his brother Frank Costello's bourbon the previous evening, spotted the black Ford roadster carrying two quite obvious hoodlums who had also been shadowing Lorenzo all day.

Costello had 'tooled' his brother up with a sawn-off shot gun that was secreted neatly underneath that tatty trench coat and a powerful automatic Luger pistol tucked into a shoulder holster.

'You fuck with my boy,' growled Castigla to himself as he eyed that sinister Ford roadster rolling along the freeway 200 yards behind the limousine carrying Lorenzo, '...and you fuck with me.'

Giovanni had killed three times before and like the old gunslingers of the Wild West would not hesitate to add a fourth notch against his name.

CHAPTER 24

Street-wise Giovanni Castigla knew that the two hoodlums who had trailed Lorenzo Berni in their Ford roadster from New Jersey to his hotel in downtown New York had not much time to make their play if they were to heist Lucky Luciano's quarter of a million bucks the lad was carrying back to Italy, only a few hours later.

He guessed that the pair of gorillas would try to make the 'hit' that evening and he also was sure that they wouldn't be too worried about whether Lorenzo was injured or killed when the robbery took place.

But who were they? Who were they working for?

To find out the answer to those two questions, after Lorenzo had gone back to his room to get ready prior to catching an early flight to Rome that night, Castigla found a pay phone in a drug store that was open day and night opposite the hotel and rang his brother, gangland boss Frank Costello.

Costello, who was a well organised big-shot with eyes and ears all around the city, rang brother Giovanni back on the drug store pay phone quarter of an hour later.

'Bad news brother, real bad,' said Costello. 'Those two torpedoes are Jack I Dragna and James Ragan. But they work for Bugsy Siegel. I certainly can't involved because Bugsy Siegel is a well connected chief in Unione Siciliano and there is an unwritten law that we never move against another member of the mob unless he is put on the spot by the Capo di Tutti Capi, Charley Luciano.'

It emerged that Bugsy Siegel, who was an original member of the young Lucky Luciano's East Side gang with Meyer

Lansky and Costello, against tradition, was holding out and refusing to hand over a racing wire service in California, which he had founded and owned, to Unione Siciliano's nationwide wire service.

So far, because of his long connection with the mob, the Unione chiefs had been lenient with Siegel and merely tried to persuade him to put his California wire service into the communal pot. But their patience was running out and there were people arguing that Luciano should order that Bugsy Siegel should be taken for a one way ride.

It was an important issue inside the organisation. The mob's wire service broadcast over its nation-wide network essential information to bookmakers all over the country about jockeys, horses, sudden switches in the betting odds and the transmission of racing results to prevent dishonest betting coups.

Siegel's insubordination by refusing to hand over his California wire service was costing the mob money. It was a situation that couldn't go on much longer.

Siegel figured that his best chance of winning this battle of wills was for a change of men at the top of the organisation. He reckoned he had as much right as Lucky Luciano to be the Capo di Tutti Capi. If he could undermine Luciano's authority and embarrass him by stealing his annual quarter of a million dollar pay-off then the rest of the mob might think it was time for a new and stronger leader to be appointed. It was a desperate throw of the dice on Siegel's part! Although Costello reiterated that he could not himself move against Siegel he would see that his brother Giovanni Castigla was provided with the right weaponry to deal with Bugsy's two 'heavies'.

'I'll send over a car with a Thompson "typewriter", a few boxes of slugs and a couple of grenades,' Costello said. 'The driver will meet you outside the drug

store in 30 minutes. Oh, brother make sure you don't
fuck this job up.'

*   *   *

Castigla moved quickly in the knowledge that there was
less than three hours left before the taxi was due at the
hotel to take Lorenzo to the airport. The gun men Jack I
Dragna and James Ragan, he figured, would either make
their play before Lorenzo got into the taxi or wheel their
Ford Roadster alongside the cab on the freeway and riddle
it with their tommy guns.

Either way Bugsy Siegel's two thugs would not be over
bothered whether Lorenzo Berni was in the line of fire as
long as they grabbed the metal-lined case containing the
$250,000 destined for Lucky Luciano in Italy.

Castigla walked briskly a few blocks from the hotel where
he had spotted a shop that sold army and navy surplus
goods and other odds and ends. He bought a brightly
designed windcheater with the Brooklyn Dodgers' baseball
logo and distinguishing white hoops on the sleeves. It was
a garish garment and he had bought it because he knew it
would be noticed.

He also bought a long blonde wig to cover his own crew cut
brown hair and a pair of dark sunglasses.

'Now I am ready to teach those two fuckin'
bastards a lesson,' he said to himself. 'May their fuckin'
souls burn in 'ell.'

*   *   *

When the time came Giovanni Castigla acted with the
timing and ruthlessness of a professional killer. Jack I
Dragna and James Ragan sat drinking coffee from paper
cups and smoking an endless chain of cigarettes in the

Ford Roadster as they waited for Lorenzo Berni to appear at the entrance of the hotel. They had parked some thirty yards back from where Lorenzo's taxi would pull in.

Their hardware, two automatic pistols and a tommy gun lay handy at their feet. Both were too engrossed in their coffee and deep inhalation of their third pack of Camels to notice the little guy in a Brooklyn Dodgers windcheater with a holdall in his hand, obviously worse from booze, tottering along the side walk past the hotel entrance towards them.

The action was sudden, violent and traumatic.

The wee man in the Dodgers' windcheater stepped off the side walk in front of the Roadster and, lifting the holdall, let blast with his Thompson machine gun through the lining of the soft case. The first salvo shattered the Roadster's windscreen in a million fragments, spilled Dragna's brains across the side window as he sat behind the steering wheel and reduced Ragan's face to a gory pulp.

Yet, as if by some ghastly fluke, there was still some life in the two would-be hit-men, Castigla pulled the ring off a hand grenade and tossed it through the shattered front window of the Ford.

Castigla, sped away as the car exploded and burst into flames, discarding the colourful windcheater in a conveniently cruising trash van and the wig and sunglasses in the pig-swill bin outside a Chinese restaurant.

Strolling now, in order not to attract attention, he calmly walked to the nearest subway station where he caught a train to Lexington Avenue and transferred to a taxi which took him to the airport.

Meanwhile a curious Lorenzo Berni wondered, as he left the hotel to catch his own taxi to the airport, what all the fuss and activity was a few yards down the street where half a dozen police cars and a fire truck, roof lights rotating, were lined up in a semi circle around the smouldering wreck of a car, and why patrolmen had taped the area off.

*   *   *

As he enjoyed his dinner aboard Pan American Flight 216 and sipped the accompanying glass of Barola, his favourite Italian wine, Lorenzo looked across the aisle and idly pondered where he had seen the little man in the brown suit before.

It was just after midnight when they landed at Rome where Lucky Luciano had arranged for his lieutenant, Tony Scarpone, to meet Lorenzo and drive him back to Naples. As they sped southwards through the night Giovanni Castigla found a pay phone and put in a call to the Turistico Hotel in Naples and spoke to Luciano, who had already been informed over the Transatlantic line that the morning newspapers were all reporting in lurid headlines of a double gangland slaying in New York.

After hearing Giovanni's report of what had happened Luciano put in lengthy calls to New York to old buddies Frank Costello and Meyer Lansky. The result of those two long distance phone calls was violently definitive.

Just 48 hours later Bugsy Siegel was relaxing on the Regency sofa in the Beverley Hills apartment he had set up for his mistress Virginia Hill who was away in Paris, France.

A masked gunman poked his pistol through the ornate drapes and blew a hole in the back of Bugsy's head,

101

making a gory mess of the Regency sofa that had been Virginia's pride and joy.

There was a big turnout of Unione Siciliano gang chiefs at the funeral, including Lansky and Costello. But the biggest floral tribute of all, a massive array of white Lillies, had been commissioned by 'old and close friend-Charley Luciano'.

As for Virginia Hill, who had decamped to Paris after being chastised by the late and lamented Bugsy for chinning another lady in the powder room of Siegel's Flamingo Room in Las Vegas, having quaffed the best part of two bottles of whiskey, she was sad.

So sad at the loss of that elegant sofa.

CHAPTER 25

On arriving at The Turistico Hotel, Naples in the early hours of the morning Lorenzo was taken up to Lucky Luciano's suite by Tony Scarpone where he handed over the oilskin package containing $250,000.

He had no idea how near his important mission had come to disaster amidst a hail of machine gun bullets.

Lucky, always a generous man when someone had done a good job on his behalf showed his gratitude by pushing five $100 bills into the delighted young man's hand. It was the most money Lorenzo had ever owned in his life and already he was hooked on the way of life the Unione Siciliano mobsters were able to lead.

The silk suits, tailored and monogrammed shirts, crocodile skin shoes and pearl grey fedoras sported by Lucky the Boss attracted him. He hoped that more work for the organisation would be put his way so that he could carry his own pistol, travel around Naples in a flash car, go to expensive nightclubs and top restaurants. In fact Lorenzo a former orphanage boy wanted to follow his father in the underworld-the Unione Siciliano's Big Boss who was still unaware that the lad was his son.

Lorenzo arrived back in the bordello at 8am after Luciano had ordered Tony Scarpone to drive him there.

Madam Tara was pleased to see him and ordered breakfast for two to be brought to her office so that he could tell her all about his trip. She was absolutely delighted with the powder compact, a coloured picture of the Empire State Building in enamel on the lid, he had bought for her in a souvenir shop just off Times Square. It was a gift that Tara would treasure for the rest of her life although her jewel box, locked away in the office wall safe, contained diamonds, pearls and several emeralds.

But her 40-minute talk with the lad revealed that her beloved Lorenzo was a young mobster in the making. It was hardly strange that a kid brought up in poverty without the help of parents, educated in the clinical and austere atmosphere of an orphanage run by monks, should hero-worship such gangland big shots as his father Lucky Luciano, Meyer Lansky, Frank Costello and the other barons of crime.

Boys brought up in poverty-stricken Naples in those hard years immediately after Italy had been crushed to defeat, alongside their Axis partner Germany, by the Allies had scant respect for the police or any other form of authority.

Having risen up the social scale herself on the wrong side of the law, from street prostitute, paid mistress of a US Army of Occupation colonel, to call girl and to her present position as Madam of Naples most exclusive brothel, Tara accepted the inevitability that Lorenzo's talents would be channeled towards criminalita organizzazione.

CHAPTER 26

Lucky Luciano's quarter of a million dollars annual cut from the combined coffers of the USA branch of Unione Siciliano was only the tip of the iceberg of the Capo Di Tutti Capi's vast fortune estimated to be $50 million in cash.

His Italian enterprises alone were also a nice earner bringing in another $1 ½ a year. Most of it was from criminal activities although he also controlled legitimate activities in confectionery and real estate.

But his lifestyle obviously had to be continually boosted by mammoth injections of folding money. Having become bored with the confinement of his luxury suite at the Hotel Turistico he bought a penthouse on 'Millionaires' Row' high up in Vomero towering above the city of Naples.

A luxury villa on the Isle of Capri was added to his portfolio, where he met and befriended the famous English singer and stage star Gracie Fields. He also owned the mortgage on a similar playboy property situated along the sun-kissed shores of the Tyrrhenian Sea.

Hard-hitting American newspaper columnist Walter Winchell reported at one time: 'Lucky Luciano has more United States greenbacks than anybody in the whole of Italy-probably more than the Italian government.'

Narcotics, vice, gambling machines, casinos, bookmaking throughout the Italian peninsula were all in the clutch of Luciano's talons despite the close surveilliance of the Carabinieri. Lucky had obviously brought with him from America his amazing talent for buying 'protection' from the cops.

He was always on the lookout and ready to recruit promising young criminals into the mob. Not as full blown members of Unione Siciliano, but on the organisation's payroll as mercenaries.

Into that category now fell young Lorenzo Berni, following his successful mission across the Atlantic.

One of Luciano's most profitable criminal ventures was the control of smuggling across the whole of the Mediterranean area. It was in this particular nefarious exercise that Lucky suddenly figured that Lorenzo could be useful to him again.

He had bought a fleet of fast boats that were smuggling much-wanted American goods into war-stricken Italy, Spain and France and making vast profits for the organisation. These countries, all with miles of coastline round the Mediterranean Ocean, trying to redeem some of their national wealth lost during World War II, charged high import duties on luxuries from the USA such as cigarettes, nylon stockings and electrical appliances.

Luciano's fleet of speedy seagoing craft, many of them war-surplus motor torpedo boats, would collect their valuable cargo of such American goods from the free port of Tangier where the gangster boss had arranged for them to be shipped from various USA harbours and secured in bonded warehouses. All perfectly legal up to that point! Luciano's flotilla would then rendezvous with cooperative fishing boats, coastal colliers, and cargo ships a few miles outside the territorial waters of Italy, Spain or France where they would be smuggled ashore and sold on the vibrant black markets in all those war-torn countries. All very illegal.

A 20 pack of Lucky Strike would cost 300 lire in official tabaccherias, including customs duty, Luciano's 20th Century smuggling organisation could afford to sell them on the streets at 200 lire a pack and still make 100% profit! But customs officials in those countries, angry at the badly needed revenue their heavily in debt governments were losing, decided to hit back. Using fast naval craft, and even spotter planes, they began patrolling the parameters of their territorial waters to stop and search every suspicious vessel.

Luciano, used to such harassing tactics from the cops when he was the USA's leading bootlegger during Prohibition days, decided to adopt various counter measures. One idea that came to him was to have an extra container welded to the bottom of his smuggling boats, which carried the contraband goods. A container that could be jettisoned by pulling a lever and sent to the bottom of the sea if stopped by a customs vessel.

'OK!,' figured the gangster boss. 'If we are caught we'll lose the cargo, which is only a fuckin' normal business write-off. But we won't have to pay a fuckin' fine or have our boat impounded.

It was at this point Lucky Luciano remembered the kid with welding skills who had served him so well, eight months previously, when he sent him as a 'mule' to collect quarter of a million bucks from the USA.

'Get hold of that kid who works as a porter at Tara's and ask him to come and see me at the villa,' was the terse instruction Lucky gave to his assistant Tony Scarpone.

*   *   *

Lorenzo was delighted at being put on the mob's permanent payroll! It was, he dreamed, the first step to becoming a gangland boss like his father Lucky Luciano.

But back at the bordello Tara was sad to lose him yet, at the same time, proud that her protege was moving up in the world! She was also pleased that with the $500 a week basic salary Lucky was paying him Lorenzo could afford to rent a compact one-bedroom apartment only just round the block from the brothel. He promised to visit Tara regularly which also helped to ease the pain she felt over his departure.

*   *   *

Luciano spelled out what he needed Lorenzo to do! He wanted his six boats converted with a quick release welded cage fitted to the hull to carry the contraband cargo of Lucky Strike, Chesterfield and Camel cigarettes, crates of nylon stockings in every shade, electric kettles, toasters and coffee makers.

The cage had to be fitted with a release lever in the wheelhouse of the boat so that it could be ejected to the bottom of the ocean if stopped by customs patrol vessels.

It was a mammoth task for a young man still not 18 years of age. But he had been taught well and absorbed brilliantly the lessons conducted by engineering tutor, Brother Thomas, at the Franciscan orphanage.

Luciano provided him with a warehouse, forge and anvil, block and tackle, dry dock facilities and all the tools he asked for. Lorenzo, shrewdly, paid a courtesy visit to the orphanage where, without divulging what the task he was embarking on was going to be used for, he asked Brother Thomas how he would set about making such a cage or basket. He hinted that it would be used on a fishing boat to keep the catch fresh until it returned to port.

Brother Thomas, who had been a highly qualified ship's engineer before entering the religious order, warmed to the request from his former pupil and drew a plan, with specifications of the necessary materials, for Lorenzo to follow.

Remembering that Brother Thomas had a sweet tooth Lorenzo showed his gratitude by presenting the kindly friar with a box of caramellas he had bought at the local negocio di dolcium earlier that morning.

*   *   *

Lorenzo studied the specifications, as laid out by Brother Thomas, and multiplied the quantity of materials required by six, and ordered them from the foundry to be delivered within the week to his warehouse workshop.

By the time the truck load of metal arrived Lorenzo had set up his forge and got it working. It took him three weeks of ten hours a day hard toil to cut the bare metal to size, shape it and weld into the six cargo cages or baskets required.

He then worked out a cable release system that would jettison the cage and its contents to the bottom of the seabed with a pull on a lever in the boat's wheelhouse.

Lorenzo asked Luciano to arrange for the six boats to call into his warehouse workshop one at time where they would be dry-docked for four or five days to have the cages fitted. It took him just over three weeks to complete the task and Lucky was pleased with the result! Lorenzo then ordered extra metal from the foundry and made several more cages as spares.

One day Lucky Luciano invited Lorenzo to join him on one of the boats to test the equipment. A couple of divers in wet suits dived under the boat in turn filling the cage with rocks as a stand-in for the contraband cargo it would normally carry.

Skipper, Umberto Mazza, steered the boat at speed several miles beyond Italy's territorial waters where, without another vessel on the horizon, Lucky tapped the sailor on the shoulder- a signal to pull the lever. It worked perfectly and , as they looked over the side of the boat, they could not see a ripple or bubble as the cage sunk slowly to the bottom of the ocean.

'Now the fuckin' cops won't be able to pin anythin' on us,' laughed Lucky illustrating that, to him, all government officials, customs, treasury, FBI or narcotics, were all 'fuckin' cops'.

CHAPTER 27

Lorenzo had done such a good job making and installing the cages that Lucky Luciano asked him if would like to work on one of the boats for a while to gain some experience.

'I would like that very much Signore,' Lorenzo told his father. 'In fact I had been thinking about taking an evening course in engineering at the Napoli Technical College in engineering.'

That statement pleased Luciano. It was a plan that could be more than useful to the mob's smuggling activities.

'That is a good idea,' said the delighted gang chief. 'In fact I will not only pay your fees to take the course but I will give you a bonus of one thousand bucks if you pass your exams and get your degree.'

Lorenzo, needing no incentive to study a subject he was intensely interested in, that morning went along to the Technical College to enrol in the engineering course that was due to start the following week. It was a two year course that would demand several evenings a week attendance, leaving little time for girls, dancing or other pastimes most young men were interested in.

*   *   *

Lorenzo was signed on as crewmember of Luciano's smuggling vessel, the Annunciare Bianco (White Herald), under the command of Skipper Umberto Mazza and was immediately involved in a multi-million dollar business.

Inevitably a racket that produced a profit of $15,000, for each voyage across the Mediterranean from Tangier to just outside the territorial waters of Spain, France or Italy, was not without problems. With six boats, making at least one trip a week, fully loaded in the release cages fixed on the hull, the organisation was grossing $4 ½ million dollars a year from smuggling. Lucky Luciano's personal cut was around $1 million.

So whatever the risks, they were worth taking. Although it was the crews of his boats who were taking the risks rather than Lucky who, as usual, covered his tracks so no official finger could be pointed at him.

There were still a number of independent racketeers working the Mediterranean smuggling route until Lucky Luciano decided to take over! Just as the old Mafia gangs established a monopoly in rum running in the USA during Prohibition, Luciano, a top bootlegger himself in the 1920's, set about eliminating any competition in the smuggling racket.

There was no question that the Capo Di Tutti Capi would use legitimate business methods to wipe out the opposition. He had a much more permanent solution.

That is why every crewmember, from skipper to deck hand, on his six smuggling boats was armed. Like the rest of his shipmates Lorenzo was issued with a pistol while in a locked cupboard in the captain's cabin a rack of assault rifles, tommy guns and grenades were stacked.

*   *   *

For some months Lucky Luciano had received intelligence that Oasis, a 260 ton freighter, under the captaincy of Jack Connor, renegade Irish sailor who had once run guns to the Republican army in the bloody Spanish Civil War, was profitably plying the Mediterranean smuggling routes.

Unione Siciliano spies reported to Lucky that the Oasis was on permanent charter to Signore Bernardo Jiminez, already a wealthy man in the export-import business, who was doing very nicely with smuggling on the side.

Lucky sent his emissary Tony Scarpone to Tangier to persuade Signore Jiminez that he was foolish to compete with the organisation in smuggling operations across the Mediterranean region. Scarpone made it clear that Signore Luciano was annoyed that the Oasis was trading contraband in Unione Siciliano territory. This had to stop forthwith or Signore Jiminez might suddenly learn the freighter he charted had suddenly sprung a leak and sunk with all its cargo to the bottom of the 'Med'.

Arrogantly choosing to ignore Luciano's warning, Jiminez ordered the Oasis's normal load of building materials to be boosted by more profitable 'goodies' from the USA. This increased the value of the cargo, bound according to the ship's papers for Malta, by a mind boggling $20,000.

It was easy to understand why Unione Siciliano could not simply ignore such blatant defiance of what they considered to be their monopoly.

The sailing of Oasis, ostensibly on a legal voyage but with her hold half full of contraband goods, was relayed to the furious Luciano who immediately busied himself giving instructions over the phone.

Luciano chose his smuggling craft Annunciare Bianco, with Lorenzo aboard, as the clenched fist to put Bernardo Jiminez, the defiant charterer of Oasis, in his place. It was to be a gory lesson to anyone else thinking of challenging the long and powerful arm of Unione Siciliano.

The Oasis was knifing through becalmed Mediterranean waters a few miles off the coast of Spain in the early hours of a dark July night. Except for those on watch most of the crew, including skipper Jack Connor, were asleep in their bunks below. Even the gritty-eyed lookout failed to see the sleek shape of the Annunciare Bianco, showing no navigation lights, sliding alongside the larger vessel.

After slinging boarding ladders over the side of the Oasis, Umberto Mazza, led all but one of the crew of Annunciare Bianco, armed with tommy guns, and took over the rival ship by storm.

Two men were despatched below and brought up Captain Jack Connor and the sleeping watch at gunpoint. Mazza and the other men, including Lorenzo, rounded up the duty watch. There was only one show of resistance when German Kirk Gurke, who was at the wheel while his skipper slumbered below, reached for the pistol that was secreted in a drawer in the wheel house.

Lorenzo, who had never fired a gun in earnest before and had only practised by shooting at floating pieces of flotsam from the side of the Oasis, spotted Gurke's knee-jerk action and instinctively let loose a sharp burst of fire from the tommy gun slung round his shoulder.

Gurke, who took the whole salvo in his stomach, stood for seconds, eyes glazed in disbelief at what had happened, was dead before he slid slowly down the wheel house wall to the floor.

Lorenzo was dumbstruck with shock and horror at what he had done! He felt nauseated, as most men do when they have killed for the first time. His stock in the opinion of his boss and unknowing father, Lucky Luciano, would go up several notches. Any young man who could kill callously and quickly, at the twitch of an eyebrow, was an excellent recruit for the mob.

Skipper Mazza ordered his men to tie up the entire Oasis crew and lock them in number two hold. Then came the task of transferring all the contraband cigarettes, nylon stockings, electric toasters and coffee machines to Lucky's boat, which was secured alongside the Oasis. It took hours to get all the goods aboard the smaller vessel. The legitimate cargo Oasis carried in number one hold, of cement, bricks, roof tiles and scaffolding, all bound for Malta, was left untouched as the Annunciare Bianco did not have enough capacity to carry such a heavy load. Lorenzo, still shaking from the thought he had killed a man for the first time, was totally aghast at the next order he and the other members of 'Bianco's' crew received from their captain.

'There are 20 drums of kerosene tied aft,' growled Mazza. 'Pour it all over the ship below and above deck, in the companionways, galley and engine room.'

The smell of kerosene was overpowering as Captain Mazza ordered his men to get back on board Annunciare Bianco, tied alongside. With, throttle on full ahead, the grinning Mazza pulled out a signal pistol and fired at the deck of Oasis. A line of flame quickly sped from fore to aft of the stricken ship. Then, as a final evil gesture, Mazza pulled the firing pin on two grenades and tossed them aboard the blazing Oasis. The accelerating Annunciare Bianco, prow lifted above the water, powered clear of the deafening explosions that followed.

'Holy Mother of God,' agonised the traumatised Lorenzo to himself. 'That makes ten men dead-including the guy I shot.'

There was little time for recrimination as Captain Mazza pointed Annunciare Bianco towards the island of Majorca only 20 miles away, while on the horizon, as dawn broke across the placid waters of the Mediterranean, there was only a fading wisp of smoke to show that Oasis ever existed.

Skipper Mazza, after a lengthy ship to shore radio telephone call, steered Annunciare Bianco into waters just outside the Balearic island's picturesque Puerto Andraxt where, by arrangement, they rendezvoused with a huge motor yacht originally registered in Southampton.

More than 300 cases of Lucky Strike cigarettes and five crates of nylon stockings were put aboard the yacht in exchange for two suitcases crammed with English five-pound notes. Within two hours Mazza had pointed 'Bianco's' prow out to sea before the Spanish police, customs officials or coastguard officers had a chance to catch up with them to enquire the purpose of their visit to Majorca.

Now Lucky Luciano could add 'piracy of the high seas' to his portfolio of criminal activities yet, as usual, he had not been within several hundred miles of the terrible destruction of the Oasis and the terrifying deaths of all her crew.

The next port of call for Annunciare Bianco was the island of Corsica where the remainder of the contraband, taken from the ill-fated Oasis, was transferred to a Portugese fishing vessel in exchange for a sack full of escudos.

*   *   *

Later on the very morning that the blazing inferno that was once the good ship Oasis sank slowly to the bottom of the ocean a messenger handed in a parcel at a top Tangier hotel addressed to Signore Bernardo Jiminez.

When Jiminez, still in his gaudy silk pyjamas, curiously and impatiently tore away the brown paper wrapping he dropped the parcel in sheer horror and fright! There, spreading an ugly stain across the delcately embroidered quilt, was the bloody head of a sheep slaughtered a few hours earlier at the local mattatoio. The lolling tongue

116

added to the macabre scene-it was severed in half. The message accompanying the gruesome package was clear enough: 'Do not fuck with us again or your tongue will be the next to feel the knife.'

Jittery Jiminez was in doubt, as he rushed to bathroom to vomit, that the gory dono had come from Lucky Luciano the powerful head of Unione Siciliano. He decided there and then to retire from the export-import business and immigrate to Brazil.

Port authorities in Tangier, Interpol and insurance investigators from Lloyds of London could not find a shred of evidence towards solving the mysterious disappearance of the Oasis with all hands.

It was not until nearly three years later that a charred lifebelt, bearing the blurred letters ' *AS *S', washed ashore, ironically, in Palma-de-Mallorca did a possible clue emerge-by then it was too late.

If Lucky Luciano could not exactly claim the name Neptune he was now widely acknowledged as the menacing Monarch of the Mediterranean.

CHAPTER 28

Young Lucky Luciano and his best pal Frank Costello were playing 'hookey' from Public School 19 in the teeming Lower East Side of New York and discussing a story that had appeared in a brightly coloured boys' comic.

'This guy Robin Hood was an outlaw in Nottingham, England, years ago, who used to steal from the rich and give all the money he had stolen back to the poor people,' said Costello.

Luciano retorted sarcastically: 'the guy must have been a stupid 'crum'! What fuckin' hood would be fool enough to give away the loot he had just stolen? I tell yer Frank I just don't fuckin' believe it!'

Costello, angry that Luciano should doubt the yarn, argued: 'Believe it or not but this guy Robin ran such a powerful mob that the Sheriff of Nottingham put a big price on his head. He was Public Enemy Number One over there in England-that's how fuckin' real he was!'

* * *

No one will ever know whether the yesteryear legend of Robin Hood the outlaw sparked a train of thought in the agile mind of gangster chief Lucky Luciano when he was having a drink with half a dozen local Unione Siciliano mobsters in Palermo, Sicily, five decades later.

Aldo Caramusa, a chief from the bandit-infested hills in the north west of Sicily, told the rest of the assembled party of gangsters how the owners of the sulphur mine, near the town of Lercara Friddi, where Luciano had been born in 1897, collected the cash to pay the miners' wages from the local bank. They would then lock away the lire

119

equivalent of $70,000, in a steel cabinet every Friday night, guarded only by an ageing night watchman.

'The bastards must be fuckin' mad,' said Caramusa, who was in his cups after quaffing nearly two bottles of chianti and several glasses of grappa. 'If it wasn't for the miners, who God knows are poorly enough paid as it is, I'd take my lads and hijack that pay roll one night! But it would only hurt the families of the town who are struggling to get enough to eat!'

It was then that Lucky Luciano came up with an inspirational idea that would have tickled the imaginations of the legendary Little John, Friar Tuck, Robin Hood and the rest of the merry men of Sherwood Forest.

'Aldo, amico mio, you've just given me an idea,' grinned Lucky. 'I owe that fuckin' blood-suckin' sulphur mine a kick in the testicolos. Mio padre worked for those bastardos nearly 60 years ago and didn't earn enough to pay the steamship fares to America for the family, though we all travelled in the sweatholes of steerage class. So he had to go heavily in debt to borrow the money for our tickets and had to work hard in America to pay the loan back. So I really owe those motherfuckers!

'The ordinary people of this island of Sicily have always been supportive of those of us who belong to Unione Siciliano-they never squeal on us when the cops come asking questions! They know we all come from the same stock as them and have all, at one time, felt the pangs of hunger and the humiliation of unemployment and slave wages when we did find a job!
'I say we of the Unione should repay the loyalty of the people. Let's heist that payroll, boot the owners of the sulphur mine up the ass and use the money to buy food, drink and luxuries for the good people of Lercara Friddi!'

There was a buzz of excitement amongst the hard-nosed bunch of thieves, murderers, kidnappers, smugglers and drug dealers!

Aldo Caramusa, the local bandit who had sparked off the vibrant discussion, chipped in again: 'My men learned that the old night-watchman begins his tour of the mine at nine o' clock every night.   It takes him 90 minutes to do the tour of premises and sheds where the sulphur is assessed and sorted.   He locks the office, where the steel cabinet, which holds the payroll over night, is kept, before setting off on his rounds.

'Any gang doing the heist would have to get through the office door which is secured by two Chubb locks, and then break into the strong steel cabinet which is held by two metal bars in brackets and four strong padlocks.   All that in 90 minutes if there is to be no confrontation with the nightwatchman who is 64 and due to retire in three months. It would require the skills of a good locksmith to work that quickly!'

Lucky considered Caramusa's assessment carefully, then, thinking of Lorenzo, he said: 'I have just the lad who could do that job.   He's clever with locks and using an acetylene torch and proved his worth to the mob when he chilled one of our enemies with a Tommy gun recently.

'As Aldo said the job would need to be done in 90 minutes.   I wouldn't want any harm to come to that old night watchman.   He'll be in enough trouble with those bastardo mine owners any way, in which case it will be up to us to give him a nice nest egg for his forthcoming retirement!'

Aldo Caramusa, obviously approving of Lucky's usual shrewd planning, added: 'It's a deal Charley Luciano! You supply the break-in artiste and I will give you four of my toughest men and a fast getaway car to back him up.'

Then, with a wry smile and a wink to every man in the room, Caramusa said: 'although I must say it is the first caper I have ever participated in and given the entire haul away. I wouldn't want the word to get round or it might spoil my reputation!'

So in the smoke filled back room of a Palermo tavern the blue print of one of the most unusual robberies in the history of the notorious and sinister Unione Siciliano was drawn up. Back in Naples, where that evening he was attending his engineering class at the local technical college, Lorenzo Berni was unaware that another chapter was about to be added to his curriculum vitae of crime!

CHAPTER 29

There was never a question that Lorenzo Berni would travel from Naples to Sicily by a normal public transport route requiring a traceable ticket-that applied to both airline and sea ferry services.

It was real cloak and dagger stuff when Lucky Luciano's aide, Tony Scarpone, drove him in the boss's new Lincoln limousine, imported from the USA and still carrying California plates, to an isolated beach a few miles along the coast from Naples.

There he was put aboard a fast former British motor torpedo boat to make an equally clandestine disembarkment on a lonely shoreline on the northwest corner of the island of Sicily. Aldo Caramusa sent a car and two of his hoods to collect Lorenzo and his heavy luggage which included a portable acetylene burner and a set of tools.

He was quickly sped to the bandit chief's hideout in the Sicilian hill country. A former hunting lodge, the hideout was well appointed, with every modern convenience possible, and secreted in a wooded area that the police had so far never discovered. The theory amongst the bandits was that the cops, who had lost several gunfire battles in the hills, were frightened that trying to storm Aldo Caramusa's heavily defended citadel would prove to be too costly for the forces of law and order.

Lorenzo was extended lavish hospitality. A dinner of wild boar, shot the previous day, roasted slowly over a spit and accompanied by sweet potatoes and wild asparagus was washed down by an excellent Sicilian wine.

After dinner Caramusa showed Lorenzo a plan of the sulphur mine's offices which would be raided around 9 pm the following evening after the night watchman had started his rounds.

'We don't expect any problems but bring your "rod" with you, just in case,' said the bandit chief. 'My men are all experienced shots and will be carrying tommy guns and pistols. But Lucky Luciano said you know how to use a gun yourself and have already made your mark working for the organisation.'

Lorenzo had long since recovered from the trauma of killing the sailor during the piratical hijack of the ship Oasis and now actually enjoyed the kudos that he had earned amongst other members of the mob for his impromptu action.

After a hearty breakfast of ham, from the same wild boar on which he feasted the previous night, and a plateful of fried eggs, Lorenzo spent the rest of the day checking his tool kit was in order for the work ahead.

*   *   *

With headlights switched off Lorenzo and his four rugged bodyguards, Gino, Rafael, Umberto and Giovanni, drove to within a mile of the sulphur mine.

The driver, Umberto who was ordered to stay with the car and have the engine warmed up half an hour later, had parked it in a convenient coppice which was concealed from the roadway.

It took Lorenzo, with the other three of Caramusa's men helping, to carry his gear, quarter of an hour to reach the fence that surrounded the sulphur mine. Eight snips from Lorenzo's wire cutters and a hefty push made an opening large enough for the four raiders to crawl through. As they crouched behind one of the railed trucks that were used to cart the mined sulphur they were delighted to see the elderly night watchman leave the company offices to begin his regular security round.

They had just less than ninety minutes to complete their mission. It took Lorenzo fifteen of those precious minutes to pick the two especially strong Chubb locks on the office door. Once in the office Lorenzo viewed the steel cabinet where the payroll was kept. He quickly decided that the fastest way to gain access into the cabinet was to cut away the brackets that held the metal bars complete with their four padlocks. Out came his acetylene burner and 30 minutes later the cabinet doors were opened and there, in front of their eyes, were the piles of lire notes to the value of USA $70,000. Half of their allotted time had gone so the three bandits flung the money into the three mail sacks, they had carried with them, while Lorenzo packed his tools.

It took the four men another nail-biting 20 minutes to carry the sacks loaded with money and Lorenzo's heavy tools to get to the hole in the fence and cover the 200 yards to the appointed spot where Umberto had the car, engine purring smoothly, waiting for them.

With time to spare, quarter of an hour later they had put ten miles between them and the sulphur mine. Within another ten minutes they arrived at the beach where it was arranged that Lorenzo would rendezvous with the boat that sped him, and the night's haul, back to Naples.

They had pulled off the most 'gallant' heist in the violent criminal history of the notoriously murderous Unione Siciliano without harming a soul. A caper that would have warmed the hearts of the Merry Men of Sherwood Forest.

The good people of the sulphur mining town of Lercara Friddi were in for a very pleasant surprise that would make the mine owners, the local police and the Carabinierie a laughing stock for many years to come.

CHAPTER 30

Josef Gabbadini had been Sindaco of the Sicilian sulphur mining town of Lercara Friddi for the past four years.

Four years since he had retired from the local bank, where he had worked as office boy, clerk, assistant manager and finally manager for more than 40 years, apart from serving for a short period in the pay corps of Mussolini's army before being invalided out of the military because of recurring stomach ulcers. His election as Mayor by the vast majority of the town's fourteen thousand inhabitants was the final jewel in his career of service to the public of which he was very proud. It emphasised that he was liked and trusted by business men, shop keepers, local farmers and the calloused miners who worked hard under atrocious conditions for so little pay. It was his sympathy with the downtrodden working men that fired his understanding of why so many of them had turned their back on toiling for a pittance to enhance the mine owners' wealth, and then to take up crime.

The fearless local hoodlums and bandits of the Unione Siciliano trusted him. They knew they would get a fair deal and confidentiality when they 'laundered' stolen money through his bank. The mob showed respect for him by placing the elegant three bed-roomed villa he built on the outskirts of town out of bounds to any burglar, safe cracker, petty thief or kidnapper in the ranks of the otherwise ruthless Unione Siciliano.

Sindaco Josef Gabbadini was in the civic offices looking through the town's ailing finances one day when his phone rang.

'Signore Sindaco I think you will recognise my voice as we have met a couple of times in the past...' said the person on the end of the line, speaking in the Italian language with a distinguishable American accent, before being interrupted by the distinguished civic dignitary.

Throwing all caution to the wind His Honour, Mayor Gabbadini, excitedly blurted out: 'Signore Luci....' before being interrupted abruptly himself.

The hoarse voice with the American accent barked back: 'Signore Sindaco-no names please. At no time must my name be associated with the matter I am about to discuss with you! This is a Unione Siciliano affair and the organisation would not take kindly to anyone who compromised their cover.

   'Four lorry loads of food, drink and luxury goods will be delivered to the Mayor's Office in Lercara Friddi in one week's time I would like you to organise the distribution of these things, on an equitable basis, to every adult person in the town. If the police ask questions, the donor wishes to be anonymous. Capisce?

   'One other matter Signore Sindaco a messenger will be delivering five thousand U.S dollars to you in a few days time. Please see that this is given to the old night watchman who has just been so unfairly sacked by the sulphur mine owners. Tell the old chap this is to help in his retirement.'

Lucky Luciano had made the phone call to Sindaco Gabbadini only a few hours after being arrested, questioned, and released for the lack of evidence as the criminal suspected of master minding the sulphur mine robbery in Lercara Friddi.

   'Why should I want to organise a heist for a fuckin' miserable seventy grand?' Luciano angrily asked Inspector Berti Di Giacoma of the Guardia de Finanza-Italy's post war Secret Service. 'I lose more than that at the race track every year.'

There was nothing unusual about Lucky being the main suspect when a major crime was committed in those days. As usual, the cool Capo Di Tutti Capi of the powerful Unione Siciliano had covered himself with a cast-iron alibi. On the very night of the sulphur mine payroll robbery Luciano was seen by several influential people dining in Capri, at a high-class restaurant, with Ex-King Farouk of Egypt.

At a nearby table sat popular British music hall star, comedienne and singer Gracie Fields with three friends. The head waiter could have testified, if necessary, that Signore Luciano, with a typically gracious gesture, ordered three bottles of Krug champagne to be sent across to Gracie's table with his compliments. At the table with Lucky and the obese ex-ruler of Egypt was a police inspector, seconded by the Rome government to protect Farouk while he was on Italian soil, and his own gigantic Ethopian personal bodyguard.

Later that evening, in the privacy of the villa the ex-king had rented for himself and his royal entourage, Luciano had struck a business deal with Farouk who agreed that the Unione Siciliano boss could 'launder' his 'hot' earnings from crime through the former royal's Swiss bank account. After the deduction of a reasonable amount of interest, of course.

Questioned by newspapermen after his arrest and release the indignant Luciano told the world: 'The fuckin' cops keep trying to pin something on me but they can't. I know nothin' about any fuckin' robbery in Lercara Friddi. My lawyer says that the next time the cops try to frame me I should fuckin' sue them.
　　　　'I might fuckin' just do that.'

CHAPTER 31

Josef Gabbadini, the highly respected Sindaco of Lercara Friddi, moved quickly into action only minutes after receiving the phone call from Lucky Luciano, the town's benefactor whose name he had sworn not to disclose.

He rang the local printer and ordered 3,000 hand bills-one for each household in the town-stating that he was declaring a Festa on the Thursday of the following week when there would be gifts for everyone, dancing, singing, feasting and drinking in the town square.

He then arranged with the local school for 30 of their ten-year-old pupils to deliver the handbills throughout the town the following day. For the next seven days there was an air of expectancy throughout Lercara Friddi.

Up at the sulphur mine the owners, still smarting about the payroll robbery, objected to the Mayor declaring a Festa without first consulting them as the biggest employer in the town. As far as they were concerned no miner would be given the time off to enjoy the festivities so high-handedly organised by Sindaco Gabbadini. In fact they pompously proclaimed that any of their workers who did not report for work on that day would be immediately fired! The owners of the sulphur mine had made an error of judgement which would light a fuse of militancy amongst their down trodden employees who, at a meeting in a local school hall, decided that for the first time they would act in unison.

They would take the day off en masse.

One out all out–was the unprecedented decision of the 246 miners present underlined by the chairman of the meeting, who said: 'As for threatening us all with the sack let's see how the bastardos manage to run their mine without any workers.'

So the seeds were sown of the first ever trade union of workers employed by the Lercara Friddi sulphur mine. Life would never again be so easy for the penny pinching slave masters who owned the mine.

*   *   *

The town square was ablaze with bunting that only ever appeared on New Years Day, the Festa Tre Re on 6 January each year, Easter Day, and the town's Patron Saint's Day.

Trestle tables were laid out like a military parade across the square, with chairs lined up each side. In one corner the town's four bakers had set up an enormous pan in which they had collaborated in making the 'biggest pizza pie ever seen in Lercara Friddi.'

There were delicious tortas of every flavour, apple, chocolate, apricot, cream and jams. Wine was set up in huge barrels.

The bambinos, always central players in any Sicilian family party, were not forgotten. There were lollipops of every shade in the rainbow, popcorn, bubble gum-real American bubble gum-candies, chocolates and sherbert.

Some of the older women even put on their traditional Sicilian national costumes to mark the occasion. On the steps of the town hall and civic offices the local band played popular airs and later music for dancing in the square when the trestle tables and chairs were cleared.

But the highlight of the whole event was the Grand Draw featuring a huge revolving drum, turned manually by handle, containing the number and street of every house in the town.

It took nearly two hours for the Mayor to complete the draw and there were gasps of joy and amazement as each house was drawn and matched against an identical drum containing a list of prizes which were drawn by the parish priest. What magnificent prizes they were too.

There were huge uncooked hams, and mouth watering cured Parma prosciuttos, bottles of tomato paste, all varieties of dry pasta, spaghetti, lasagne, vermecilli, gnochhi and macaroni. There was flour by the sackful for those who preferred to make their own pasta. There were plump chickens, pheasants ready for plucking and a parade of fattened turkeys that would have softened the heart of Scrooge in Charles Dickens' novel.

There was a fanatasy of formaggio! Gigantic cartwheels of Parmesan, the crowning glory of the great pasta dishes; truckles of gorganzolas as blue-veined as any entry in Debrett; ceramic bowls filled with the unique masacarpone, a full-fat soft cheese often used for desserts.

There was fruit from the four corners of the Italian peninsula. Apples, grapes, plums, pears, peaches, oranges and grapefruit all were oozing the goodness of Italy's lush farmland and orchards.

There was asparagus by the bundle, strings of fat garlic cloves, onions clad in white, red and brown wafer thin skins and every herb that any Italian cook could desire to add spice to their work.

There was a veritable flood of the best vino. Out of the drum were drawn tickets that sent bottles, from some of Italy's finest vignetos, of Barolo, Valpolicella, Frascatti and the delightful, and well named Est Est Est, to humble homes where normally only the cheapest and roughest peasant wines were drunk.

But the biggest oohs and ahs were for the electrical goods, all made in the USA, as they were drawn out of the drum. The new owners of electric toasters, kettles and food mixers would be the envy of their neighbours in this poverty stricken Sicilian community.

Finally, when Sindaco Gabbadini made the final speech of gratitude to the anonymous benefactor who had footed the bill for the magnificent Festa, the name Signore Lucky Luciano was whispered from person to person despite the presence of the local police.

The hard working people of Lercara Friddi were not stupid and had no doubts that Signore Luciano, the Comendare of Unione Siciliano, was the man they owed their thanks to. Who else? The irate owners of the sulphur mine were in a terrible quandary when their entire work force failed to turn up for three days. In the end they had to meet the miners' leaders and agree to withdraw the threat of dismissals and pay the men for the three days they had absented themselves, in recompense for an immediate return to work.

Lucky Luciano, mobster, murderer, drug dealer, smuggler and brothel keeper, had struck a blow for industrial relations in the town where he had been born! Two months later Luciano was delighted with the package he received from Mayor Josef Gabbadini. It contained the tiny gold and enamel badge of the newly formed Lercara Friddi Sulphur Miners' Union and the message from the Sindaco saying: 'I have been asked to pass this emblem on to you as a token that you have been elected as the Honorary President of the new Union.' Lucky wore that little badge in his lapel with great pride for many months afterwards.

CHAPTER 32

Lorenzo Berni was surprised to get a call from Tony Scarpone early one morning to say that the boss wanted to see him immediately at the villa.

There was a further instruction that Lorenzo was to take an overnight case with him.

'Hi there kid. How ya doin'?' was the warm greeting when Tony Scarpone escorted him to the dining room where Lucky Luciano was eating his breakfast of ham and eggs. The Boss was obviously in a good mood! 'Sit down! Have some coffee.

'We're going to Sicily on the midday ferry. OK kid? Tony will drive the Lincoln and take it on the ferry with us. Tonight we'll stay at a hotel in Palermo and Tony will drive the three of us to Lercara Friddi.'

Lorenzo's eyes lit up with curiosity as he eagerly asked: 'Another job Boss?'

'Not really kid!' smiled Lucky. 'This will be more like a pleasure trip, although we will be doing some business while we are there.'

After breakfast Lorenzo was ordered to help Tony Scarpone and the gardener to hoist a heavy bale into the huge trunk of the Lincoln limousine. They only managed to squeeze it in by securing the lid of the trunk down with electric flex.

Lorenzo was inevitably curious what the bale contained but he knew better than to ask questions.

The trip to Palermo was uneventful. A calm ferry crossing from Naples followed by an excellent dinner in their hotel saw them motoring up to meet their old friend, local

Unione Sicilano Don and bandit chief, Aldo Caramusa, at his mountain hideout.

Caramusa welcomed Luciano and Lorenzo warmly and said: 'Let's go and take a look what is going on down at Lercara Friddi today. It's the day of their big Festa and the day when we will see our reward for the payroll heist at the sulphur mine.'

Aldo Caramusa joined Lucky, Tony Scarpone and Lorenzo in the Lincoln while his two guardi del corpo followed in a Fiat sedan. They stopped at a ledge, just off the, road where they had a clear view of the festivities going on below in the Town Square at Lercara Friddi.

Scarpone produced two pairs of powerful US Army field glasses from the glove cupboard in the dashboard. Lucky was delighted with the sight of the townspeople enjoying the luxuries that had been provided with the cash from the payroll robbery.

'There you are kid,' said Luciano, handing Lorenzo his field glasses.

'Take a look at what you and Aldo's men made possible with that smooth heist at the sulphur mine! At the same time we taught those fuckin' mine owners a lesson they will never forget.'

Lorenzo was elated with what he saw through the field glasses and felt proud that Luciano and Caramusa now treated him as a fully-fledged member of the mob. He realized that he liked being a member of the gang and thought to himself that he had never liked a man as much as he admired Lucky. He wondered that maybe he should have ignored Tara's advice not to reveal to Lucky Luciano that he was his son.

*   *   *

Later that evening at Aldo Caramusa's mountain hideout Luciano ordered that the huge bale in the trunk of the Lincoln limousine be carried into the house for their host to see.

'This is a new racket which will bring us in a lot of quick bucks and I want you to handle the Sicilian end of it.' Lucky told Caramusa.

The sacking and waterproof paper covering the huge bale was ripped away and the contents strewn across the floor. They were all old clothes, men's, womens' and childrens' clothes-only some of them were not so old even although they were all hand-me-downs from the USA.

Luciano smiled wryly, Lorenzo was puzzled, Aldo Caramusa so dumbfounded that he could only blurt out: 'What the hell? What fuckin' crum is going to pay a million bucks for that crap–it's only worth a place on the trash cart.'

Lucky, still grinning broadly, added to the confusion when he said: 'I've had 5,000 of them bales shipped over from the States.'

Then, without further ado, he illustrated just why he remained the all-powerful Capo Di Tutti Capi, on both sides of theAtlantic, of the sinister Crime International organisation known as Unione Siciliano.

During the austerity post war years in defeated and poverty-stricken Italy there was a desperate shortage of clothes, he explained, particularly amongst the lower class poorer people in the south of the country.

Luciano, with his shrewd mind for business, saw the opportunity for the mob to make a quick financial killing by capitalising on the desperate shortage of trousers, shirts, jackets, dresses, blouses and skirts. In fact any garment that could be worn by adult or child.

'You ask who will buy those 5,000 bales of second hand clothes which cost me two hundred bucks a bale,' said the gangland boss. 'Well, I'll tell you who is going to buy them at $500 a bale it is the market traders all across Italy. They are going to buy them and make a profit for themselves and us.

'The traders will put the old clothes on their stalls and let the public rummage for bargains at five dollars a time. Working girls about to get married could find a dress for their trousseau, the street corner lads will search and will sometimes find a hand-sewn jacket discarded by some New York dandy, mothers with several kids will rovistare through the stalls looking for junior sizes at knock-down prices. Some bales will be better than others-but that will be a matter of luck.

'Of course there is the possibility that some second hand clothes traders might not want to accept our offer. If that is the case they must be "persuaded" by a rap across the napper with a baseball bat, a pistol slug behind the knee cap or by torching their stall if they are really stubborn. Word will soon get around that we mean business.

'As I have said you, Aldo Caramusa, and your men, will take care of all the street markets that are held on different days of the week in Sicily. While you Lorenzo will be in charge of this matter throughout the Italian peninsula with the help of three of the mob's heavies.'

Lorenzo was delighted with his promotion and rise up the echelon of the organisation. He felt rather like a student aviation pilot who, after month's of dual control flying with an instructor next to him in the cockpit of the training 'plane, was sent up to make his first solo flight. He knew he would be judged on his performance.

Bandit chief Aldo Caramusa made no secret of his admiration for his Capo Di Tutti Capi and said: 'Don Luciano, I raise my hat. You are the master planner! It is a great scheme.

'Most market traders will jump at the chance to earn extra money particularly if we offer them protection and a promise to "discourage" rival second hand clothes dealers. If they don't we'll lean on them.'

*   *   *

Luciano, once again meticulously careful to distance himself from a racket that he had schemed, had the shipment of five thousand bales of second hand clothing from the USA stored in a massive warehouse the organisation owned on the Naples water front.

Lorenzo, who had developed something akin to hero worship for his father, began the operation to supply the market traders with bales of cast-off American gear the following week.

Luciano had provided him with a Mercedes limousine, which although not new was still an impressive vehicle in a war ravaged land where rusting wrecks were the norm and new cars almost a rarity.

There were pockets of resistance, of course, but within three months he had placed 2,500 bales, at $500 a time, around the country. It was how he dealt with any market trader daring, or foolish, enough to buck the tough Unione Siciliano that he would be judged by his father and the other Dons who ruled the mob under Luciano.

There were no problems in the city of Naples where many people regularly caught glimpses of Lucky Luciano the legendary Capo Di Tutti Capi with the fearsome reputation.

139

Lorenzo set off on his tour over the rest of Italy accompanied by one of the three heavies assigned to him by Luciano. The other two mobsters followed in a huge covered lorry stacked from floor to roof with bales. The first sign of dissent from the market traders came in Milan where the local czar of the second hand clothes trade Frederico Mazza said that his business was doing alright without taking a chance on what might or might not be in the bales Lorenzo was peddling.

Mazza spit on the ground in the market place when Lorenzo warned him that Unione Siciliano would be very displeased at his defiance. That night the warehouse where Mazza stored all his stock for the Milan markets was torched-not one garment escaped the blaze not even a single sock! That same morning a scruffy Milano urchin delivered a package to the distraught Mazza containing the gory tongue of a dead sheep-the time honoured warning, handed down from the Mafia days, that anyone who 'squealed' on Unione Siciliano would not have long to live.

The following day the frightened Mazza renewed the stock he had lost in the fire by handing Lorenzo a bundle of grubby lire bills. They represented $1,500 USA, for three bales of American hand-me-downs that were delivered inside the hour by Lorenzo's rugged assistants.

There was an amusing sequel to this when a week later the chastened Mazza, having quickly sold the contents of the three bales and made a good profit, contacted Lorenzo and asked if he could buy another supply of cast off American clothing.

'Yeah, sucker, it's good that you've seen sense,' snarled Lorenzo. 'I'll get one of the boys to drop you over four more bales. But this time it's going to cost you $750 a bale. Take it or leave it but, if you know what's good for you, don't fuckin' leave it or you'll be needing a call from the fire fighters again.'

Lucky Luciano roared with laughter when he heard how his protege, Lorenzo, had turned the table on the dissenting Milan hustler Frederico Mazza. The kid was shaping up well Luciano told his aide Tony Scarpone, adding: 'the time has come when we can trust him with the bigger jobs. He's got a mean streak in him-that's good.'

By now the word had spread amongst the market traders around the country that the mob meant business and, in any case, the bales of second hand clothing from the USA produced a useful profit on the market stalls.

It was not until Lorenzo and his entourage arrived in Rome did they encounter really serious opposition. There Lorenzo came face to face with Gaetano Boi, head of the Italian capital's small time crooks known on the streets as Il Re dei Delinquentes-King of the Thugs-who in a delusion of grandeur imagined he was bigger than the dreaded Unione Siciliano.

'I don't want any shitty rags of clothing from Unione Siciliano,' growled Boi. 'I run things here in Roma, tell that to your fuckin' boss Signore Grande Luciano-now get your ass off my market stall. Tell Luciano not to send his monkey with a message, next time I'll only talk to the organ grinder.'

Then with a totally unnecessary show of petty violence Gaetano Boi gave Lorenzo a backhanded slap across the face! Rome's King of the Thugs had made a serious mistake. Unione Siciliano had been insulted and would inevitably take terrible retribution.

Lorenzo knew, as he walked away from that stall in a large street market only five minutes walk from St Peter's Square, what he had to do. In fact it was what he wanted to do-kill a man for the second time. But finishing off that

141

bastardo Boi would be the first time he had murdered in
cold blood.

*   *   *

Tomas Sartora arrived to open his delicatessen shop on the
outskirts of Rome at 7 am one morning. As he poised
before turning the key in the lock of the front door he
noticed the lid had fallen off one of the two garbage bins
waiting for the sanitation truck due that morning.

As he stooped to retrieve and replace the garbage bin lid
his eyes nearly popped out of their sockets. He tried to yell
for help but his throat muscles had seized up with fright.

The glazed eyes of the corpse, jammed into the garbage can
several hours earlier, stared sightlessly at him. The pallor
of death and the rigidity of rigor mortis had long since
taken over.

The neat hole in the forehead was encircled by a macabre
halo of congealed blood.   The .38 calibre slug had been
propelled at close quarters through the back of the head,
through the skull and out through the forehead.

It had the hallmark of a gangland slaying.

*   *   *

At Rome's imposing police headquarters it did not take
detectives long to identify the body, which had been
trussed like a chicken with hands behind the back tightly
roped to the ankles.   The police were well acquainted with
the evil Il Re Dei Delinquente, Gaetano Boi. Whether the
cops could not find any clue to who was the killer of
Rome's King of the Thugs, or they were not too bothered
about finding the murderer of a villain they were well rid
of, is anybody's guess.

142

Three days after Gaetano's funeral, which was attended by many members of Rome's fraternity of petty crooks, one of his market trader rivals, Francis Logi, handed over $2,000 to Lorenzo in exchange for four bales of American hand me downs.

Six weeks later Lorenzo and his three hoods had disposed of the remaining 5,000 bales of second hand clothing that their Capo Di Tutti Capi   had shipped over from the USA.

Lucky Luciano was delighted with the way his protetto, Lorenzo Berni had handled the caper.

Lorenzo had matured into one of the most useful and ruthless hoods on his payroll. The kid had chilled that fuckin' pig Gaetano Boi for his lack of respect to Unione Siciliano and brought the whole thing to a happy and profitable conclusion.

The inspired venture into the 'rag trade' had grossed $1 ½ million for Unione Siciliano in little more than three months. This meant a bonus of $250,000 to swell the balance at Luciano's Swiss bank.

As for Lorenzo he was elated with the ten grand that Lucky had slipped into his jacket as he headed off to Naples' biggest car dealer where he bought the English Jaguar car he had been eyeing for some time.

CHAPTER 33

Lucky Luciano had been a known drug trafficker since 1916 and when Prohibition ended in the USA, as head of Unione Siciliano, he made up the loss of earnings from illicit booze by ensuring narcotics became the mob's main racket.

USA Narcotics Bureau investigators were sure Luciano was the mastermind of the pipeline of drugs that flooded from Italy to America after his exile in 1946.

Drug convictions of men under 21 years of age in the USA mushroomed from 712 in 1946 to a staggering 2,482 in 1950-521 of under 21's.

Luciano was filed at Interpol headquarters in Paris as Europe's Mr Big in the sordid business of international drug trafficking. In 1952 USA Narcotics Bureau conducted a mass onslaught on the sale and distribution of hard drugs in America . It was tagged as "Operation Big Sweep" and resulted in the indictment in San Francisco of 23 traffickers in a coast-to-coast drugs cartel.

'Those 23 villains were distributing dope from one source and that is the illegal Italian traffic controlled by Lucky Luciano,' alleged George Cunningham the Assistant Chief of the Narcotics Bureau.

Top brass of Guardia de Finanza, Italy's Secret Service, bridled at that statement from the USA Narcotics Bureau and considered it was a slur on their own policing methods.

An angry Guardia de Finanza spokesman, noting that the Narcotics Bureau had not come up with a shred of evidence to support the allegation, said tartly: 'If Luciano is running a world wide narcotics ring, he is doing it by some of the cleverest remote-control operation we have ever seen.'

But remote control was Lucky's modus operandi as he always distanced himself from the rackets he controlled be it drugs, prostitution, smuggling or murder.

Despite intensive investigations and frequent grilling of the Capo di Tutti Capi in Rome, Naples and Palermo the Italian cops failed to find any evidence of drug trafficking to haul Luciano in front of the courts.

*   *   *

Lucky Luciano intended to keep his Unione Siciliano in top place as the world's biggest trafficker in hard drugs. He just did not subscribe to the theory that competition is good for business.

He killed off all opposition-in fact 'killed-off' was literally true when business rivals refused to move aside! He never hesitated when his men failed to 'persuade' an opponent to give ground.

'Chill the fuckin' stubborn bastardo,' he would instruct his hit man, making sure that he was himself several hundred miles away at the the time the murder was committed.

The Great White Road of cocaine and opium from the poppy fields of Turkey and the Balkans to the USA via Italy was under the stewardship of Luciano and his mob.

So it did not require much imagination to understand Lucky's blind fury when he received a trans-Atlantic'phone call from his old buddy Frank Costello saying that a French connection, not associated with Unione Siciliano, had shipped a huge quantity of heroin to New York.

'Thirty three fuckin' pounds of uncut 99 per cent pure H,' roared Costello. 'The fuckers have rounded up some East Side kids and are undercutting us for price by selling it at a dollar a shot on the streets. It's gotta be fuckin' stopped at your end Charlie or we're in fuckin' trouble.'

Lucky Luciano's calculating brain quickly figured out that 33 lbs of pure uncut heroin cut and re cut with milk sugar, would produce several hundred thousand shots to be sold on the streets. The take could be as much $300,000.

'These French pigs have gotta be stopped fuckin' quick,' Luciano said to himself as he picked up the phone to speak to his Unione Siciliano contact in Paris.

Lucky did not like what he heard from Mario Tomalli, a Sicilian who ran an Italian bistro on the outskirts of the affluent 8th Arrondisment of Paris.

'The Paris underworld is now controlled by the Hubert twins, Gaston and Louis,' reported Tomalli. 'They are a new breed of mobsters who like fast cars and bright lights. They took over Paris a few months ago after they arranged the assassination of our old Unione ally Harry Vandermulder!'

Luciano had already heard that the 56-year-old Vandermulder, the last of the old style Paris gangsters, had been shot as he sipped a bottle of acqua minerale in a high class betting shop off the Champs Elysees.

Born in Marseilles to a Flemish father Vandermulder held dual Belgian and French passports. He progressed in the underworld from a pimp in the red light district of Paris before becoming boss of a mob that ran heroin to America on behalf of Unione Siciliano.

It was Vandermulder and his evil gang that inspired the Gene Hackman film the French Connection more than a decade later.

The Hubert brothers made sure of Vandermulder's demise when their two hit men rode up the Champs Elysees on powerful motor cycles, their faces obscured by crash helmets, and fired eight bullets into him, plus the traditional gangland close range shot to the head.

The Hubert brothers, who were likened to London East End's murderous Kray twins because of they way they cared for their widowed mother, had eliminated Vandermulder to make quick headway into the world of international drug trafficking.

The evil brothers' one error of judgement was thinking they could evade the long arm of Unione Siciliano and fly solo in the supersonic altitude of global heroin dealing.

The master of malevolence, Lucky Luciano, was about to clip their wings and declare a gangland war.

CHAPTER 34

As an avid reader of military history Lucky Luciano knew that to gain an advantage over an adversary it was essential to acquire good and reliable intelligence.

He had learned this from the biographies and historical accounts of war about great tempo di guerra strategists such as Montgomery, Rommel, Macarthur, Hannibal, Wellington and Napoleon.

Lucky also had his own experiences to draw on from the battles he had conducted and won against rival bootlegging mobs during the tough and rumbustious days of Prohibition in the USA.

His first decision against the forthcoming punitive campaign against the arrogant and rebellious French hoodlums, the Hubert twins of Paris, was that it would have to be waged on their territory. The scene of battle would, he decided, have to be Marseilles, a tough and rough seaport similar to his own base, Naples.

It was from Marseilles he knew that the narcotics exported to the USA by the Hubert twins would begin their journey. Luciano decided that he would have to send, what later in the century military chiefs would call, a task force to deal with the French renegades in their own citadel.

He decided also the commander of that task force, against the violent Hubert brothers, would be the highly intelligent Lorenzo Berni. The 19-year-old Lorenzo had steamed through every course he had taken at the Technical College in Naples. He had degrees that certified he was a highly qualified engineer, an offshoot of that was he was Unione Siciliano's best safe and lock man and a hot shot on security and electronics. Added to those qualifications

Lorenzo had performed impressively in the smuggling racket, and the Lercara Friddi pay roll heist, and, as leader, the second hand clothing caper during which he had killed two men on Unione Siciliano business.

So within days Luciano despatched his two closest aides, Lorenzo and Tony Scarpone, to France on a spying expedition to find out everything they could about the plans of Gaston and Louis Hubert.

Lorenzo was sent by sea, in one of the fast boats in Luciano's smuggling fleet, while Scarpone flew to Paris for a liaison with Unione Siciliano's man on the spot Mario Tomalli.

*   *   *

Lorenzo booked himself in to an inconspicuous hotel near the Marseilles waterfront, on a corner directly opposite a warehouse, which was used by the Hubert mob. He cased the goings and comings at the warehouse for several days making jottings in a tiny notebook. Entry to the warehouse was by an electronic keypad.

It looked as if there was one four figure code to open the small door for a person on foot and another four figure code to open the up-and-under gates to admit vehicles, of which there was a steady flow during the day. The electronic entry codes off a simple ten-digit keypad would be easy to bypass.

Security at night began at ten o'clock when two of the Hubert's young hoods acted as guards until 7 am the following morning! It looked as if the Hubert twins relied on muscle rather than go to the expense of a sophisticated electronic alarm system.

The only outsiders who appeared to visit the warehouse and gain entry without using the electronic entry system were the garbage men who arrived at 10 am every morning , rang the doorbell and waited for one of the hoodlums inside to press the button to open the up-and under gate. Ten minutes later the garbage van, manned by four Paris Council employees, would reverse out of the up-and-under gate, full of empty and flattened cardboard boxes.

Lorenzo noted the fleet number of the van and later spoke to its four man crew at a little café opposite the garbage depot.

The garbage men gasped with glee after their chat with Lorenzo and jumped at the chance of earning the $1,000 he offered them. In return one of them would lend Lorenzo their bright orange boiler suit and allow him to switch with him when the van called at Hubert's warehouse the following day.

*   *   *

Lorenzo was oblivious to the dangerous situation he would be in should he be discovered helping the three bona fide garbage men to flatten several hundred cardboard boxes and fling them on the van. Surreptitiously he took numerous photographs of the interior of the warehouse with a tiny camera he had secreted in his boiler suit.

He noted that the warehouse was full of gambling machines, one-armed bandits, and pinball machines-a racket that had taken over from prostitution as one of the Hubert twin's main sources of income. It was a scam with which Unione Siciliano and their Capo Di Tutti Capi, Lucky Luciano, were well acquainted.

Luciano had no objections to the Hubert's interest in the slot machines as long as it was confined to France. But running narcotics from Europe to the USA was a different matter. That was Unione Siciliano's exclusive business and they intended to keep it that way.

151

Lorenzo noticed that there was a gallery running completely round the warehouse and the Hubert's had detailed three men armed with sub-machine guns to patrol it all the time. Apart from the two electronic doors that opened on the wharf side of the waterfront there was a back door, leading to the street, which was secured by a massive Chubb lock.

As the van reversed out of the warehouse and drove off towards the garbage depot Lorenzo knew that the Hubert twins warehouse could be breached if the raid was well planned. But it would not be easy and there would surely be strong-armed resistance.

*   *   *

On the other side of France Tony Scarpone, with the help of Unione Siciliano ally Mario Tomalli, had trawled the Paris underworld seeking information about the latest developments in the Hubert twins involvement in the narcotics trade.

By pressing a few $100 bills in the right hands Scarpone learned that the Huberts were collecting in the duty- free city of Trieste an 880lb consignment of raw opium from a Yugoslavian poppy grower.

The Huberts planned to ship the dope out to the USA, via their waterfront warehouse in Marseilles two week's later. This huge consignment was heading for Kansas City where scientists were waiting in a well-equipped laboratory to process it before it was sold on the streets to junkies.

The raw opium would be taken from Paris to Marseilles in two fast Citroen limousines accompanied by the Hubert twins and four of their armed 'soldiers'. There would be four more of the Hubert's locally based gunmen added to the security force before the deadly cargo was shipped to the States aboard a Marseilles registered freighter.

The opium would be concealed in plastic bags down in the hold amongst a cargo of tons of rice destined for the kitchens of some of New York's hundreds of Chinese, Indonesian and Japanese restaurants. It would be almost impossible to detect by customs or Narcotic Bureau officials.

The street value of this sizeable shipment would eventually reach $1.2 million! A consignment that would seriously undermine Unione Siciliano's domination of drugs trafficking in the USA.

It was a situation that Luciano was determined would not happen.

'Organise the heist on those French bastardos warehouse in Marseilles,' the irate Capo Di Tutti Capi ordered Lorenzo. 'Take as many of our men as you need to catch those French fuckers red-handed! Wipe the motherfuckers out; make sure those Hubert shits are the first to die, nab the dope for ourselves and burn the fuckin' warehouse down.'

Never had a more vitriolic declaration of war been made.

CHAPTER 35

Lorenzo Berni had ten days only to assemble, equip and train the group of nine Unione Siciliano mobsters he reckoned would be needed to successfully storm the Hubert twins Marseilles warehouse.

Through Lucky Luciano's impressive list of contacts all across the globe he acquired three former US Navy inflatable boats with powerful outboard motors.

Again through the Capo Di Tutti Capi's influence, he was able to obtain a dozen Czechoslovakian made automatic rifles with a plentiful supply of ammunition.   From the same source came 20 hand grenades-10 of the stun variety and 10 of the fragmentation sort.   Each of the ten men on the raid, including Lorenzo himself was also equipped with a brand new Bereta pistol, still packed in its greased paper from the factory.   This formidable array of armaments, he learned, had been secreted in a Unione Siciliano hide-out near Naples awaiting shipment to the IRA, an organisation whom they regularly did business with.   On this occasion the aggressive Irish Republican Army would have to wait for their consignment of weapons to fight the British, as the Unione's own affairs took precedence.

Lorenzo decided that the expedition would set sail from Sicilly.

It was not only a convenient point of departure for a voyage across the Mediterranean but the mountainous island was an ideal place for his squad to train and familiarise themselves with the new weapons.   He received every support possible from local Unione Siciliano bandit chief, Aldo Caramusa, who, at Lorenzo's request, supplied four of the men in the squad.

By the time the party was ready to leave, with all their equipment stowed aboard Lucky Luciano's smuggling boat, Annunciare Bianco, Lorenzo's men were fit, wound-up and ready for battle.

*   *   *

The three inflatable boats, slipped away from the Annunciare Bianco, which was anchored two miles offshore. As they neared the Marseilles waterfront Lorenzo signalled for them to switch off their outboard motors and silently use their oars to glide towards the dockside.

Tony Scarpone was one of the other three men in Lorenzo's boat. He had pleaded with his boss Luciano to be allowed to join the caper. Lorenzo was in fact happy to have him aboard because he liked Tony very much.

The ten raiders disembarked quietly and moored the inflatable boats securely at a dockside spot suitable for a quick getaway, if necessary.

As they tip-toed towards the warehouse, keeping to the shadows, Lorenzo, in the lead, spotted something through his ex-US Army night binoculars that he had not anticipated. The canny Hubert twins had left a 'sentry', armed with a sub machine gun, on patrol outside the warehouse entrance. His weapon was concealed beneath a raincoat, in case the gendarmes passed by, but Lorenzo could see the bulge.

Lorenzo quickly decided that the 'sentry' had to be taken out as quickly and silently as possible! In the few days that his squad had trained together in Sicily Lorenzo had spotted Gino Peronace, one of Aldo Caramusa's bandits, was an expert with a throwing knife.

Lorenzo beckoned the Sicilian forward and, with hand signals, indicated that he wanted the sentry taken out silently.

Peronace, hugging the wall, crept within range and as the 'sentry' turned in his direction he hurled his knife. The deadly stiletto plunged to the depth of the handle guard into the luckless sentry's Adam's Apple. The only noise was the thud of the dead man's sub-machine gun, which was muffled by his raincoat!

Lorenzo patted Peronace on the back and a whispered 'well done' as he crawled forward himself towards the electronic pad that would open the warehouse door. He knew from the couple of hours he has spent watching that door through binoculars during his spying mission a couple of weeks earlier that the entry code then was 3-5-7-9.

He held his breath knowing they held the advantage of surprise if the Hubert mob had not changed that entry code. He touched the buttons and sighed with relief when he heard the door click open. The die was cast! All that was needed now was quick and definite action. He signaled the team forward. By arrangement at an earlier briefing Lorenzo's squad split into two sections, five men to the left of the building and five men to the right.

Taking the initiative as leader, Lorenzo, tossed two of the stun grenades into the centre of the warehouse to create confusion. Then leading the fire with his AK47 he immediately took out two of the four Hubert mobsters, patrolling the gallery, in one devastating salvo. That left eight of the French hoodlums, including Gaston and Louis, the Hubert twins. In fact he spotted the Hubert brothers taking cover with two of their men behind a bank of gambling machines. He signalled his team to spread out wide before starting to close in on the French mobsters. The battle was far from over.

The firefight became intense as the Hubert twins and their henchmen grouped towards the rear of the building. Shells ricocheting off the stone walls of the warehouse were a danger to both sets of combatants. Lorenzo realised that the tiny back door of the warehouse could provide an escape route for Gaston and Louis Hubert and their priceless sacks of raw opium. He countered that possibility decisively by despatching two of Aldo Caramusa's Sicilian bandits round the building to cover the back door.

'Blast any fucker who comes through that fuckin' door to hell,' was Lorenzo's tense order.

Grouping their men together proved to be a tactical error by the Hubert brothers. Although it concentrated their firepower it also left Lorenzo with one big target instead of several smaller ones.

Lorenzo barked instructions for five of his team's stock of fragmentation grenades to be hurled from different directions at the Hubert huddle. It was an explosive intrusion that immediately took out four of the remaining eight enemy 'soldiers'. One of the Parisian hoods was killed outright with multiple wounds in his stomach, one lost an eye, and two went down with shattered legs!

It was then the Hubert's decided that retreat was the only way out of their dilemma. With their two remaining henchmen they hoisted the sacks of raw opium on to a hand truck. The two hoodlums were ordered to give the Hubert's covering fire as they made for the back door in an effort to wheel the truck and its valuable load to safety.

In the ferocious barrage of machine gun fire the law of averages suggested that at least one of Lorenzo's men would pay the price. It was Tony Scarpone who took a burst of eight bullets in his chest. Lorenzo saw at once how bad it was for Lucky Luciano's loyal and long-serving body guard.

Blood poured in a torrent from the gaping wound as the doomed Scarpone tried to say something. If the words had been intelligible they would have still have been his last words. Only a last gasp gurgle from a man drowning in his own gore was emitted.

*   *   *

As the perspiring Hubert brothers unlocked the back door and pushed it open with the front of the opium laden hand truck, aiming to reach their Citroen DS limousine parked outside in the street, they were literally cut in half by a savage hail of shells from the two AK47 toting Sicilian bandits waiting outside. Both the French villains died instantly.

Hearing the machine gun fire behind them, and realising what had happened to their two bosses at the back door, the two remaining members of the decimated Hubert gang threw down their own guns and stepped from cover of the shell riddled gambling machines with their hands held above their heads.

Surrender, however, was not an option for Lorenzo who was desperately sad and angry at the death of his friend Tony Scarpone. He lifted the AK47 from the sling around his neck, took deliberate aim and ruthlessly mowed the two French thugs down. As he reached their twitching bodies he, spitefully, spit on their death throes.

Lorenzo did not forget the two other French thugs, wounded by grenades earlier, and despatched both of them with Unione Siciliano's traditional bullet in the back of the head. The caper had cost 12 lives!

All that remained was to splash gasoline from three barrels, that stood in the corner, all round the floor and set fire to the building. Carefully carrying Tony Scarpone's body between them Lorenzo and his eight men headed for the inflatable boats on the way back to board the Annunciare Bianco.

As the smuggling boat forged across the Mediterranean towards Naples, Lorenzo put in a radio telephone call to Turin, where Lucky Luciano, as always covered by a cast-iron alibi when he had masterminded a big crime, was eating breakfast in his suite at the Albergo Grandioso Torino.

'The job is done boss,' was the simple message from Lorenzo who, for security reasons, decided it was not a suitable time to tell his father about Tony Scarpone's death. Lucky finished his breakfast, lit his first Monte Cristo cigar of the day, and grinned when he noted the date on his morning giorna-14 February.

'St Valentine's Day,' he chuckled. 'A fuckin' good day for a massacre!'

CHAPTER 36

Lucky Luciano, delighted with the news he had received over the radio telephone from Lorenzo about the Marseilles caper, rang room service at Turin's plush Albergo Grandioso Torino and ordered champagne despite the early hour.

He had shared the night with Gloria Grapelli a busty Italian film starlet who had been romantically linked with many politicians, bankers and actors. They had gone clubbing until after midnight in Italy's wealthy motor city dominated by the Fiat car empire and the famous Juventus Soccer team, whose star at the time was the popular Welsh giant John Charles.

They had returned to the hotel and spent the next couple of hours in bed where the silk clad Gloria still luxuriated.

A connoisseur of 'bubbly', Lucky ordered two bottles of Pol Roger White Label, the favourite tipple of his World War II idol Winston Churchill. The wine was accompanied by a generous serving of Beluga caviar bedded on crushed ice and a plate of hot toast.

After the room service cameriere had left, Lucky carried the champagne and caviar into the bedroom and climbed in between the black sheets to join the voluptuous Gloria in another raunchy romp.

His voracious sexual appetite satiated, Lucky made it clear to Gloria that he had important business to do that day and, handing her $1,000, suggested she should go 'and buy a new gown or sumpin' like that.' Patting her affectionately on the rump as she left the hotel suite he said he would see her later. Lucky rang the hotel reception desk and asked them to put in a person to person call to

161

Mr Frank Costello in New York, who at that particular point of time was holding court with two elegant Broadway babes at his favourite night club.

'Charley,' yelled Costello, using the first name Luciano preferred, as the Maitre d'Hotel' handed him the 'phone on a long trailing lead. 'How the fuck are you?'

Luciano grinned at the sound of his old school pal's gravelly voice and replied: 'Yeah, yeah--I'm OK old buddy-I just thought you'd like to know that the business with our French associates has been settled-fuckin' permanently settled. After some tough negotiations we have taken over their stock, which we will be shipping out to you in the usual way.'

Costello, with the mob's other big bosses that side of the Atlantic Ocean, had been angry and perturbed at the threat the ill-fated Hubert twins were to Unione Siciliano's multi-million dollar drugs operation in the USA, was delighted with the news that the rival French gang had been so ruthlessly rubbed out.

'Geez! That's great to hear Charley pal,' said the New York gangster. 'The organisation are going to be mighty grateful with the way you have handled the business your end. The kid you put in charge of the deal deserves a real nice bonus.'

Costello cradled the phone and handed it to the hovering waiter. Then, like his old pal thousands of miles away, he ordered champagne - two bottles of Dom Perignon was his choice.

So the corks popped on both sides of the Atlantic to celebrate the St Valentine's Day Massacre, Mark Two.

*   *   *

Later that day Lucky was not so happy to hear about the death of his trusted retainer, chauffeur and body guard, Tony Scarpone.

Deep-rooted sorrow, however, was not in Luciano's emotional repertoire and he said philosphically: 'Tony was a good guy but that's the business we're in-full or risks.'

Risks for everyone other than for Lucky Luciano, master of the cover-up, the Unione Siciliano boss of bosses who left nothing to chance. Lucky was too street-wise in the evil ways of the underworld to be overly sentimental over the loss of Tony Scarpone.

Yet he allowed himself one, out-of-character, gesture to the memory of his loyal henchman.

Scanning his favourite newspaper Giornale de Sicilia he noted the parish priest in the tiny town of San Valentino, near Salerno, where Tony Scarpone was born, was trying to raise funds to renovate the church bell-tower.

'That fuckin' St Valentine is the patron saint of the town and I reckon on Tony's behalf we owe him a hand-out!' mused Lucky as he wrote out a cheque for $5,000 as a donation towards renovating the bell tower of the crumbling church at the town of San Valentino Torio.

A bizarre memorial to a hoodlum who lost his life in a gory gangland massacre.

CHAPTER 37

Lucky Luciano moved quickly to appoint a new Man Friday after the violent demise of his chauffeur-body guard Tony Scarpone.

His choice was a 20-year-old Sicilian-born hoodlum by the name of Bernardo Provenzano who had earned his spurs from the mob as one of the gun men who pumped 112 shells into the car of Michele Navarra the local Unione Siciliano Godfather of his home town Corleone. It earned Provenzano the nickname of 'Tractor'- a mark of respect for the ruthlessness with which he mowed down his enemies.

He was destined a couple of decades later to become Sicily's Capo di Tutti Capo. He served Luciano loyally and efficiently but at the same time built up a fund of knowledge of Unione Siciliano's secrets that would eventually orbit him to the top of the organisation.

Luciano had other plans for Lorenzo Berni who he felt had done enough to be elected as a 'made man' of Unione Siciliano. If his election was approved by such organisation bosses as Frank Costello and Meyer Lansky, it would elevate Lorenzo to the status of 'wise guy' in the underworld on both sides of the Atlantic. Before making his move, to elevate his protege to the privileged position of a blood brother in Unione Siciliano, Luciano took steps to make sure that Lorenzo was eligible for such promotion under the mob's rules.

Unione Siciliano, maintaining the traditions handed down from their predecessors, the Mafia or Cosa Nostra, insisted that all blood brothers should have some Sicilian antecedents in their family history. If not actually born on the island, a Sicilian father or mother, or grandparents, would suffice. Lucky phoned his avvocato, Pierluigi

Cudicino, and asked him to research Lorenzo's background. He told the lawyer that he could begin his investigation at the orphanage run by the Franciscan monks where Lorenzo had spent most of his boyhood years.

It took two weeks before Signore Cudicino had finished his enquiries and arrived at Luciano's villa to make his report. The powerful Capo di Tutti Capo was totally dumbfounded when the lawyer revealed that the young man had been registered at birth with the name Lorenzo Salvatore Lucania Berni - father unknown; mother Signorina Gina Berni only daughter of fornaio Umberto Berni. The realisation of what was the unshakeable truth hit Lucky Luciano hard in the groin. 'The kid is my son!' he muttered to himself in sheer disbelief. 'That fuckin' baker and his bitch daughter double-crossed me. But the fact remains that the kid is my runt-no wonder he's got so much guts. That fuckin' alters things!'

Now Lucky Luciano, the boss of bosses of Crime International, Capo di Tutti Capo and master planner of the notorious Unione Siciliano, had to face some serious questions.

Does the kid know I am his father?
If so does he know what happened to his mother?
If he doesn't should I tell him I am his father?
Should I go ahead, as planned, and recommend to the Unione Siciliano that he becomes a 'made man' in the organisation?

Luciano, with the sort of cool calculation that typified the ice running through his veins, decided to play it as if Lorenzo did not know he was his father.

'What he doesn't know won't hurt him!' theorised the mobster boss. 'I'll see he is made up because he has earned it. But he'll get no special favours from me.'

But beneath the tough veneer Lucky Luciano was quite proud that he had spawned a son who had already shown that he was quite a man.

*   *   *

The inauguration of Lorenzo Berni into the secret brotherhood of Unione Siciliano was staged in a mountainous region of Sicily at, more precisely, the plush hideout of bandit chief Aldo Caramusa who, with Lucky Luciano, was one of the two sponsors, as required under the organisation's rules, of the candidate.

After taking the solemn oath of allegiance, and the binding vow of omerta which solemnly pledged he would never, under threat of death, betray any Unione brother or disclose the organisation's secrets, the time honoured tradition of mixing blood took place. Handed down from the Unione Siciliano's violent predecessors the Mafia and, even more older and sinister Italian Black Hand Gang, the ancient ritual began with Aldo Caramusa unsheathing his enormous horn-handled hunting knife and slashing Lorenzo's thumb. In an almost simultaneous action the bandit chief opened a cut across his own thumb and pressed the two bleeding gashes together.

Lorenzo was now a sworn blood brother of Unione Siciliano a bond that could only be broken by death. It meant that Lorenzo was a free agent to launch his own rackets, as long as he not only paid twenty five per cent of the profits to the mob and always available to do any work for the Unione who paid him a retainer. It also meant that no other blood brother could ever take out a 'contract' to kill or harm him without the OK of the Unione bosses. He himself had to take a reciprocal oath.

The ceremony over, Lorenzo was given a warm abbracciare and a kiss on each cheek by Luciano, Caramusa and the

167

other eight made brothers in the crowded room.   The vino, champagne and acquavite was opened, the Romeo y Juliet sigaros passed around and lit as the booziest festa ever held in that remote part of Sicily got under way.

CHAPTER 38

After Lorenzo's induction as a made man he was invited by Lucky Luciano to stay over in Sicily for a few days while the Capo di Tutti Capis completed some mob business with Aldo Caramusa and other Unione Siciliano chiefs.

One evening, in his luxury suite at Palermo's top hotel, Lucky ordered a bottle of Dom Perignon and asked Lorenzo what he intended to do now that he was free to branch out and organise his own rackets.

'Well I am coming up to my 19th birthday and I think I need to build up a nest egg for the future, Charley,' replied Lorenzo, using the Christian name Luciano preferred. 'The thing I do best is using my training as an engineer and mechanic to crack safes and break into places. I thought I would put a small mob together of two or three hoods and rob some banks and get a few thousand bucks into the kitty to finance other businesses.
'I know heisting banks is a dangerous racket but it pays well. That guy John Dillinger did alright out of robbing banks in the States back in the thirties didn't he?'

Luciano laughed out loud at his protege's passionate dissertation.

'Listen Lorenzo I knew Dillinger back in the Chicago days and he was a crum,' pronounced Lucky venomously. 'He was a mug who believed his own publicity and drew attention to himself.

'He came to us and wanted to join the mob and we turned the stupid fucker down. He was a loner who had every cop in the land, after him because of his big head. In the end he made several fuckin' schoolboy mistakes. After escaping from jail in Crown Point, where he

169

was awaiting trial for murder, and having left his fingerprints all over a bank he was robbing, he crossed the Illinois state line in a stolen car which gave FBI Chief Edgar J Hoover the authority to send in his G-men after him.

'Finally in July 1934 Dillinger was shot dead by G-men as he left a Chicago cinema after the Feds had been tipped off by a hooker called Polly Hamilton and a brothel madam by the name of Anna Sage,' said Lucky, apparently forgetting that, before his exile from the USA in 1946, he himself had pulled a 50 year sentence in the 1930's on evidence in court given by a series of prostitutes, pimps and brothel madams.

' As far as the mob was concerned we were fuckin' glad to see the back of him. His stupidity put the heat on all of us. The secret of being in the rackets is to cover up and try to make sure that the cops never hear your name or frame you. John Dillinger was nothing more than a headline grabbing crum. At the end of the day what did Dillinger make out of bank robbery except headlines in the newspapers?

' All his father and former girlfriend Billie Frechette found after he was shot dead was $250-a miserable two hundred and fifty bucks-as I have said he was a fuckin' stupid small-time crum!'

Lucky poured the champagne and thoughtfully made Lorenzo a proposition.

'Renzo if you really want to go into the bank heisting business in a serious way I am prepared to finance you,' said the most powerful mobster in the world.

'You will need three or four good men, which I can supply, getaway cars, a set of safe-cracking tools, tommy guns, pistols and other gear which I will pay for! In other words I'll set you up. In return I'll take ten points from the profits. With the 25% you have to hand over to the mob it means you will still keep 65% of the cash you make after expenses! It's a good deal from your point of view and you'll have my protection to back you up if things go wrong.'

Lorenzo knew he was being made an offer that he just could not afford to refuse! He nodded and held his hand out to the father he idolised as the Unione Sicliano's respected Capo di Tutti Capo.

Lucky smiled as he returned the handshake and gave his son some further advice.

'Remember 'Renzo don't try to be too big in the bank robbery business,' said Luciano. 'Ten small heists, planned carefully and spread over a period of time will draw less attention than one massive heist of several million bucks which would bring the national cops hot after you. The banks are insured against the smaller grabs and won't make too much fuss-but if you clear out their vaults they'll light a fuse that will fuckin' blow you to 'ell.

'My advice to you is map out your heists carefully leaving no fuckin' evidence for the cops. When you have built up a useful bank roll, pay off your mob to keep them quiet remembering to chill any fucker likely to spill the beans to the cops under pressure, and retire from heisting banks and set up in a less dangerous racket.'

* * *

Lucky Luciano, with important Unione Siciliano business to complete before returning to Naples, gave his new chauffeur-bodyguard, Bernardo Provenzano, the following day off to visit his parents who lived in the small town of Corleone in the mid-west of the island.

Bernardo asked Lorenzo if he would like to join him on the short trip from Palermo and both of them were delighted when Lucky said that they could use the new Buick sedan he had just had shipped out to him from the USA.

171

Lorenzo liked the Provenzano family as soon as he met them. Bernardo's father, Enrico, had lost a leg when forced to fight alongside the Germans, even although Italy had surrendered two months earlier, against the invading Allied troops in the bloody battle of Monte Cassino. He now had to live on the small war pension the cash-strapped Italian government paid him. Maria Provenzano, a hard-working woman, took in washing, sewing and mending for a pittance to eke out the small family budget.

Bernardo in the past couple of years, as he progressed through the ranks of the local mob, had become the main provider for the family. When the Unione Siciliano chieftains sentenced Michele Navarra, Corleone's Godfather, to death after discovering he was 'squealing' to the local Caribinieri, Bernardo's reputation rose with the part he played in the gory gang slaying. Amongst the Sicilian hoodlums he had earned the nickname 'Tractor' after he had mowed the ill-fated Navarra in two with a merciless spray from his tommy gun.

But the revelation was Bernado's sister, Sophia, who joined the family party in the afternoon after finishing work in a Corleone restaurant. She was a wonderful cook having been trained at the catering college in Palermo when she left convent school.

She beamed into the dimly lit parlour like a ray of spring sunshine with a twirl of a blue pleated skirt accentuating her voluptuous figure. Lorenzo, his experience of women limited to no more than half a dozen 30-minute sessions with one of Madam Tara's girls, was completely captivated by the shapely Sophia.

The flow of dark hair and most impressive the green eyes, uncharacteristic of the rather swarthy Provenzano family, excited him. Her handshake was cool and firm when her brother introduced them and those twinkling emerald eyes suggested that she was, at first sight, just as attracted to him as he certainly was to her.

She quickly departed towards the kitchen to prepare a meal leaving the company to talk and sip one of the half dozen bottles of Frascati wine that Lorenzo had generously brought as a gift for Bernardo's family.

Although the Provenzano family was quite poor Sophia made sure they ate well with uncooked food remnants from the restaurant kitchen she was allowed to bring home by courtesy of her boss.

In little more than half an hour she brought to the dining table a culinary miracle that everyone complimented. It was a tasty risotto of carnaroli arroz, goat's cheese, tomato in oil, chopped green rocket, and formaggio Parmesan all simmered and blended together with butter, chicken stock and half a bottle of Verdicchio wine. To follow, for dessert, she produced the lightest and creamiest zabaglione that Lorenzo had ever tasted.

By the time the two young mobsters had to climb into the Buick sedan to drive back to Palermo everyone one was in a merry mood. But it did not escape Bernado's notice that Lorenzo had kissed Sophia's hand promising, as they said goodbye, that he would get in touch with her again, soon.

*   *   *

'I like you Lorenzo,' Bernardo said as he tooled the Buick towards the city of Palermo adding. almost with menace, 'I think my sister likes you too. But I won't let her be hurt by anyone. So just remember that!'

CHAPTER 39

Lorenzo had a lot to tell Tara when he called into the bordello to have coffee with her after his trip to Sicily.

She was proud that his induction as a wise guy into the brotherhood of the Unione Siciliano emphasised the respect he had earned inside the organisation.   Yet, in a maternal way, she was frightened for him now that he was free to launch his own rackets.   He was discreet enough not to tell Tara that he planned to rob banks.   Not that he didn't trust her but he feared he might compromise her with knowledge that could create trouble if she was ever called on by the cops to answer questions about him.   Tara, as a woman, was particularly interested in how he enthused about his meeting with the lovely Sophia Provenzano.   Her experience told her that this was true love in embryo rather than the lust that drew the men who visited her brothel.

'Sophia sounds like a really nice girl,' advised Tara. 'Unless you are mistaken it sounds as if she is also attracted to you.   Remember 'Renzo, my love, that such a girl needs to be treated gently if you are going to win her and retain her love.   I would be really pleased to meet her when you bring her over from Sicily for a visit!   It is time you settled down and, if things work out right, Sophia could be the right girl for you to marry.   The love of a good woman is a blessing for any man lucky enough to earn and win such devotion.'

Lorenzo assured Tara that Sophia was the only woman he had ever wanted to marry.

She wished him luck, hoping in her mind that the affair with the attractive Sicilian girl would go well and not end in heartbreak for either or both of them.

A few days later Luciano rang Lorenzo asking him to call at his office situated in the Naples dockside area. When he arrived Lucky produced the four men he had chosen for Lorenzo's back-up gang in the bank robbery racket.

All four men were seasoned hoodlums in their twenties and had proven themselves while working for Unione Sicliano in various rackets. They had all, so far, eluded the polizia despite being involved in burglary, hijacking, kidnapping, drug peddling and other unsavoury scams.

Tomas Bertorelli, a 24-year-old Sicilian from the coastal town of Siracusa, was a brilliant car driver who had honed his skills at the wheel on the racetrack at Monza. Luigi Corbello, a 26-year-old cat burglar from Ascoli near Italy's Adriatic coast had shown on many occasions that he could master the lock on any door or window, whatever the height from the ground.

Frances Tabardini, the senior of the quartet, a 28-year-old Neapolitan, who was an expert marksman with pistol, rifle, shotgun or the deadly Czechoslovakian AK47 automatic rifle which was such a favourite with the Soviet Army, IRA and ETA, the Basque Separatist Movement. He had already killed three times on Unione Siciliano business.

Finally there was 26-year-old ex-seaman, Paulo Gabbatini, from Brindisi on the heel of the Italian peninsular, an evil wizard with a knife, rope or the gruesome garrotte wire that could decapitate a victim.

Lorenzo approved all four of the men chosen by Luciano. He welcomed them as members of his new gang but warned them that, as they would be operating under the aegis of Unione Siciliano, the penalty for careless talk about the organisation's business, or squealing to the cops, would be death.

He told the gang that, apart from the monthly retainer they would get from him, they would also receive a bonus after every bank raid they did. Finally Lorenzo promised that he would call them all together again in a few weeks time to reveal plans for their first bank-heist together.

Each man went away with a $1,000, which Luciano had donated, as a sign of goodwill for joining Lorenzo's new gang.

*   *   *

Lorenzo's strategy was to accumulate a personal bank roll of a million dollars from five bank heists spread far apart in distance and over 24 months in time.

If he was to become an underworld big-shot this would provide him with the capital to retire from the high risk business of bank robbery and branch out into less hazardous but even more profitable rackets.

Packing his suitcase in the boot of the fast and futuristic Citroen DS that Luciano had given him he set off on a 3,000 mile trip through the length and breadth of mainland Italy and even across the border into France. He carefully chose and 'cased' each of the five banks he had targeted. All five were small to medium size local banks and unlikely to attract a great deal of national media attention when robbed.

He knew that these smaller banks were insured against loss up to $250,000 and would not raise too much fuss, avoiding security fears amongst their customers. Against that the insurance companies would certainly appoint private investigators to the case and Lorenzo was aware that he and his men would have to be careful not to leave a trail behind them.

Only five weeks after their initial meeting Lorenzo called his gang together and told them he was ready to take them on their initial bank raid but first they would spend two weeks together training in Sicily for the big job.

CHAPTER 40

Sophia had been the pride and joy of the hard-working Provenzano family ever since her days at the Corleone Convent School where she excelled.

Respected by the teaching nuns and her fellow pupils she was, by popular choice, elected as the school's Head Girl in the final two years before she graduated.

Hard work and academic excellence earned her well-deserved scholarship at Palermo's highly rated catering college where she gained honours and a rating as a Cordon Bleu chef.

Like many modern teen-aged girls in the post war world, Sophia had a childhood boyfriend. Luigi Viera, who lived with his family a few doors away from the Provenzano's, adored her, carried her books when he walked her home from school and, with the blessing of her loving parents, escorted her to the local cinema once a week where they snuggled up on the back seats and watched the latest offerings from Hollywood.

But to Luigi the affair, if that was what it was, assumed a greater importance than it ever did to the lovely Sophia, particularly when she moved into lodgings in Palermo after being enrolled in the Catering College. Her meetings with Luigi were reduced to a few stolen hours when she returned to Corleone at weekends.

Despite the considerable amount of homework demanded by the hard taskmasters at the catering college Sophia still found time to join her fellow students, many of them attractive young men, at a nearby coffee house a couple of times a week. Meeting much more cultured and educated lads of her own age made the thoughtful Sophia realise that the coarse-mannered Luigi had to be told that he should no longer consider her as his fiancee. She would like to remain his friend but would tell him that she no longer wanted to inextricably tie herself to him.

Luigi, a muscular 20-year-old slaughter man who had worked at the Corleone abattoir since he had left school, did not receive Sophia's decision very graciously.

'I suppose some snotty-nosed Palermo student has been sniffing up your fuckin' knickers,' he yelled as he slammed out of the Provenzano kitchen with the parting crack: 'I'll slit the pansy's throat if I find out who he is! I'll tell you this my pretty signorina, after six years going out together, no other fucker's going to have you if you dump me like an old boot.'

*   *   *

It was an odd stroke of fate that ten days after giving the resentful Luigi his marching orders Sophia should walk into her parents home in Corleone to be introduced to the handsome Lorenzo Berni by her adoring brother Bernardo.

She had read in girlie magazines that love could strike like lightning but never thought it would happen to her.

It was a fortuitous meeting so soon after the painful and stormy split with Luigi and one that left her with a penetrating personal pledge that Lorenzo Berni was the man she would share the rest of her life with. She had fell in love at first sight and as far as Lorenzo was concerned the feeling was profoundly mutual.

*   *   *

Sophia was not at all worried that Lorenzo, the man she had instantly fallen for, was a mobster like her beloved brother Bernardo. Like all Sicilians over the past two

180

centuries, steeped in the violent traditions of the Unione Siciliano and it predecessor the murderous Mafia oppressed and over-taxed by Mussolini's Facist regime and before that by the Italian Royal Family and the aristocratic landowners, she hated government and all forms of officialdom, including the police.

Everyone on the island knew who the Unione mobsters were and where they could be found but the cops looking for evidence against the gangsters and bandits were hard pressed to find anyone prepared to break the code of omerta.   The silence and lack of information about the sinister Unione from the ordinary citizens was deafening.

Lorenzo was much too professional to have chosen Sicily as the venue for his newly formed gang of potential bank raiders purely because of the opportunity to see Sophia so soon again.   The fact was the rugged island with its isolated mountainous regions, the hideout of so many local bandits, was an ideal site where his men could practise their skills away from prying eyes. Yet he could not deny the thrill of seeing the lovely Sophia again.

Local gang chief Aldo Caramusa, the main sponsor of Lorenzo's induction into the Unione Siciliano, provided excellent accommodation for Lorenzo and his four henchmen during their stay on the island.   It was a four-room log cabin fitted with rural cooking facilities and bunk beds.

Lorenzo was determined that his team should be as fit and prepared as possible before their onslaught on the banks began.   For the first two days he led his men out on a gruelling cross-country run.   In the succeeding days they sharpened their skills with pistol, rifle and knife.   In the evenings they joined Caramusa's men for a drink and boisterous games of playing cards.

During the third day of their training soiree Lorenzo telephoned Sophia at the restaurant in Corleone, where she worked as the head chef, and arranged to meet her when she finished work at 9 o'clock that evening. He collected her in his sleek Citroen DS saloon car and they drove to a country inn she knew where they drank the local wine and enjoyed a simple supper of home made bread and goat's cheese.

Their love affair blossomed as they met every evening and either drove out to a country inn or sometimes spent the evening at the Provenzano house where she would cook for him and the rest of the family.

It was obvious where they were heading. It was no surprise to Sophia that, with only a few days left before he left Sicily for the mainland, Lorenzo asked her to marry him. She agreed without hesitation and her mother and father gave them their blessing.

They quickly arranged with the local parish priest, Father Roberto Tomassi, they would be married in the Corleone church two days later.

News of the forthcoming wedding between the popular Sophia and the up and coming Unione Siciliano mobster spread quickly around the neighborhood and was well received by everyone but the rejected and brooding Luigi Viera who embarked on a wild drinking orgy in an unsuccessful attempt to ease his bitter pangs of jealousy.

* * *

Lorenzo's stag party, held in a bustling Corleone tavern, was a boisterous affair attended by the four members of his newly formed gang, local bandit chief Aldo Caramusa and three of his henchmen, Sophia's brother Bernardo and Lucky Luciano who had only arrived on the island earlier that day.

Lucky had been surprised, but delighted, to be invited to be the best man at the wedding of the young man who, the mobster big-shot mistakenly believed, was still unaware that he was his father.

The celebrations had been going on for nearly two hours when the irate Luigi Viera, his jealous anger stoked up by a copious intake of fiery grappa, entered the bar and strode purposefully across to confront Lorenzo.

'So you are the mother-fucker who has stolen my girl?' stormed the burly slaughterman so recently rejected by the lovely Sophia. 'I suppose you think you are a tough guy with your pistols and fuckin' bodyguards?'

Lorenzo, Lucky, Caramusa and the rest of the party were dumbstruck with surprise at the ferocity of the verbal attack from the wrathful Luigi, who continued: 'We'll see what kind of a man you are if you step outside and fight with a knife-we'll see what stomach you've got for cold steel!
'Personally I think you're a fuckin' yellow vigliacco......'

Viera finished his vitriolic tirade, in which he had branded Lorenzo a coward, by spitefully spitting straight into his rival's face.

There was a tense moment when Luciano, Caramusa and several of their men reached for the revolvers nestling in shoulder holsters and belts! Lorenzo, picking up a table napkin to wipe the vile spittle from his face, held out his arm to restrain his friends.

He had been challenged, his courage doubted. His pride was hurt-Italian pride! There was only one answer to that.

183

'Hold it,' Lorenzo told his friends. 'This is my fight. I'll give this crum satisfaction if that is what he fuckin' wants!'

Then, eyeballing the irate Luigi, he barked: 'Outside you fuckin' creep-if you want a fight I'll give you one in the square outside. If it's a knife fight you want that's OK by me-we'll fight the way the zingaros' battle!

The zingaro-gypsy- style of knife fighting laid down that the two contestants must each hold between their clenched teeth the end of a one metre length of leather strap while they stabbed and slashed at each other. If one man let go of the leather strap in an attempt to gain an advantage he would be shot by the man appointed as the arbitro of the fight.

If a man went down because of a wound the fighter left standing had the right to finish him off without any interference from the arbitro. It was the deadliest form of close range knife fighting.

CHAPTER 41

There was an air of excitement as the bar emptied in anticipation of the gory duel that was about to be enacted outside in the tiny Town Square of Corleone.

Just one problema had to be settled before the knife battle could begin. The local off-duty policeman, Tomas Petronelli, was in the bar. The street-wise Aldo Caramusa, however, knew how to deal with that difficulty.

'Look Tomas, mio amico, you don't want to compromise yourself or cause trouble by trying to stop the fight,' said Caramusa persuasively. 'I know a duello is against the law so why don't you go home and forget about what is about to happen here?'

The policeman had been born and reared in the town of Corleone and, as a shrewd Sicillian, knew when it was politic to turn a blind eye to a situation, particularly one that concerned members of the powerful Unione Siciliano. As Officer Petronelli turned away to head for his home on the other side of town Caramusa pushed several bank notes into the top pocket of his tunic and said: 'Take your wife to the shops in Palermo and buy her a new dress. Just forget what happens in the square tonight!'

As the excited customers poured out of the bar they formed a human ring outside in the Town Square while the two combatants, Lorenzo and Luigi, in the true gypsy fighter's tradition, stripped to the waist.

As Lorenzo did not carry a knife one of his new gang Paulo Gabbatini, an expert with the blade, came to his rescue and loaned him his own deadly coltello, which had already tasted the blood of six men he had killed. It was a slender stiletto, balanced perfectly, and honed to a keenness that a man could shave with.

'Viera will be fighting with a much heavier knife,' advised Gabbatini. 'But you will have the advantage of reach because the stiletto I have lent you is nine centimetros longer than his weapon and much lighter and easier to wield.'

A former merchant seaman and smuggler, who became a mobster, Gabbatini was feared and respected as the most expert knife-fighter in the Italian underworld.

'Like most men who fight with knives Viera will defend his midriff and face, the targets most opponents aim for,' cautioned Gabbatini. ' So try to harness the element of surprise and attack a less well defended, but nevertheless vulnerable part of your rival's body.'

* * *

It was mutually agreed by the two contestants that Aldo Caramusa, armed with a loaded revolver, would act as the impartial 'arbitro' of the fight with the power to shoot either man if he released the leather strap clenched in their teeth in order to gain an advantage.

Caramusa took Lorenzo aside and cautioned him: 'Although it is against the laws of Unione Siciliano to kill a brother without the sanction of the Council you have chosen the path of honour. If you break the rules of the fight I must treat you the same as I would deal with your opponent Luigi Viera in the same situation if he cheats. You were challenged and called a coward-you had no choice but to fight even although this is your wedding day.'

Caramusa then briefed each man jointly of the rules under which the knife battle would be fought. If either of them released the leather strap between their teeth to gain an advantage he would shoot that man. If a man went down wounded, and could not continue, his opponent had the right to either kill him or spare his life. But either way that would be the end of the vendetta.

*   *   *

The crowd from the bar bayed as they encircled the two bare-chested combatants, knives clutched in their hands, the one metre stretch of leather strap clenched firmly between their teeth.

As the two men sparred for an opening Viera's many years experience working in the local abattoir meant he had the advantage in knife skills. The slaughter-man flicked his heavy hunting knife expertly from hand to hand leaving Lorenzo guessing from which flank he could expect an attack.

Viera feinted to his left, the leather taut between two sets of clenched teeth. Lorenzo tried to pull away evasively. Viera switched his knife to his right hand leaving Lorenzo's left side vulnerable. Viera's slashing blow was slightly off-target but nevertheless opened up a bleeding gash from Lorenzo's cheek to chin.

It was to leave Lorenzo with a permanent scar down his face that quite eerily matched the one borne by his father, Lucky Luciano, since the violent days of Prohibition in the USA.

Lorenzo, if he had any previous doubts, was now aware that he was in a fight that would probably end in death. The taste of blood as it trickled down his cheek into the side of his mouth fired Lorenzo into a frenzy.

The watching Luciano, alarmed that Luigi Viera had drawn first blood, yelled at his son: 'Watch it kid!'

Lorenzo, the adrenalin rising, countered by switching his own blade to his right hand. He took a sharp pace forward to slacken the leather strap and dipping his left knee took Luigi totally by surprise with the bold manoeuvre. Lorenzo's upward backhand thrust caught Viera on the inside of his right arm just above the wrist. Lorenzo swept his thin blade in a searing arc that opened up Viera's arm to the bone like a fishmonger filleting a huge salmon.

Viera, horrified by the sight by the two gory flapping hinges that had once been his right arm sank to the ground. His eyes glazed.

Caramusa stepped forward and bent over the traumatised Viera and inspected the injured right arm, almost bisected from wrist to armpit, the oozing blood forming a scarlet pool of mud on the paving of the town square.

'He's done for!' ruled the arbitro. 'It's your shout Lorenzo, either chill this fuckin' creep or spare his useless life!'

Lorenzo hesitated, his knuckles whitening as his grip tightened on the handle of that deadly stiletto. For a split second he readied himself to slit Viera's throat. Lorenzo's hesitation only lasted a couple of seconds until he summoned up a morsel of mercy from his conscience, and snapped: 'Oh! What the fuck? Let the cock suckin' creep live. Take him to the doctor and get his arm fixed!'

Caramusa took the leather strap that had been used for the fight and crudely applied it as a makeshift tourniquet to stem the blood spouting from Luigi's lifeless arm.

Ten minutes later in his tiny surgery just behind the town square local medico, Dr Roberto Pucio, performed an even more professional job to stop the bleeding before calling an ambulance to transport the unfortunate Viera to hospital in Palermo.

188

'One thing for sure Luigi Viera will never use that right arm in a knife-fight or at work in the abattoir again,' opined the worthy Dottore Pucio. 'That is apart from the most likely chance that the surgeons in Palermo will decide to amputate.'

Then turning to Lorenzo the doctor said: 'Now then lad, let's look at that gash on your face and patch you up for your wedding this afternoon.'

CHAPTER 42

Sophia was stunningly beautiful as her father, Enrico, who lost a leg while serving in the Italian army during the World War II, proudly helped her into the white Mercedes limousine that would take her to the church.

Her spectacular dress, of 'Gypsy' cream and soft gold Jacquard bodice, with full tulle skirt and matching gloves that stretched to six inches above the elbows, had last been worn by her mother. It had been handed down from Sophia's maternal grandmother, who had received it as a gift for her own wedding nearly a century previously from the wife of her employer, a wealthy rancher in Cordoba, Spain, who bred pedigree fighting bulls for the rings in Madrid, Barcelona and Seville.

Sophia's dark hair and green eyes were highlighted with a jewelled tiara, which was also a family heirloom.

The remainder of the Provenzano family, Sophia's mother, Maria, and brother, Bernado, had left earlier in another car.

At breakfast that morning Bernardo had told the family about the duello Lorenzo had been forced into against Sophia's former boy friend, Luigi. He also described how Lorenzo had courageously triumphed and then mercifully refused to kill Luigi.

Sophia was, of course, relieved that her future husband had been victorious and had come out of the knife fight with no serious injuries.

There were gasps of approval and admiration from the congregation in the crowded Chiesa Santa Maria as Sophia arrived on her father's arm. Lorenzo, dressed in a white tuxedo and maroon trousers and bow tie, was waiting at the altar with Lucky Luciano, his best man, at his side. Sophia was a little alarmed when she first glimpsed the long strip of plaster stretched down the left side of Lorenzo's face from cheek to jaw. It hid 30 stitches, neatly inserted by the deft and skilled fingers of Dottore Pucio, whom she had already spotted in church.

A little more than half an hour later the parish priest Padre Matteu pronounced Sophie and Lorenzo 'uomo e moglie' – man and wife.

They kissed passionately, Sophia proud to have become the new Signora Berni while Lorenzo believed he was the happiest man on the island of Sicily.

The reception for more than 100 guests was held at the restaurant where Sophia worked. She had personally chosen the buffet menu.

There were six varieties of hot pasta. Fish in abundance - arogostas, gamberetos, and salmone. Copious quantities of meat, hot and cold - carne di marzo, agnello, carne de maiale. Mounds of pane, white, brown and crusty, produced at the local panneteria. There were large brightly coloured porcelain dishes overflowing with every kind of fruit - melas, arancias, prugna, melones, uvas, fragolas, and lampones. Then there was wine – hundreds of litres of it in pitchers and traditional straw covered bottles - Valpolicella, Barola, Frascati, Chianti and Champagne.

It was a feast fit for the assembled barons of the Unione Siciliano and their ladies – married and unmarried.

In keeping with Unione tradition the guests brought with them wedding gifts in brown bustas_containing large denomination lire and dollar bills. These were handed into the top table where Lorenzo and Sophia were seated at the side of a four-tiered torta de matrimonio, which would later be cut and sliced ceremoniously.

Each gift was acknowledged with a kiss from the bride. At the end of the soiree Signor and Signora Berni were richer to the merry tune of nearly $50,000.

But there were two very special surprise gifts. One came from Lucky Luciano and the other from Tara. During the reception Lorenzo had noticed Lucky in deep conversation with the ageing Rafael Casiraghi, owner of the restaurant and Sophia's boss. After a long discussion Rafael and Lucky repaired to the restaurant office for half an hour.

Towards the end of the evening Lucky came and sat beside Lorenzo and handed him a thick buff envelope containing documents.

'These are the deeds of the restaurant,' explained Lucky. 'Rafael Casiraghi told me earlier that he planned to retire – he is 70 years of age, you know – so I bought the business as a wedding present for Sophia and yourself. Sophia is the best chef in Sicily, one of the best in Italy if it comes to it, and will be able to run the restaurant as good if not better than Rafael. As for you Lorenzo it will give you a legitimate business standing and will be excellent cover for your other activities.'

The newly-weds were delighted with the gift and for Sophia the dream of one day owning her own restaurant had come true.

Tara's wedding present was equally generous and when they opened the two slim crocodile skin covered, velvet-lined presentation boxes they discovered 'his and hers' matching gold and diamond encrusted Cartier wrist watches.

The wedding party finally came to end at 9 pm when a chauffeur driven limousine arrived to take the bride and groom away to a top Palermo hotel where the bridal suite had been reserved for the night.

Before they departed Tara kissed them both warmly with the blessing: 'Good luck, my darlings, in your married life. Look after each other.'

The honeymoon had to be short because Lorenzo was about to start on the first of his planned bank raids with his new gang. It meant he would periodically be separated from Sophia early in their marriage but as they both agreed it would give her the opportunity to build up the restaurant business.

CHAPTER 43

Only two days after the wedding Lorenzo called his gang of four men together for a briefing on how he had planned their first bank raid.

He had explained the situation to Sophia without divulging any secrets about his scheme. It was best that she knew nothing if ever she was questioned by the police. But as a good Sicilian wife married to a Unione mobster she never asked about his movements.

'Our first target will be a bank in Trieste,' Lorenzo told his men, who were now eager for action after their spell of training in Sicily. 'It is a busy bank which handles a lot of money for the shipping companies that use the free port.

'It is situated in the Piazza dell' Unita next door to the Peschiera, which is one of the finest aquariums in the world.

'We will split up into two groups, which could confuse the cops if they follow us after the raid. Luigi Corbello, Frances Tabardini and Paulo Gabbatini will travel by speedboat across the Golfo di Trieste, while I will travel in the Mercedes with Tomas Bertorelli at the wheel.

' It will serve as a getaway car for everyone should Luigi, Frances and Paulo be unable to get to the speedboat after the raid.

' However if everything goes well, and I see no reason why not, half the money, which we will stuff into sacks will be loaded onto the speedboat while the other half will be put into the trunk of the Mercedes. That way if any of us are caught the cops will only get half of the stash.

'The speedboat can be tied up in the marina at the Stazione Maritimo where it will not attract attention amongst the dozens of other leisure craft moored there.

'Security inside the bank is nothing to be frightened of. There is one guard – an ex cop who is turned 60 years of age. He carries an old Beretta pistol but I doubt that he has ever pulled it out of the holster in anger. We certainly don't want any shooting so it will be your job Frances Tabardini to rap him over the head and keep him out of action.'

Lorenzo had chosen the target well. Trieste was a bustling free port dealing with millions of tonnes of legitimate cargo being exported to all quarters of the globe. This in addition to being the main link in the evil supply of heroin from Italy to the USA – a trade in which Lucky Luciano was the main organiser.

It followed that the local bank would always be holding vast amounts of cash in many of the world's currencies.

*   *   *

Lorenzo had decided that Sophia would continue to live with her family until the local builder had renovated and decorated the apartment over the restaurant, which the previous owner had used as a storeroom.

When completed with luxury bedroom and en suite bathroom the apartment would be their love nest when Lorenzo returned to Sicily between bank raids.

Nevertheless they were both sad when he left with his gang for the mainland.

*   *   *

They travelled on the ferry from Catania to Reggio di Calabria, on the toe of Italy, that night where they split up into two parties. Lorenzo with Tomas Bertorelli at the wheel travelled in the Mercedes while Luigi Corbello, Frances Tabardini and Paulo Gabbatini picked up a van which would also carry the tools they thought they would need.

Their next rendezvous was in the exquisite city of Verona, the setting for Shakespeare' plays 'Romeo and Juliet' and 'Two Gentlemn of Verona'.

It was not, however, for any romantic reason that Lorenzo chose the 13th century building in Via Capello, which houses the famous balcony where the lovely Juliet is said to have stood listening to Romco, as their meeting place! They checked into a small hotel situated in the Campo della Fiera, which is claimed contains Juliet's tomb, where Lorenzo gave his men their final briefing before the raid.

*　　*　　*

The following morning Lorenzo and Tomas set off along the autostrada to Trieste while the other three cut off to Venice where they transferred the gear from the van to the speedboat that Lorenzo had arranged to be left for them. They would then skim across the placid Golfo di Trieste where they would all meet up again before the bank raid.

On his reconnaissance trip a few weeks earlier Lorenzo had spread a few $100 bills amongst local government officials in Trieste and had managed to get hold of the town building plans. He had carefully worked out that it was quite possible that access to the bank could be gained overnight through the connecting wall of the neighbouring Peschiera.

It was a job ideally suited for the nefarious talents of former cat burglar Luis Corbello.

He would hide in the toilet of the aquarium after it closed to the public at 8 pm, then lay low until the town had quietened down after midnight. Then he would unlock the front door and admit Lorenzo and the rest of the gang.

Lorenzo had worked out that only a small explosive charge would be needed to weaken the connecting wall so that it would be easy to break through to the bank.

Providing Lorenzo's calculations were correct the gap in the connecting wall would take them straight into the bank's strong room where the money was kept. It would be up to Corbello to use his skills with locks to open the strong room door from the inside allowing access into the main hall of the bank where Frances Tabardini would quietly put the elderly night guard out of action.

*   *   *

Lorenzo's plan worked perfectly.

The speed boat, one of the vast fleet of smuggling craft owned by Lucky Luciano for his rum running, drug peddling and contraband cigarette dealing, was waiting fuelled and ready at the marina in Venice.

Corbello, Tabardini and Gabbatini made smooth passage across the Gulf to Trieste and were on time for their tryst with Lorenzo and Tomas Bertorelli who had enjoyed an uneventful journey in the Mercedes.

En route Lorenzo had asked driver Bertorelli to pull off the autostrada and call in at the villiage of Latisana where he bought provisions for the day at the local negoziante di generi aimentari.

He purchased three kilos of prosciutto, three whole salamis, pane and two kilos of formaggio and several bottles of wine and mineral water.

After leaving the Mercedes in a public car park Lorenzo and Bertorelli strolled leisurely to Trieste's 14th century cathedral and there, as arranged, amongst the magnificent 12th century frescoes and mosaics they met up with Corbello, Tabardini and Gabbatini who, having safely tied up the speedboat at the Stazione Maritima, had also meandered through the town.

After collecting the Mercedes they spent the day in a nearby forest where they picnicked on the provisions that Lorenzo had bought and dozed the time away in the hot afternoon sun.

At 6.00pm Lorenzo drove Luigi Corbello into town and dropped him near the Peschiera

The former cat burglar spent the next couple of hours wandering through the many spacious rooms of the dimly lit aquarium. He spotted a broom cupboard where he was sure he could safely hide when the aquarium closed to the public at 8 pm. He also spotted that a portable tank of tropical fish was handily situated against the connecting wall with the neighbouring bank.

That was good-after he had breached the wall and admitted Lorenzo, and the other gang members at midnight, they would be able to pull the fish tank back in place to hide their forced entry.

He spent a couple of hours viewing the exhibits in the aquarium and was particularly fascinated with the impressive collection of sharks. But his favourite part of the exhibition was the section containing the different specimens of sea horses from all the world's oceans.

*   *   *

At 7.45 pm most of the public had already drifted out of the aquarium and, making sure he was not spotted, Luigi

Corbello selected one of the skeleton keys he carried on a ring and slipped into the roomy broom cupboard. It was a tedious wait until 10 pm when he let himself out of the cupboard and made sure all the staff had left.

Lorenzo had thought that a small explosive charge would be needed to break through the connecting wall from the aquarium but when Luigi began hacking away with his heavy knife he found that the cement had rotted over the years and the bricks came away easily. In just under quarter of an hour he had opened up a cavity in the wall that the gang would easily be able to clamber through.

As the clock, in the nearby church tower, struck midnight Luigi slipped the lock on the front door of the aquarium to admit Lorenzo, Frances Tabardini and Paulo Gabbatini while Tomas Bertorelli would be waiting in the getaway Mercedes in a turning opposite the bank waiting for their signal to hopefully pick them all up with a haul of stolen cash.

Lorenzo was the first through the gap in the wall and gasped with joy to see the bundles of paper money stashed along the shelves of the strong room. He told the men to concentrate on dollars and English sterling pounds and forget the Italian lire. They crammed 12 naval type canvas kitbags full of folding money inside half an hour.

Luigi Corbello had meanwhile figured a way to unlock the strong room and, by snipping a few electrical wires, avoid triggering off an alarm. Tabardini, efficiently, took care of the ageing security guard with a sharp rap on the head with his cosh.

Luigi, making sure that the front door of the bank was not wired to an alarm, opened it up and signalled with his torch to Tomas Bertorelli to bring the Mercedes. They all piled in quickly, squeezing the 12 kitbags into the trunk of the car.

Bertorelli quickly sped to the waiting speedboat where six of the kitbags were loaded for the quick trip across the Golfo di Trieste also carrying Corbello, Tabardini and Gabbatini.   They met up with Lorenzo and Bertorelli, who carried the other six kitbags, in the Mercedes, at the city of Venezia later that day.

*   *   *

The gang's rendezvous in a Venice restaurant that evening was a merry get together although Lorenzo had warned them against any ostentatious spending spree which would attract the notice of the police. Strangely there had been no news over the radio or in the evening press about the robbery and Lorenzo guessed the bank were trying to keep the raid secret.   But he knew the insurance investigators would try and pick up their tracks. They collected the van they had left the previous day and ordered Bertorelli to drive the 12 kitbags full of bank notes to Naples where Lucky Luciano had already arranged for it to be 'laundered' through various business contacts in the city.

A quick count-up in their Venice hotel room revealed that their haul had come to the equivalent of $180,000 (USA).   Even allowing for the $18,000 that Lorenzo was obliged to hand over to the Unione Siciliano, via Luciano, it was a haul that matched up to anything that they had anticipated.

Lorenzo decided there and then that the gang would quickly strike again while the iron was hot before the insurance investigators got on their trail.

 He called his four men together in Naples four days later and told them that they would launch another raid the following week and that their target would be a bank across the border in France.

CHAPTER 44

Lorenzo Berni had proved what a shrewd tactical leader he was with his immaculate planning of the sortie against the bank in Trieste.

He surprised the members of his gang when he informed them that their next raid would be against a bank in the French university city of Grenoble, which straddles the junction of the winding rivers of Isere and Drac.

A city with a number of wealthy inhabitants, including influential academics connected to the university, Grenoble featured many architectural gems. Tourists came from all over the world to see the Church of St Laurent with its 6th century crypt and the 12th century cathedral, which boasts an exquisite altar canopy.

Standing in the wooded heights that surround Grenoble is the Carthusian monastry of La Grande Chartreuse, founded by St Bruno in 1084, where the famous green and yellow liqueurs originated.

Lorenzo had shrewdly figured that with so many tourists milling through the city that the local bank would be holding a huge quantity of foreign currencies.

The raid on the bank in Grenoble would be a tricky operation entailing the gang crossing the border under the eagle-eyed French customs, immigration and police officials. Five men all showing Italian passports at one border crossing would attract attention that Lorenzo aimed to avoid.

He knew he could not afford any organizational errors in his planning for the complicated mission into foreign territory. He had already worked out, to confuse the

French authorities, that he and his gang would have to cross the border using four different methods-sea, air, road and rail. That way the gang would not leave a pattern of entry into France that the authorities would pick up quickly-if at all.

The escape route after the raid would also be vital! It would have to be designed, Lorenzo decided, to put the police off their trail, particularly until they had crossed the border into Italy.

Lorenzo's entire strategy for the Grenoble project was based on the mob's link with the Mineo Tile Company of Naples.

They were a company with a close connection with Unione Siciliano, with whom he had liased during an undercover trip to the USA on Lucky Luciano's behalf some years previously.

In fact he chose the target in France after learning that the Mineo Tile Company were designing, manufacturing and delivering a special consignment to a building site adjacent to the campus of the Grenoble University who were erecting a new sports, theatre and assembly complex.

The firm's high-sided lorry, when specially adapted, would make an ideal escape vehicle that would not attract the curiosity of the French gendarmerie after the hoist on the bank in Grenoble.

Using Lucky Luciano's influence with the Mineo Tile Company-in fact the gangster chief was the major stockholder in the firm- Lorenzo had arranged for a carpenter and a panel beater to install a false compartment to the interior of lorry. A compartment where three men and the stolen loot could be secreted while the vehicle crossed the Francese-Italiano border.

All five of his gang would carry false passports created by Unione Siciliano forgers. Lorenzo and Tomas Bertorelli would man the lorry carrying documents identifying them as driver and mate, long serving employees of the Mineo Tile Company. They would drive the lorry on the long haul from Napoli to the University building site on the outskirts of Grenoble. Help the site workers to unload the consignment of tiles before booking into an inconspicuous boarding house for the night prior to the return journey to Naples.

In fact they would meet up with the other three members of the gang in the early hours, raid the bank and all make their escape in the lorry, hopefully crossing the border into Italy before a hue and cry could be raised.

The gang would rendezvous at the town of Vizelle, only a few kilometres from Grenoble. Luigi Corbello, it was decided, would fly from Rome to Lyon, changing planes in Paris. From Lyon he would either purchase or hire a car or van for the 90-minute road journey to Vizelle. Frances Tabardini would travel by sea in one of Lucky Luciano's smuggling boats from Genova to Nice and then by coach to Grenoble. Leaving the final member of the gang Paulo Gabbatini to travel by train from Rome to Grenoble, changing trains at Gare de Lyon in Paris.

There would be no pattern for the gendarme's, flics or insurance investigators to trace.

'Security at the bank in Grenoble during the night is similar to what we found at the Trieste bank,' Lorenzo briefed his gang. 'It is the responsibility of one guard. But there is one chink in the Grenoble bank's armour! I don't know if the manager is aware but his night guard let's himself out of the bank at 11 o'clock every night and walks 100 metres down the road to the local bar for a few drinks and a sandwich.

'I know all this because I monitored his movements over several nights when I did my reconnaissance for this caper. Furthermore I don't give a fuck whether or not the manager knows that his night guard slips out for a drink but it gives us an easy chance to get access without having to break in to the bank. This should be an easy heist. All we have to do is ambush the night guard on his way back from the bar. We will take his keys and let ourselves into the bank.

'We will tie him up and leave him bound and gagged after we leave the bank with the loot. That way he will not be discovered, and no alarm raised until the manager comes to open the bank at 8.15am the following morning. By that time we will be several hours drive away from Grenoble and safely over the Italian border.

'Tomas Bertorelli and I will leave the Mineo Tile Company's lorry parked overnight in the village of Vizelle where we have booked a room for the night. We will use the car or van Luigi Corbello has hired in Lyon as an escape vehicle that will take us from the bank to Vizelle where we will transfer into the lorry. We will then dump or torch the hired vehicle to destroy any evidence that might help the cops.

'This could be an even simpler heist to pull off than the Trieste caper was.'

*   *   *

The Berni gang converged on the sedate city of Genoble from all points of the compass. Lorenzo and Tomas, alternating at the steering wheel, the lorry, almost fully laden with decorative ceramic tiles, drove at a steady speed to avoid the attention of the traffic cops in Italy and France.

At the French border their documents passed the scrutiny of immigration and customs officials, who also inspected and approved of the load the lorry was carrying. All the papers and the manifest of the load conformed to regulations laid down by the French government for the import of building materials into the country.

Lorenzo and Tomas broke their journey with an excellent meal in a little restaurant on the outskirts of Genoa before driving on to the university of Grenoble. There, with the help of the construction workers, they took two hours to unload the lorry.

The boarding house, where they had decided to stay overnight, was owned and run by a delightful middle aged French speaking Swiss lady who fussed over them plying them with coffee and chocolate cake.

They paid Madam Annette Foincet in advance, adding a generous tip to the amount she had asked for. They explained they would be making an early start the next morning.

There would be no need for her to get up from her bed at 4.am to see them off. She thanked them for their consideration and said she would leave a pot of coffee for them to heat up and a packet of chicken sandwiches for them to take on their long journey.

After thanking Madam Foincet again, they informed her they would be going out for a drink later that evening.

The other three members of the gang all turned up for the rendezvous with Lorenzo and Tomas within two hours of the appointed time at the local bar in Vizelle. They had found rooms in another part of town where they would rest until late in the evening when they would meet up again before their raid on the bank.

Luigi Corbello had bought an old Fiat van in Lyon and they would use that to transport them from Vizelle to Grenoble and back to Vizelle after the robbery. It was decided that when they did get back to Vizelle and the lorry that Corbello would dump the van in some secluded spot. It could not be traced back to them because Luigi had used a forged passport when the salesmen took down his details as he bought the van.

*   *   *

Lorenzo outlined the plan for the evening's raid on the bank and ordered his men to meet him again at 9 pm when they would all travel in the van to Grenoble.

They set up the ambush to waylay the bank's night guard after he left the bar where he had several drinks and a plate of sandwiches. The guard was a little unsteady on his feet as he returned to the bank well after midnight. He was too merry and mildly inebriated, to sense danger or to even suspect that he would be attacked.

Lorenzo gave the responsibility for immobilizing the guard to Paulo Gabbatini, who quietly stepped out from a clump of bushes before rapping him twice over the head with a leather-covered cosh. Frances Tabardini and Luigi Corbello helped Paulo to truss and gag the guard and relieve him of the large ring of bank keys, which hung on a short chain from his belt to his trouser pocket.

They bundled the unfortunate guard into the van and carried him with them as Luigi let the gang into the bank with the front door key.

The whole operation took less than 45 minutes as Luigi selected the correct key to admit the gang to the bank's strong room where they were dumbstruck with the neat piles of French francs, English pounds, Italian lire, and, most important of all, US dollars.

Out came the naval type kit bags that had served them so well in the recent exploit at Trieste – all fifteen of the canvas made bags with a piece of draw-rope at the top were quickly stuffed with bank notes to their capacity.

So excited were Lorenzo and his men, at the sight of what would be their richest haul yet, that all five men were momentarily oblivious to the night guard they had left trussed up in a corner of the bank's main hall.

The rap over the head from Paulo Gabbatini's cosh had sobered him up by the time he started to regain consciousness. Fury mounting that he had been careless and would certainly lose his job, he started to work and niggle at the cord that Paulo had tied around his wrists and legs.

Finally, by sheer persistence and the convenient proximity of the metal corner on a coffee table, he managed to free his right arm. He loosened the other arm and his ankles and surreptitiously stretched his fingers down to his right sock where he had secreted a flick knife that had been carelessly missed when he was ambushed. This stealthy move, unfortunately for him, was spotted in the nick of time by Paulo, who had been deputed to keep a watch on the guard.

The irate bank employee was just sighting up to hurl his deadly flick knife at the inviting back of Lorenzo who was intent on stuffing a kit bag with bundles of $100 bills.

Paulo almost certainly saved Lorenzo's life as he instinctively, from a distance of five metres, flung his own Bowie knife at the agitated bank guard. It hit the target and there was an audible gush of air as the vicious blade buried itself to the hilt in the doomed guard's windpipe.

Lorenzo looked behind him, horrified at the danger he had been in! He walked over to the twitching man, his own Luger pistol suddenly appearing in his right hand. But as he stood over the prone figure, a fountain of gore spurting from the horrific gash in the luckless guard's throat, Lorenzo could see it was all over.

'The bastard's dead.' Lorenzo said. 'But thanks Paulo, it might have been me. But it's put a difficult edge to this caper. We had better get the fuck out of here and get on the road back to Italy as soon as possible. With a bit of luck this fuckin' carrion will not be found until the manager opens the bank early tomorrow morning.

'That should give us seven hours start if the flics get on our trail. With a lot more luck we should be safely over the border in Italy by then.'

They quickly piled the bulging bags, full of bank notes, into the van that Corbello had hired the previous day in Lyon and sped off to Vizelle where they transferred the stolen cash into the Mineo Tile Company's lorry.

Luigi Corbello drove in front of the lorry in the van as they headed towards the Italian border. About 20 kilometres from Grenoble, following Lorenzo's orders, he wheeled the van into a side lane and set fire to it.

'That way all traces that could lead to us, like fingerprints, will be destroyed,' said Lorenzo who later, after a quick count of cash they had stolen, as the lorry sped on its way, came up with an estimation that their haul was more than $1.3 million – much of it in USA dollars, the most wanted currency in the world.

But their greedy delight was dampened by the thought that they were not only bank robbers but also cold-blooded murderers. Lorenzo warned them they would have to be careful because they would now certainly attract the attention of such high powered law enforcement agencies as Interpol, who had their headquarters in Paris, America's FBI and Italy's secret service Guardia de Finanze.

CHAPTER 45

Getting across the frontier presented no problems to Lorenzo and his gang apart from the butterflies that fluttered around their stomachs as French and Italian border officers scrutinised the lorry.

On the French side the gendarmes waved the unladen vehicle through after a cursory look inside. Luigi Corbello, Frances Tabardini and Paulo Gabbatini held their breath in trepidation, trigger fingers poised on their pistols, inside their secret compartment.

Lorenzo, perched up in the driver's cab alongside Tomas Bertorelli, cleverly diverted the attention of the caribierni on the other side of the frontier. The broad shouldered Italian cops, all of them over the mandatory 6ft 2inches or taller, were delighted with the two bottles of Napoleon brandy handed down from the cab window.

'Don't get too ubriaco boys,' grinned Lorenzo. 'We ought to have brought a couple of those French prostitutas and had a party.'

The sergeant caribienieri came back with his own brand of humorous repartee.
'If you had we would have locked you up for being pimps.' he laughed.

Within minutes they were ceremoniously waved through and the lorry powered southwards towards Napoli. A few kilometres inside Italian territory Tomas pulled the lorry into a lay-by to allow the three other stiff-limbed members of the gang to clamber out of the stifling confines of their secret compartment and stretch out in the spacious back of the lorry.

They stopped once on the five-hour journey for a meal, washed down with three bottles of vintage Barolo, at a roadside café just off the autopista at the town of Magliano Sabina.

Resuming their journey after the break Lorenzo switched on the radio in the cab and they heard the first flashes of news about the bank raid in Grenoble.

Inevitably the murder of the bank guard was at the top of the story. Information about the robbery was skimpy but a spokesman for the bank claimed that nearly $2 million had been stolen. There was no suggestion that the bank robbers were Italians but the report said the French police were staging a nationwide search for the criminals.

By the time they drove into Naples later in the day all five men were dog-tired after all the adrenalin they had released in the previous 24 hours.

Lorenzo told his men they would have to lay low for a few weeks to allow things to quieten down. He handed them $2,000 apiece but warned them about going on a spending spree that would alert the cops. Finally he told them they would get together on the island of Sicily four weeks later to prepare for their next bank job.

*   *   *

Lucky Luciano was delighted with the report that he received about the bank raid at Grenoble when Lorenzo called at his Naples villa the following day.

The mob boss shrugged aside Lorenzo's worries about the consequences of killing the bank guard.

'In our line of business these fuckin' things happen,' said Lucky philosophically. 'It's a risk we take. Don't worry about it. If it presents a problem we'll deal with it.'

214

Lucky then said he had an important job that he wanted Lorenzo to organise for Unione Siciliano.

'The fuckin' government have appointed a new Public Prosecutor in Palermo,' he explained. 'He is causing the organisation a lot of grief.

'He has already arrested three of Aldo Caramusa's men who are facing charges of armed robbery, hijacking and kidnapping. This cocksucker has got to be chilled quickly. I don't care how it is done as long as you don't leave any leads that can be traced back to us.

'Word has got back to our brothers in the USA who have a lot of family and friends in Sicily. Frank Costello has put out the word that he wants this matter attended to as soon as possible.'

Lorenzo said he would look into the situation promptly and would report back to Lucky as soon as he had come up with a way to eliminate the troublesome lawman.

As he left the villa he spotted his cognato Bernardo Provenzano polishing the new Bentley limousine Luciano had recently shipped over from England. After they had embraced and kissed each other on the cheeks Lorenzo told Bernardo that he would be travelling to Sicily the following day to see his sister Sophia.

'Don Luciano has obviously told you the organisation over there is having problems from the new Public Prosecutor – a shit-arse called Giorgio Fiore,' said Bernardo, adding a warning. 'So watch your step. The bastard has already nabbed some of Aldo Caramusa's men and the newspapers are saying that he has been sent from Rome to wipe out the Unione Sicilione.'

Lorenzo thanked Bernardo for the words of caution and said that he hoped he might see him over in Sicily in the next few weeks.

'You never know with Lucky,' Bernardo said. 'A couple of months sometimes go by and he never mentions the island. But then one morning over breakfast he will tell me to pack the suitcases and get the car ready and that we would be travelling to Sicily on the afternoon ferry. You just never know with the boss...'

Luciano had been warned that the FBI were liasing closely with the Italian police and the appointment of a tough line public prosecutor, Giorgio Fiore in Sicily, the very heartland of the Cosa Nostra, almost surely meant he was being watched closely. As Lorenzo drove out of the villa on the outskirts of Naples he noticed that two of Lucky's mobsters were posted at the huge wrought iron entrance gates. Lorenzo figured that the FBI was trying to crack down on the pipeline of hard drugs travelling via Italy to the USA. A sinister pipeline organised by the world's biggest trafficker in cocaine and other drugs – Lucky Luciano.

*   *   *

Lorenzo took the Mercedes with him on the ferry to Sicily the following morning and drove immediately to meet Sophia at their restaurant in Corleone.

'Can the restaurant get along without you for few days mi amore?' Lorenzo asked after embracing her passionately. After Sophia explained that her cameriere capo-head waiter-could manage the business as long as she phoned him every day while her assistant cucinare could cope in the kitchen as long as she left him a list of menus to follow.'

216

'That's great because I have hired a penthouse suite overlooking the sea at the town of Marsala for five days.' Lorenzo said, grinning as he gave his new wife the news. 'It will be our honeymoon. We did not have much time together after the wedding.'

After organising things in the kitchen and a long talk with her assistant cook and Head Waiter the excited Sophia joined Lorenzo at one of the restaurant tables where they shared a lobster dinner and a bottle of Dom Perignon champagne.

'Although I will probably be on the island for a few weeks more after we have had this short break I will be very busy,' Lorenzo warned his wife. 'So let's make the most of this holiday mi amore.'

The following day the couple packed their cases into the trunk of the Mercedes and set off on the short journey to Marsala on Sicily's south coast.

Sophia and Lorenzo enjoyed an idyllic five days vacation. They lazed about soaking up the Mediterranean sunshine during the day, cooling off occasionally with a dip in the penthouse pool. They found a small but delightful restaurant just outside the town where the owner Signora Gina Rossano cooked such wonderful pastas that Sophia asked her for some recipes to take back with her.

But the holiday was too soon over and they were both a little sad as the Mercedes headed north towards Corleone.

*　　*　　*

Lorenzo got down to work immediately the following day planning ways how to follow Lucky Luciano's instructions and deal with the danger to Unione Siciliano by the inquisitive Public Prosecutor Giorgio Fiore. He drove up into the mountains and met local bandit chief and Unione capo Aldo Caramusa.

'This bastardo Fiore is at the moment spending a lot of time in the port of Siracusa, in the east of the island, trying to sniff out how we ship the heroin to the USA,' said Caramusa. 'As a result we have to clear our warehouses and suspend all shipments of drugs to the USA. This fuckin' cop is a pain in the arse. He's already got three of my men in gaol but they have all refused to talk and our avvocato thinks the mother fucker Fiore will not be able make any charges stick.'

Lorenzo considered Caramusa's obscene outburst carefully. Unione, Siciliano, through their capo di tutti capo, Lucky Luciano, had entrusted him with a particularly lethal contract.

CHAPTER 46

Lorenzo knew that his reputation in the mob was at stake to make this one of the most perfect gang-hits of all time.

The cover-up for himself, and whatever helpers he drafted into assist with the caper, had to be one hundred per cent foolproof. The chilling of the troublesome Giorgio Fiore had to be precise, clean and flawless. This asshole of a Public Prosecutor had to disappear off the face of the earth without trace.

A bungled job would bring down a heap of trouble for Unione Siciliano both sides of the Atlantic and, even though he himself was a made man in the mob, it would mean that his own throat would be cut. The organisation suffered failure badly.

He would also have to bear in mind the necessity of a cast-iron cover up for Lucky Luciano and Aldo Caramusa, who, in the eyes of Italy's Guardia de Finanze and the USA's narcotics bureau, would be the first suspected of organising the assassination in Sicily of Signore Fiore.

Lorenzo's choice of modus operandi would be vital. A car bomb would be too messy, leave too many clues and would be open to a disastrous misfire.

His man Paulo Gabbatini's gruesome garrotte would be a fitting end for the crum Fiore' but it would point the finger at the man considered to be the best in Italy at twisting that barbarous wire around a pop-eyed victim's neck.

A knife in the back thrown by the dead-eyed Frances Tabardini might produce a noiseless end for that pig of a

Public Prosecutor but again there would be a margin of error. If Tabardini's uncanny accuracy with the blade was even a fraction off target Fiore would survive to wreak terrible revenge on Unione Siciliano.

The end for Fiore, Lorenzo decided, had to be swift and sure without leaving the slightest trace of forensic evidence.

*   *   *

Fortuitously Lucky Luciano celebrated his birthday with a huge party for nearly 300 guests at his villa in Naples. Several marquees were erected in the vast grounds of the villa and an army of 200 caterers, chefs and waiters employed. More than 50 Unione Siciliano armed 'soldiers' took care of security. The party provided the backdrop for the perfect cover-up for not only was Lucky Luciano prominent as host but Aldo Caramusa would be a guest as one of the mob's leading Dons.

The vital factor, from the point of view of the perfect cover-up, was that many of Napoli's leading citizens, from the city's civic and legal authorities were at Lucky's birthday party. Even the Chief of Police, a man who had been on Unione Siciliano's payroll for several years, was amongst the guests.

*   *   *

Lorenzo started the planning for one of the most important mob murders in the bloody history of the ruthless Unione Siciliano by calling his gang member Tomas Bertorelli from his family holiday in Siracusa, the very Sicilian town where the Public Prosecutor had based himself.

Tomas was ordered to monitor Fiore's every move and to come up with a detailed pattern of the Public Prosecutor's daily habits. He did the job conscientiously, his report emphasising that for nine hours every day Fiore was accompanied by two plain clothes policemen as he trawled Siracusa's docks and warehouse district trying to lift the lid off the mob's trade in narcotics.

But at nine o'clock each evening his two police aides left him to return to their lodgings for supper while Fiore went to a local waterside restaurant for dinner. Having dined on his favourite pasta and bistecca controfiletto Fiore said goodnight to the restaurant owner Rafael Panetti and strolled along the dockside to his hotel.

Tomas Bertorelli assured Lorenzo that Giorgio Fiore did not carry a gun as he considered it inappropriate for a Public Prosecutor to walk around 'tooled up' like the common hoodlums he was chasing. A brave, but foolish public servant trying to pit his wits against a ruthless enemy who had no scruples.

Restaurateur Rafael Panetti, ironically, had been in the pay for many years of the mob who had used his cellar on numerous occasions as a store house for tons of raw opium and heroin before it was secreted aboard cargo and passenger ships bound for the USA. He would have willingly cooperated with Unione Siciliano if Lorenzo had decided the hit would take place in his restaurant.

Appealing as that idea was, Lorenzo, carefully assessing the situation, concluded that it would inevitably point the finger at the organisation. If Fiore disappeared off the face of the map without trace the cops could think what they liked but would be without any evidence to put before the courts.

*   *   *

Lucky Luciano's birthday party was the most opulent 24 hours soiree since Mount Vesuvius erupted so many

221

centuries past disrupting the extravagant social whirl of ancient Pompeii.

Whole suckling pigs, baby lambs and an ox were roasted on a span of spiralling spits manned by a coterie of chefs. Lorenzo, with the beautiful Sophia on his arm, moved around the milling guests stopping here and there to chat with Tara and other old friends. He had a long conversation with Pietro Tamolli, Naples Chief of Police who had been collecting $5,000 a month from Lucky Luciano to smooth the way for any of the Unione Siciliano brotherhood who might fall foul of the law.

The sumptuous buffet continued all day being replenished with fresh supplies by the chefs and watchful wine waiters.

The afternoon hours were taken up with a travelling circus in one of the large marquees. Lorenzo and Sophia particularly liked the bare back riders performing ballet movements as their jet black Arab mounts pranced around the ring.

With all the champagne, wine and spirits that had been freely flowing for hours no one noticed Lorenzo slip away from the party in late afternoon. He had prepared Sophia, who was staying with him as Lucky Luciano's houseguest, for his departure saying: 'Mi amori. I have some important business to attend to but I don't want anyone to know I am leaving the party. If anyone asks about me just say I have gone to my room for a shave, shower and a change of clothes.'

As the sister of one mobster and the wife of another Sophia knew better than to question what Lorenzo had said. She just kissed him passionately and said: 'be careful mi caro. Remember I love you.'

Less than half an hour later Lorenzo lay flat in the back of Lucky's Bentley, so as not to be seen, while Sophia's brother Bernardo drove him to a small field two miles away where a helicopter was waiting with rotors turning to warm up the engine.

Just over two hours later, Lorenzo was met by Tomas Bertorelli as the helicopter landed on farmland just north of Siracusa. They drove towards the city and a kilometre from the outskirts they liased with the other three members of the gang, Luigi Corbello, Frances Tabardini and Paulo Gabbatini who had arrived by sea, in one of Lucky Luciano's ex-British navy torpedo boats, earlier in the day.

Gabbatini, the garrotte expert, was chosen to waylay Giorgio Fiore as he left the waterside restaurant after his dinner. Stepping from an alleyway he slugged him with a leather-covered cosh. Tabardini and Corbello helped to carry the unconscious Public Prosecutor to where Lorenzo and Bertorelli were waiting on the dockside.

Bertorelli had a mobile cement mixer revolving, it contained a mix of sand, cement and water as between them they bundled the comatose Fiore's body into a large oil drum.

Lorenzo now took charge of the proceedings. Leaving nothing to chance he bent over the oil drum and pushed his Uzi machine pistol roughly against the lolling head of Fiore and emptied a full magazine into the doomed public prosecutor. Having completed his deadly task Lorenzo then spat on the gory mess that was Fiore's cranium and muttered: 'Rest in fuckin' hell you mother fucker.'

Lorenzo then tossed the pistol alongside Fiore's body before Bertorelli wheeled up the mobile mixer up and poured the viscous concoction of cement, sand and water to the very brim of the drum. The doomed Fiore's head was completely covered with the cement mix that had turned pink as his death blood oozed to the top.

Lorenzo's final chore, calling on his former experience as a blacksmith, was to weld the lid tight on the oil drum using a portable welding kit that Bertorelli had also brought.

Without further fuss Corbello, Tabardini and Gabbatini manhandled the oil drum onto a hand truck and pushed it towards the dock where they had moored Lucky Luciano's smuggling boat.

Lorenzo and Bertorelli drove speedily to the waiting helicopter and were soon airborne enroute for Naples and an appearance at the final celebrations of Lucky Luciano's birthday party.

Meanwhile as the helicopter whirred towards Naples, down below, the evil three-man crew of a former Royal Navy torpedo boat unceremoniously consigned a heavy oil drum to the deep blue waters of the Mediterranean, without so much as a prayer to send the gruesome remains of the former Giorgio Fiore on its way.

CHAPTER 47

Lorenzo's stock was now high in the upper echelons of the Unione Siciliano and there was no doubt that the organisation's Dons, on both sides of the Atlantic, perceived him to be a possible heir-apparent to the ageing Lucky Luciano, as the capo of the mob's operations in Europe.

Word came by messenger from the delighted boss in America, Frank Costello, to Luciano suggesting Lorenzo should be given a bonus of $100,000 for the ruthless and professional way he had handled the demise of the hated Public Prosecutor Giorgio Fiore.

'It lets the FBI and the Italian cops know that we have a long arm,' Costello said in the letter he sent by hand to Luciano. 'Lorenzo is a good professional and, as far as I am concerned, no job is too big to trust him with.'

Lorenzo was delighted with the handout the organisation had given him. He gifted the four members of his gang Tomas Bertorelli, Luigi Corbello. Frances Tabardini and Paulo Gabbatini $5,000 apiece for their part in the Siracusa caper but, as always, warned them not to draw attention to themselves by going on a wild spending spree.

Lorenzo's wife, Sophia, was making a success of running the restaurant Lucky Luciano had bought for her in Corleone and it was now showing a good profit. He was already a millionaire and had decided that the next bank raid would be the last before the gang concentrated on less hazardous, but just as profitable, capers.

Once again Lorenzo did his homework carefully. After much consideration he chose Lecce, a prosperous city in

225

Southern Italy on the heel of the peninsular, as the target venue for the gang's swan song in the precarious business of robbing banks.

A road and rail junction in a busy agricultural region the city housed thriving factories producing cigarettes, toys, pottery, glass, furniture and wine. In particular the brassware and wrought iron manufactured in the city was outstanding. With a population of nearly 100,000 the city of Lecce, built mainly in the 16th and 17th centuries when it was part of the kingdom of Naples, attracted thousands of tourists from all over the globe to view its cathedral built in 1670, Bishop's Palace, Seminary, Governor's Palace and 16th century castle.

It figured that the local bank would not only be loaded with lire but would also have in its safekeeping currencies from all parts of the world.

But what really excited Lorenzo was the information he gathered during an incognito three-day, reconnaissance trip that on the last Thursday of every month the bank handed over the local cigarette factory's payroll, in cash, to two of the firm's wages clerks.

The collection of nearly $120,000 in used, mainly large denomination, lire notes was undertaken by these two unarmed men who took the sacks of cash from the bank and piled them in the trunk of a waiting car driven by a company chauffeur.

Lorenzo hit on a brilliant plan to fox the local police in Lecce. A double heist that would send the cops scurrying like scalded cats in abortive circles

Three of the gang would hold-up the bank within minutes after the tobacco company's two representatives had collected the wages and had driven off in the car towards the cigarette factory on the outskirts. Three kilometres out of town Lorenzo and Frances Tabardini

226

would hijack the car with their sacks of cash packed into the trunk.

Luigi Corbello and Paulo Gabbatini, with Tomas Bertorelli in charge of the caper, would hold up the bank. Bertorelli would drive the specially tuned Mercedes get away car and liase with Lorenzo and Tabardini at the spot where they had hijacked the car! The problem was how to take care of the two pay clerks and the chauffeur of the Company car.

Lorenzo, with his meticulous attention to detail, decided that the four members of his gang and himself would each be armed with the traditional American mobsters' weapon - the extremely portable, deadly at close range, Thompson machine gun.

A burst or two from one of the 'Tommy's' would quickly stifle any resistance inside the bank, which was guarded by only one security man carrying a holstered light calibre pistol.

As for Tabardini and himself they would use an old subterfuge of faking a road accident to bring the company car transporting three men and the tobacco factory payroll to a halt. Here again the Tommy guns could be easily concealed yet possess formidable fire-power at close quarters.

*   *   *

As usual Lorenzo went to extraordinary lengths to arrange a cover up for himself and his four men. Paulo Gabbatini took Luigi Corbello to stay with him at his mother's house in nearby Brindisi in the week before the caper in Lecce. Having established a reason for being in the area they created an alibi by spending much of the morning in the steam room of a local Turkish baths. In fact, in collaboration with the manager of the baths – a man who had helped the mob before – they slipped out of a side door and returned a few hours later as if they had never left the steam room at all.

Tomas Bertorelli drove to Lecce in the Mercedes, which would outpace any police car, and speed the whole gang from the area. Lorenzo and Frances Tabardini took the train from Naples to the city of Foggia in southern Italy where they established an alibi by ordering 100 cases of the highly rated local wine for Sophia's restaurant in Sicily. Under cover they then flew on to nearby Brindisi in a tiny plane, piloted by a former Italian air force officer who, in the past, had completed several smuggling trips for Unione Siciliano.

*   *   *

All five men rendezvoused, as arranged, at a little bar opposite Lecce's 16th century Chiesa Sant'Irene.

The raid on the bank at Lecce went as smoothly as the freshly greased wheels on the express steam train that had conveyed Lorenzo and Tabardini so swiftly from Naples to Foggia.

Lorenzo's organisational genius was once again in evidence with the evil and innovative ploys he planned in the two-tiered caper in the ancient city of Lecce.

Using Unione Siciliano's vast list of contacts he arranged for a brightly painted red van to be parked outside the target before and during the raid.

Several eyewitnesses remembered seeing the red van parked outside the bank and told the police so when questioned.   The van was in fact on bona fide business and was enroute for a further delivery of locally grown potatoes at Taranto some 80 kilometres away. This red herring, set up by the astute Lorenzo, sent the police off on

228

a time-wasting wild goose chase. By the time the harassed policemen had caught up with the van two hours had elapsed after the bank raid.

Two hours which were invaluable in Lorenzo and his gang's escape from the crime scene. The cops' faces were as red as the van when, after the abortive chase, the driver produced his manifest to prove he was on legitimate business delivering a consignment of potatoes to restaurants in the ancient town of Taranto. Thanks, again, to Lorenzo's shrewd planning, Corbello, Gabbatini and Bertorelli were probably the first ever bank robbers to use the new-fangled full faced motor cycle helmets modelled on the metal headgear worn by pilots of the modern jet-propelled fighter aircraft that had displaced the petrol-driven ME 109's, Spitfires and Hurricanes of World War II.

The three bandits strolled into the bank after watching, from across the street, the two wages clerks load the cash for the cigarette factory workers' payroll into the company car.

Pulling down the visors on their gaudily painted crash helmets they held up the bank's customers, staff and it's solitary security guard with their menacing Tommy guns.

Within quarter of an hour they had stuffed more than $300,000, in USA and various hard European currencies, into sacks and made off at speed for their rendezvous with Lorenzo and Frances Tabardini.

Half an hour earlier Tabardini had spread-eagled himself across a road four km out of town with Lorenzo bending over him as if there had been an accident.

The payroll vehicle braked and the driver and two wages clerks got out to see if they could help. To their utter astonishment and dismay they found themselves staring into the ugly and intimidating snouts of two Thomson machine guns.

A spray of bullets from Lorenzo's 'Tommy' was enough to curb any thoughts the three cigarette factory employees might have had of offering resistance. With Lorenzo's gun covering him Tabardini trussed up the three men with wire cable and manhandled them into the trunk of their car after they had been first curtly ordered to transfer the sacks of cash into the rear seats.

Just over half an hour later, a jubilant Corbello and Gabbatini drove up in the souped-up Mercedes, with Tomas Bertorelli at the wheel, to join Lorenzo and Tabardini. There followed a few minutes of excited chatter as the mobsters gloated over their haul of more than half a million dollars from the double-headed caper.

But Lorenzo sharply brought his men down to earth with the rasping reminder: 'If you stupid fuckers don't stop gossiping like a bunch of washer women at the fountain the cops will soon be coming up this road in a few minutes after us....'

Lorenzo heard tapping from inside the trunk of the hijacked car. He walked to the rear of the vehicle lifted the lid of the trunk and shouted at the three trussed up hostages: 'Shut up. You fuckin' crums.'

A muffled voice pleaded from the trunk: 'Let us out. We can't breathe...'

Lorenzo grinned evilly! To the complete astonishment of his gang he pointed his Tommy gun and with a flamboyant spraying movement pulled the trigger for several moments until the magazine was empty! A few piteous groans were followed by deep silence as blood began to ooze through the blanket that had been slung over the three doomed hostages.

The eerie silence spread from the gory mess in the trunk of the car to Lorenzo's four aides who were, for the moment, shell-shocked with the speed and viciousness of their chief's violence.

Tomas Bertorelli was the first to regain his equilibrium and he stuttered: 'But what are we going to do with them?'

Lorenzo smiled and said truculently: 'I've already made arrangement for that also. We are going to drop the three fuckin' stiffs and their fuckin' heap at a farm 40 kms up the road on the way back to Napoli. It is owned by a man known to the mob as – di impresarii di pompe funebri – the undertaker! He is an allevatore di maiales – a pig breeder!
'He'll take care of those three lumps of fuckin' carrion – or to be more precise, his 200 pigs will. He'll also get rid of the fuckin' car for us!'

Less than an hour later the Mercedes, driven by Lorenzo, pulled into a farm just outside the town of Brindisi. It was closely followed by the hijacked car and its grisly load, with Bertorelli driving. Lorenzo greeted the farmer warmly, slipped him $5,000 in stolen bills and said: 'You know what to do Pinot?'

The bearded farmer nodded and promised: 'Don't worry those three cadaveres will be dinner for my pigs, and their fuckin' car at the bottom of the Adriatic Sea, come tonight.'

As Bertorelli tooled the powerful Mercedes out of the farmyard Lorenzo and his four men could hear the rattle of a chain saw doing its macabre work on the three bullet-ridden corpses.

They stayed that night en route to Naples in a hotel near the city of Benevento in the Campania region.

As they sat down to a sumptuous dinner Lorenzo joked: 'I think we should start with prosciutto – after all we have got an interest in the pig meat trade.'

It was a gory end to the gang's depraved venture into the risky profession of bank robbery.

Chapter 48

Lorenzo Berni, blacksmith, brothel porter, bank robber, gang boss and multi-murderer, decided that he needed a vacation.

The mob killing of the hated Public Prosecutor Giorgio Fiore in Syracusa followed by the training for, and completion of, the bloody bank heist in Lecce, meant that it was a month since he had last seen the lovely Sophia.

Having bade farewell to the four members of his gang when they arrived back in Naples, following the caper in Lecce, he told them to enjoy themselves as he did not want to see them again for two weeks.

Before taking the ferry to Sicily, the following day, for a romantic reunion with his wife, Lorenzo visited his capo di tutti capi, Lucky Luciano, and his long time friend Signora Tara the brothel madam.

*　　*　　*

At his palatial villa, overlooking the tranquil Bay of Naples, Luciano warmly welcomed his protégé and ordered bodyguard Bernardo to bring a bottle of champagne in an ice bucket to the side of the swimming pool while he talked business with Lorenzo.

'Congratulations on the success of the job in Lecce,' grinned Lucky. 'As always, you organised well and the local police seemed to have been completely baffled by your tactics. What is more a haul of half a million dollars was very acceptable and I know the Unione Dons will be pleased with their cut.

'But that might well be chicken feed compared to what the capos in the USA are going to call on you soon to handle for them. The heat is on the mob Stateside,

233

because of the cock-sucking US Attorney-General Robert F Kennedy, the brother of the President.   Bobby Kennedy is conducting a serious crackdown on Mafia and Unione Siciliano activities.

'But Angelo Bruno, the mob's capo in Philadelphia, is sitting on $5 million worth of stolen, instantly negotiable, bearer bonds. Yeah, five million bucks. But they are shit scared to sell them in the States because Bobby Kennedy and his team of prosecutors are waiting to nail them.

'Bruno has passed the word down to me that, the only short-term solution to the problem is to sell the bonds in Europe,and that he would be prepared to accept 50 cents on the dollar to get rid of the bearer bonds. I don't need to spell it out Lorenzo, amico, but that would gross us a profit of two and a half million greenbacks.

'All these bearer bonds have certificates of origination and it will be up to you to persuade bank managers in Italy, France, Switzerland and England to change them into their local currency at the up to date rate of exchange. Angelo Bruno has particularly asked that you be put in charge of the operation.

'As I have said the organisation in the States only see this as a short term solution and they know the long term answer will be to ice Bobby Kennedy or his brother President John F Kennedy, or both.'

Lorenzo was quite excited about the important task that was being handed to him, but said: 'I was rather hoping to get a couple of weeks vacation with Sophia. I haven't seen her for a month...'

Lucky interrupted: 'don't worry about that Lorenzo my lad. Angelo Bruno is sending his chief bodyguard, Eddie Pucci, over from the States on the Queen Elizabeth with the bearer bonds. It will be ten days from now before the Queen Elizabeth docks at Southampton so it will be nearly two weeks until he reaches Naples.'

234

The arrangements suited Lorenzo admirably and, as he said goodbye, he told Luciano that he would be travelling to Sicily to join up with Sophia the following day. That evening Lorenzo called at the bordello and was disappointed to find that Tara was feeling unwell.

'It's nothing to worry about darling,' Tara said after giving him a warm embrace and a kiss on the cheek. 'I have just got a pain in my stomach – it's not that bad. A touch of indigestion I think! My, you are looking handsome. It's good to see you.'

Tara and Lorenzo talked until well after midnight when he left to grab some sleep at his apartment in the centre of Naples. To Tara he was still like a well loved son and she would never have believed that he had become such a vicious killer. The following morning he drove his open-topped Mercedes sports car to the ferry terminal on the first stage of his journey to be reunited with his beloved Sophia in Sicily. But just before he left the apartment he received a phone call from Luciano.

'I have placed my yacht at your disposal for the next 14 days,' said Lucky. 'I have instructed my skipper Gustav Holden – he is Swedish and you will like him – to take the yacht to my berth in Termini Imerese, which is only about a half an hour's car journey from Corleone. I have told Captain Holden to provision the yacht for a two-week cruise and he will take Sophia and yourself wherever you fancy going. Make sure you both enjoy yourselves.'

*   *   *

Sophia was delighted to see Lorenzo when he walked in to her restaurant at Corleone later that evening.

'It seems like years since I last saw you caro, mio,' she smiled and kissed him passionately. When Lorenzo told

235

her that Lucky Luciano had given them the use of his yacht for the next two weeks Sophia was ecstatic.

'That's wonderful innamorato,' she said, tears of joy welling up in her eyes. 'I will have to arrange a few matters here at the restaurant before we go, but I'll be ready to leave after breakfast in the morning.'

*   *   *

Just after midday the next day Captain Holden, with the help of his crew of three, plus a ship's cook, had cast off and the yacht Rosa Bianco put on course for Vulcano in the Aeolian Islands.

That evening the skipper skilfully moored the Rosa Bianco off the islet of Vulcano that takes its name from the volcanic ructions and the mountain that rarely erupts, unlike the more famous one on the neighbouring island of Stromboli.

Sophia and Lorenzo were taken ashore by one of the crew in the yacht's rubber dinghy fitted with a powerful outboard motor. They asked the sailor to collect them at midnight before they strolled around the little island where they gazed in wonder at the spouting geysers, smoke holes and bubbling mud baths. Another feature of the islet of Vulcani that intrigued them was the black volcanic sand.

They found a restaurant where they enjoyed a superb dinner washed down with a bottle of the, richly heavy, local wine.

Sophia and Lorenzo were deliriously happy as they clambered again into the rubber dinghy and returned to the Rosa Bianco. Even then they decided to prolong their idyllic evening when they spent an hour stretched out on the moonlit deck of the yacht sipping brandy.

236

It was the night their child was conceived.   Hopefully it would be a boy, which Lorenzo planned to have named Salvatore Berni – Salvatore had been the given name to Lucky Luciano when he was born in the Sicilian mining town of Lercara Friddi six decades earlier.

For the next seven days the Rosa Bianco leisurely cruised around the other Aeolian Islands including Stromboli and Lipari.   They spent an unforgettable weekend ashore on the island of Panarea, the smallest and least known of the Aeolian Islands.   Leaving the yacht for 48 hours they booked into Panarea's small, and romantic, hotel, the Raya, a favourite with honeymooners.   They spent the whole of one morning on the Hotel Raya's terraza sipping chilled Camparis, watching the Rosa Bianco swaying at anchor quarter of a mile away and the volcano of Stromboli, in the distance, erupting every 15 minutes or so.

They decided to spend the second week of their vacation cruising around their own fantasy island of Sicily.   They stopped off at Cefalu, a charming town with one of the loveliest squares in Italy with graceful palm trees in each corner providing a suitable guard of honour for the sublime Norman cathedral.

They stopped off at other seaside resorts such as Erice, Selinute, Agrigento and Taormina where they spent their last night aboard.   Sophia decided that as a gesture of gratitude to Captain Holden and his crew she would cook a special dinner for everyone aboard.   Even for a cordon bleu chef like herself, cooking dinner for seven people in the yacht's minute galley was quite a challenge.

The Chinese cook, Ling Ling Hui, was unhappy at first about handing over his galley to 'Missy Sophie', but when he realised that it was meant as a compliment he grudgingly fell in with the arrangement and even offered to assist as Sophia's kitchen porter.

Ling Ling went ashore in the rubber dinghy with Sophia and carried the ingredients for the meal she was going to cook. What a truly delicious meal it was with a main course of tonno fagioli, Sicilian-style tuna marinated in fennel, chillies, garlic and the zest of fresh lemons.

She made everyone sit down at the table in the main saloon of the yacht while she served them all personally. Lorenzo did the honours with the drinks making sure everyone's glass was kept full with a non-stop flow of Vapolicella and Frascati.

The entire company laughed when the Chinaman said appreciatively: 'Missy Sophie a velly, velly good cook. Ling Ling give her job in his galley any time.'

But it was over all too soon and the most fantastic two weeks of their lives had ended. For Lorenzo the nightmares of the blood he had shed so evilly in the past year had evaporated in Sophia's passionate embraces.

Yet as the euphoria died he was aware that he now faced his most daunting assignment for the powerful Unione Siciliano. An assignment that would make or break him as one of the organisation's big shots.

CHAPTER 49

As Lorenzo Berni pointed the sleek Mercedes sports car towards the Sicilian ferry port of Catania, en route to Naples, $5 million worth of stolen bearer bonds were steaming across the Atlantic in the custody of a vicious hood known in the American underworld as Eddie 'Coyote' Pucci.

Although Pucci's main job was bodyguard to evil gambling guru Angelo Bruno, Unione Siciliano's capo in Phildelphia, he was also a mob enforcer. God help any welshing punter, having lost a pile on Bruno's roulette wheels, blackjack or crap tables, or in one of his horse parlours, and failing to pay-up, who received a visit from the bloodthirsty Pucci.

Pucci was the only man in US criminal history to have been released from Death Row after winning an appeal on a legal technicality against what the FBI believed was a cast-iron indictment for a gangland killing. Once Pucci, nicknamed 'Coyote' early in his criminal career as a nocturnal petty thief, handed him the bonds, Lorenzo would be on his own with the problem of how to dispose of that vast fortune in instantly negotiable bearer bonds. The danger was that the huge financial sums involved, filtered into the post war economies of various European countries, would arouse the interest of Italy's secret Guardia de Finanze, USA Treasury agents and Interpol.

It was a formidable and, possibly, dangerous assignment.

Lorenzo phoned Lucky Luciano as soon as he arrived back at his apartment in Naples. Thanking Lucky for the use of his motor yacht he told the Capo di Tutti Capi how much he and Sophia had enjoyed the vacation.

'Eddie Pucci, the hood Philadelphia boss Angelo Bruno has chosen to act as courier for the bearer bonds, phoned when he landed at London's Heathrow airport last night,' Luciano told his protégé. 'He will arrive at Napoli airport at six o' clock this evening. I told him you would meet him. He will hand over the bonds to you and fly back to New York via Rome the following morning. From then on the bonds will be your responsibility.

'It would be courtesy to our American cousins if you laid on some hospitality for him tonight.'

Lorenzo had already alerted the four members of his gang to report back after their two weeks vacation and meet for a briefing over lunch at the Trattoria di Vesuvio near the Naples waterfront.

Lorenzo told them that Tomas Bertorelli would be at the wheel of the big Mercedes when he met the American mobster, Eddie Pucci, at the airport.

Aware that top security was necessary to protect the shipment of bonds, he ordered Bonds, he ordered Luigi Corbello, Frances Tabardini and Paulo Gabbatini to ride shotgun in a second car and follow the Mercedes when it left the airport with Pucci and himself.

Tomas Bertorelli would lead the convoy to the palatial villa owned by Lucky Luciano, who had agreed that the bonds could be locked away in his electronically secured strong room.

As usual Lorenzo's planning was immaculate and everything went off smoothly. The bonds deposited securely in Luciano's strong room, Lorenzo checked Pucci into the most expensive suite of a top Naples hotel and laid on a night of entertainment for his American guest.

Lorenzo arranged for two busty showgirls to join Pucci and himself at the nightclub table when they dined.

'Gee! That's great my buddy 'Renzo – I'm partial to a bit of Italian pussy,' said Pucci who kept everyone at the table enthralled with anecdotes about the six months he spent incarcerated on Death Row.

'I'll go down in history as the only guy to walk away free from that fuckin' situation,' he boasted.

'A fuckin' cell on death row, which allows you only six paces in any direction, prepares you for anything. Nah, I wasn't fuckin' scared just fuckin' bored. The only reading matter you are allowed on Death Row is the bible and a law book. I had a smart mouthpiece who beat the rap and saved me from being fried like crispy bacon in the chair, but I was guilty as 'ell of chilling those two crums. May they both rot in 'ell'

During what turned out to be a merry party two bottles of Dom Perignon champagne were brought to the table for Lorenzo's party.

'With Signor Luciano's compliments,' explained the cameriere as he popped the corks, filled the four glasses, and placed the remainder of the champagne in the ice bucket.

Lorenzo and Eddie Pucci, looked across the room where Lucky Luciano was sat at the usual table with his mistress, Igea Lissoni, a former night-club entertainer, and raised their glasses in salute.

When Lorenzo, Pucci and the two show girls were ushered out of the club by the flunkied doorman, in an emerald uniform so ornate that it might have been designed by the late, and unlamented, Mussolini, Tomas Bertorelli was waiting at the wheel of the Mercedes limo.

He drove them to Pucci's hotel where they all went up in the elevator to his suite.

Strangely, despite his time working for Tara as the porter in the bordello, Lorenzo's knowledge of women was not extensive. His only love had been Sophia and, apart from a couple of liaisons with Tara's prostitutas he had no other experience of sex.

When Pucci produced some cannabis from his suitcase and a packet of cigarette papers it opened up a new world of perversion and deviation.

'This is the best Colombian Gold hash,' said the American mobster with an evil grin, as he rolled four reefers. 'A couple of tokes of this and we'll all be flying high.'

They all finished in the jumbo-sized bed, swapping partners frequently. It was the first time that Lorenzo had experienced oral sex as one of the show girls, called Anna, got down to him.

'You like that caro don't you?' she laughed. 'Now you get down and taste my pussy.'

It was a night of depravity filled with drink, drugs and sex and the first time that he had been unfaithful to Sophia.

'What the fuck does it matter?' Lorenzo assured himself. 'Sophia ain't ever goin' to know.'

Lorenzo awakened with a massive hangover at 8 o'clock the following morning when Pucci had to leave for the airport. He gave the girls a wad of $100 bills and told them to take a taxi before he rang down to the hotel lobby where Tomas Bertorelli was already waiting.

He said farewell to the American, whose company he had enjoyed, and said that Tomas was waiting to drive him to the airport.

Now, on his own in the hotel suite, Lorenzo, after ordering a pot of black coffee from room service, realised that he now had to get down to the serious business of disposing of $5 million worth of stolen bearer bonds.

CHAPTER 50

Lorenzo Berni knew that shifting $5 million worth of stolen bearer bonds was not going to be an easy task and that he would need powerful allies if he was going to succeed.

He decided to start his mission in London, a city that competed with New York and Paris for nightlife, attracting many of the world's high rollers, since the opening of Mafia capo, Meyer Lansky's, Colony and Sporting Club, in Berkeley Square. No expense was spared to entice well-heeled punters to part with their currency at the roulette wheel, blackjack and crap tables at this opulent nightspot, which was fronted by Hollywood star George Raft.

Lorenzo was a dashing figure in his ivory-white tuxedo, ruffled dress shirt and maroon velvet bow tie as he joined three of Britain's most evil crooks at the 'Colony'. The Kray twins, Ron and Reg, accompanied by their older brother Charles, were notorious and already provided protection, on behalf of Unione Siciliano and Mafia to wealthy high rollers from the American world of entertainment, politics and big business who travelled to London to spend holidays, see West End shows, go shopping in Bond Street and Knightsbridge, and hobnob with London's elite at the Colony.

Lorenzo was accompanied by his chauffeur-bodyguard Tomas Bertorelli whom, the, astute, Kray family, noting the ominous bulge under the left armpit of his dinner jacket, was 'tooled up'.

The proposition put by Lorenzo attracted the Krays. It was a ticket to earning quarter of a million bucks. Even for the sinister twins, both destined a few years later to spend the rest of their lives behind bars as murderers, $250,000 was a very acceptable hand-out in the 1960's – with the promise of even more cash to come from the American mob.

Despite their tough reputation the Krays knew that, with the omnipotent Unione Siciliano and the legendary Lucky Luciano behind the bearer-bond scam, they would have to play square with the American wise guys. The deal was for the Kray organisation to dispose of $2 ½ million worth of the stolen, negotiable, bearer-bonds amongst their influential contacts in London's banking, insurance, stock-broking and political circles. Ron Kray, well known as a homosexual and deviant, even had under his control a prominent member of the House of Lords, for whom he procured rent-boys.

Ron, indisputably the head of the gang of East End hoodlums, assured Lorenzo that his organisation were quite capable of handling the business for Unione Siciliano.

'We'll give our elder brother, Charlie, a special assignment of distributing the bearer bonds amongst leading businessmen and politicians who owe us a favour or two!' assured Ron Kray, with a knowing wink at Lorenzo.

During the ensuing business talk Ron Kray promised that his organisation would follow Lorenzo's instructions in every detail. After the bonds had been sold they would deposit the sterling equivalent, based on the current exchange rate, into a numbered Swiss bank account nominated by Lorenzo. There was a promise that, in return, Unione Siciliano, who were busy setting up various operations concerning drugs dealing, gambling, protection and kidnapping all over Europe, would use the Kray mob to run their affairs in the UK.

Much of that business would entail 'heavies' from the Kray gang protecting wealthy clients of Unione Siciliano, particularly high profile Hollywood film stars and important business tycoons, when they visited the United Kingdom. But the American mob lost interest in the Krays when the notorious East Enders were caught, tried, convicted and imprisoned for life for the gory murders of George Cornell and Jack 'The Hat' McVitie – from that time the Krays were considered to be carrying too much baggage as far as the capos of the American underworld were concerned.

'Well, now that we have settled our business, what can I arrange to make your night out in London a memorable one?' asked the leering Ron Kray, whose sexual preference for boys and young men was well known.

Lorenzo, although appreciating that Ron Kray was only trying to be hospitable, made it quite clear that his personal liking was for females – young sexy women.

'Yeah!' grinned Ron Kray. 'I am sure we can fix someone who will whet your appetite.'

The wild night in a Naples hotel with American hoodlum Eddie 'Coyote' Pucci and two sexy showgirls had already honed Lorenzo's sexual taste buds. Now he had crossed the frontier of marital infidelity, he was quite hardened about being unfaithful to his wife.

'What the fuck does it matter?' he asked himself. 'Sophia ain't here and ain't never gonna know about it and, sure as hell, I ain't gonna to tell her.'

The girl that Ron Kray arranged to join Lorenzo at the table in the plush Colony Club was a voluptuous, emerald-eyed, auburn-haired beauty. 'A dead ringer for Rita Hayworth,' the lusting Lorenzo mused to himself.

Her improbable stage name was Sylvia – Sylvia Stardust! She was an aspiring actress who had graduated from drama school, at the age of 18, two years previously. She claimed she had played several small parts in West End theatre productions, adding that her ambition was to get into films.

'Do you know any Hollywood producers that might give me a chance to break through into the movies?' she asked, the green eyes, suggestively, blinking between fluttering false eyelashes.

Switching on his most charming smile, Lorenzo replied: 'The Italian film industry is booming at the moment. I have a lot of contacts in the business. When I return to Naples I'll make a few phone calls and see if I can arrange a screen test for you.'

It was a conversational exchange that set their relationship off to a good start and certainly did no harm to Lorenzo's cause as a would-be seducer. As a result he persuaded the luscious Sylvia to return with him to the Savoy Hotel for the night. In fact she indicated that she would have been disappointed if she had not been invited. Whether her acquiescence was because she knew, like most young actresses, the quickest route to stardom was often via the casting couch, or her first sight attraction to the handsome Italian gangster, was anyone's guess.

Tomas Bertorelli drove them in the hired Bentley to the Savoy, where one of the hotel's largest suites had been reserved in Lorenzo's name. Tomas, who was billeted in one of the small single rooms designated for the personal staff of the hotel's wealthy guests, was ordered by Lorenzo to have the car ready at 10.30am the following morning for the cross channel Dover-Calais ferry.

Once in the suite Lorenzo picked up the phone and asked room service for a bottle of pink champagne and a serving of caviar to be brought up to the suite. The waiter wheeled in a trolley, the champagne in an ice bucket and the beluga caviar nestling in a bed of crushed ice, and left the suite delighted with the crisp $100 bill he received as a tip.

*   *   *

There were no inhibitions as far as the gorgeous Sylvia was concerned. When she stepped naked from the bathroom. Lorenzo, feeling a stirring in his loins, noted that her nipples were proud and pink with anticipation. When she slid alongside him between silk sheets in the jumbo-sized bed without hesitation she grasped his engorged penis. Openly admiring its size and hardness she felt the swollen organ throb as she took it in her mouth. He hurtled towards a climax as her flicking tongue explored the formidable shaft from base to tip.

'That was magic darling,' he gasped. 'Fuckin' magic.'
He reached over the ice bucket at the side of the bed and poured two glasses of bubbly. Within a few minutes he had recovered enough to accept her crude invitation to: 'Climb into the saddle darling.'

He mounted her in the missionary position. Quickly settling into a thrusting rhythm, he had Sylvia pleading: 'Fuck me – fuck me hard Lorenzo. I want to feel you come inside me.'

They lay back, momentarily exhausted, and sipped more champagne. Significantly she was ready first to resume their raunchy romp.

'Bend over darling,' she ordered in a husky voice. Lorenzo complied, wondering what she had in mind.

Without more ado she impelled the first finger of her right hand into his anus. 'Ooh! Ooh!' he exclaimed through the exquisite pain as her probing digit worked like a piston. His penis, responding to her attack from the

249

rear, stood enormously erect as she encircled her left arm round his body and briskly stroked his manhood.

His viscous juices spurted and then oozed between her scarlet, manicured fingers.

They finished off the remaining champagne and fell asleep curled up with their arms around each other. Inside the hour she awakened him and groped for his flaccid flagpole again.

She was an expert in the arts of lovemaking. It was if she had read Kamasutra from cover to cover and memorised its ancient Hindu eroticism word for word. Within seconds her probing hand had roused his rampant rod to its full glory once more! This time she varied her attack. Climbing into the saddle she mounted him with her back towards his face.

This back to front tactic tightened the grip of her vagina on his now massive member. She pumped him into frenzy until, gasping with joy, she felt his surging spate cascade.

'Fuckin' 'ell Sylvia – that was fuckin' marvellous,' he panted.

Their all-night orgy abated in the hour and half before dawn. They wrapped their arms around each other their lust sated. At 8.30am, he roused, looked at the illuminated bedside clock, picked up the phone and ordered Eggs Benedict, coffee and toast for two from room service.

'Look, Tomas Bertorelli is driving me to Paris via the Dover to Calais ferry this morning,' Lorenzo told the still drowsy Sylvia. 'We will be staying at the Ritz Hotel for two nights before travelling back to London. You could go shopping while we do some business during the day. But my evenings will be free and we can try the top Paris nightspots.'

Sylvia, now casting aside her drowsiness, eagerly accepted the invitation even before Lorenzo had hinted that there would be a generous cash bonus for her at the end of the trip to the French capital.

She only had one problem and demurred: 'But I have no suitable day clothes with me for an excursion like that.'

Lorenzo, confident he knew how to look after a dame, assured her: 'Don't worry I will give you $5,000 to spend in the best shops in the world like Cardin, Courréges and St Laurent. At the end of trip there will another $5,000 spending money for you.'

Lorenzo picked up the hotel phone again and asked the hotel hairdresser to come up to the suite to shampoo and set Sylvia's hair. At the same time he arranged for the Savoy's barber to give him a trim and a shave.

CHAPTER 51

It was late afternoon when Tomas Bertorelli wheeled the Bentley into the forecourt of the Ritz Hotel – time enough, after they had checked in, to hire a car and chauffeur to take Sylvia on a shopping spree to Paris's leading haute couture houses.

'Be sure you buy a nice evening gown' said Lorenzo, handing her a thick wad of $100 bills. 'We'll be going out on the town tonight.'

Since Lorenzo had led the raid in Marseilles, which ended with gory death for the notorious Hubert twins, Gaston and Louis, the French equivalent of Britain's evil Kray twins, the head of France's underworld had been the sinister Papa Jean-Pierre Corbieré. It was a tryst with Papa Jean-Pierre that brought Lorenzo to Paris with a view to the French crook handling and disposing of a consignment of the stolen bearer bonds on behalf of Unione Siciliano.

Lorenzo knew that Jean-Pierre's organisation controlled many of the Bureaux de Change in the French capital's main line rail stations of Gare de Nord, Gare de l'Est, Gare de Lyon, Gare Montparnasse, Gare d'Austerlitz and Gare St Lazare in addition to those at the three main airports of Charles de Gaulle, Le Bourget and Orly.

Papa Jean-Pierre had influential contacts in Monaco and it was rumoured in the French criminal world that he also owned an interest in the Société des Bains de Mer the private company, which has operated the casino at Monte Carlo since 1898.

Papa Jean-Pierre, who had cooperated with Unione Siciliano in their drug running operation between

Marseilles and the USA, to their mutual satisfaction and financial advantage, chose as venue for the meeting with Lorenzo the noted Parisian watering hole of the Café des Deux Magots.

Situated on the corner between Place St Germain des Prés and Boulevard St Germain the café was famous as the regular rendezvous for Jean-Paul Sartre and the members of the Existentialist school of philosophy after World War II.

Papa Jean-Pierre, making the arrangements for the meeting when Lorenzo rang him from his suite at the Ritz Hotel, said he would be available for talks at the Café between 8pm and 9pm, as he would be travelling to Marseilles on business later that evening. Papa Jean-Pierre informed Lorenzo he would be accompanied by a lady friend and his bodyguard. When Lorenzo added that he would also have a lady with him and his chauffeur-bodyguard, Tomas Bertorelli, the French gangster said that he would organise two sidewalk tables one for four people and one for Lorenzo and himself some distance away so that they could talk business in private.

*   *   *

Sylvia was a very happy woman when she came back from her shopping expedition, what girl wouldn't with $5,000 to spend in the fashion district of Paris in the late 1960's? She had opted for simplicity. Classical Parisian simplicity. For eveningwear she chose a fluid crépe column dress and matching jacket. In a deep pink it had stylised satin-embroidered roses encircling a shaped neckline, the lined dress had a fishtail back and a back zip fastening. Edged in satin embroidery, the lined jacket fastened with four covered buttons and roleau hoops.

For daywear she had chosen matching co-ordinating jacket, trousers and skirt. Fastened with three buttons the beige jacket was lined and had front pockets. Also lined the skirt had a part elasticated waistband with belt loops and a back zip and vent. To ring the changes the trousers, also had a part elasticated waistband with belt loops, plus small hemline slits.

She had also bought an elegant stole to go with her evening dress and an exclusive pink supple suede jacket, with top stitching on the shoulder line, and front pockets, turn back cuffs and slide slits. She purchased elegant shoes and accessories to go with both outfits.

She bought one other item a splendid man's floral necktie in delicate blue, green and orange by Pierre Cardin.

It was a surprise gift that really pleased Lorenzo, setting the tone for a wonderful evening during which he never gave a thought to the fact that his wife Sophia, back in Sicily, was pregnant.

'I have got another present for you later,' announced Sylvia.

Lorenzo smiled as he replied: 'I think I know what it is.'

*   *   *

Papa Jean-Pierre was already waiting for them when Tomas Bertorelli slid the Bentley up to the kerb outside the Café des Deux Magots. As Tomas drove the car round the block to find a parking space the Frenchman greeted Lorenzo warmly and kissed Sylvia's hand and said: 'Enchanté Mademoiselle.'

Papa Jean-Pierre then introduced them to a dark-eyed beauty by the name of Annette and to his bodyguard Joel the Turk. He sat at the smaller table for two with Lorenzo while they talked business. Annette, Sylvia, Joel the Turk and Tomas were seated out of earshot at a table

255

several metres away. Papa Jean-Pierre then ordered champagne for the whole party saying, with a Gallic wave of his hand: 'You are my guests – Paris is my home town. You are my guests.

The French hoodlum eagerly jumped at Lorenzo's proposition and said that he would be willing to launder the stolen negotiable bearer bonds.

'It will present no problems to my organisation,' said Papa Jean-Pierre. 'How many have you got?'

Lorenzo, looked around the crowded tables making sure no one was listening and explained: '$2 ½ million dollars worth and your cut would be 10% of the gross - $250,000.'

Without hesitation Papa Jean-Pierre rejoined: 'we'll take the lot. When can you deliver? I will be back from Marseilles tomorrow afternoon. I will take delivery then and guarantee full payment in dollars or francs within a week. We will dispose of them in our six Bureau de Change outlets in Paris – if there are any remaining we will pass them through the Casino in Monte Carlo. Now tell me Monsieur Berni how and where would you would like your money paid?'

Lorenzo handed Papa Jean-Pierre the details of the numbered Swiss bank account that Unione Siciliano would like their $2.25 million for the bonds paid in either pounds sterling, French francs or US dollars at the current exchange rate of the day.

A handshake between the French and Italian mobsters was all that was required to cement their crooked deal and the conversation became more general.

'How is the dope business?' Lorenzo asked, knowing that Papa Jean-Pierre was responsible for shipping thousands of tonnes of heroin, on Lucky Luciano's behalf, for Unione Sicilliano to distribute throughout the USA.

'The supply line of H from Afghanistan is running smoothly and we have got the Afghan authorities in our pocket,' Papa Jean-Pierre told him. 'The only problem that might hit us is the political unrest in the country with Muslim fanatics threatening to overcome the King. To protect against that we are supplying the King's government forces with modern arms to fight insurrection. So we are coining from both ends of the candle, from the supply of heroin to your organisation and the sale of guns to the Afghans. I have a little gift for you and your beautiful lady friend!'

Papa Jean-Pierre handed Lorenzo an elegant phial with a minute spoon and tube attached, all made in silver, and said: 'That is the best cocaine to be found in Europe, it is made from the finest Colombian coca leaves. I promise you it will set you up for a night of passion with that glamorous Sylvia. Furthermore, tonight, I will be honoured if you will be guests at the table that is always kept for me at the Moulin Rouge – I am sorry I cannot join you but it is imperative that I travel to Marseilles tonight.'

*   *   *

Papa Jean-Pierre and Lorenzo joined the two ladies and the two bodyguards, Tomas Bertorelli and Joel the Turk, at the larger table where they finished the remainder of the champagne. They said farewell as the French gangster-chief left in a stretch Citroën limousine with his party to catch the midnight train to Marseilles promising to meet Lorenzo in Paris the following evening.

Tomas drove Lorenzo and Sylvia to the Moulin Rouge where they received a warm reception as guests at Monsieur Jean-Pierre's private table. Their dinner of prawns, followed by rack of lamb and soufflé was excellent and the famous Moulin Rouge cabaret lived up to its reputation.

Lorenzo had given Tomas the rest of the night off when he dropped them at the front entrance of the Moulin

257

Rouge and said: 'We'll take a taxi back to the Ritz Hotel after the show. Leave the Bentley at the hotel garage and enjoy the rest of the evening.'

After leaving the Moulin Rouge Lorenzo and Sylvia strolled through the colourful district of Montmartre, passing the kerbside buskers, beggars and jugglers, and called into several Bohemian bars frequented by the writers, artists and musicians of Paris. It was 2am when the taxi delivered them to the door of the Ritz Hotel.

In the suite, as they both started to undress, Lorenzo teased her: 'Now about that present you promised me earlier....'

Sylvia laughed and replied: 'Well, I know what you think it is greedy man. You wont be disappointed because you will certainly get that also but I have another gift.'

She went to the wardrobe where she had placed several plastic bags when she had returned from the shops the previous afternoon. She produced a long narrow parcel and with her perfectly manicured hands pulled out a 12 inches long phallic-shaped soap.

'A trophy for the man with the biggest penis in Paris,' she laughed. 'Although to be honest I think yours might even be longer than that!'

Lorenzo joined in the laugher and, opening the fly in his pyjamas trousers, producing his own proud phallus, drawled: 'Waal, baby. I guess aahl just havta live up to my reputation. But first let's have a little pick-me-up, courtesy of our friend Papa Jean-Pierre.'

Lorenzo brought out the silver phial of cocaine he had been given by the French hoodlum.

Sylvia carefully topped the tiny silver spoon with powder sniffed it back then repeated the action with the other nostril. She lay back and let the euphoria engulf her.

Lorenzo chose to use the tiny silver tube and laid out four lines of cocaine on a glass- topped coffee table. He took two long inhalations into each nostril. Although many male addicts found that cocaine inhibited their sex drive, as a very occasional user, Lorenzo discovered it actually aroused him.

His penis was engorged when Sylvia bent down and applied her flickering tongue to his already animated genitals. She did not withdraw her mouth as his semen spurted prompting a sigh of contentment from him. They lay back for a few minutes before he returned the compliment and explored her already wet vagina with his tongue.

It was 6am, they could hear a bell tolling, possibly from Cathédrale de Notre Dame, when they lay back on their pillows after their night of debauchery! They awakened at 11 am and Lorenzo pulled off his pyjamas and headed for the bathroom.

'Would you like to join me in the shower?' he shouted to half-awake Sylvia.

She quickly pulled herself together and replied: 'Yes – I'd love to.'

He turned the shower on to a cold, full jet that took her breath away but was immediately interested as she felt his erection pressing against her. She gasped with pleasure as she felt him enter her.

'Bloody hell it's as hard as a rock inside me,' she panted. 'You're making me come already – I can't stop it darling Lorenzo.'

Even as she spoke through the throes of ecstasy she could feel his orgasm erupt inside her.

*   *   *

They were later drinking their cappuccinos and nibbling their croissants in the suite when hotel reception rang to say a telegram had arrived for Lorenzo. Within a few minutes a uniformed bellboy delivered a yellow envelope on a silver tray. Lorenzo slipped the youngster ten dollars and slit the envelope with a stubby forefinger. The message read: Tara taken to Napoli hospital last night STOP She asks you get back to see her quickly STOP It looks serious STOP Saluto STOP Bernardo Provenzano.

The terse and foreboding message from his wife's brother spurred Lorenzo into immediate action. Tara had always been like a mother to him. Closer in his heart to his own mother who he had last seen on her deathbed in that same Naples' hospital when he was only three years of age.

He rang Tomas Bertorelli on the hotel extension and asked him to come to the suite immediately. Then turning to Sylvia he said: 'I have to go to Naples on the first available flight. I am sorry but we have to cut our holiday short. You will have to travel back to London in the car with Tomas.'

Handing her an envelope with five crisp $1,000 bills he added: 'Here Sylvia is the bonus I promised you. We'll be in touch again no doubt.' The last sentence was not delivered with any conviction for he knew that the sexy actress, with the ludicrous stage name of Sylvia Stardust, meant nothing more than a passing ship in the night to him.

He rang hotel reception and instructed them to book him on the next flight from Paris to Naples before giving his instruction to Tomas Bertorelli.

260

'Deliver the Bonds to Papa Jean-Pierre, as arranged, then return the hired Bentley to London and take the broad with you and drop her wherever she wants to go,' said Lorenzo. 'Tara is ill and I have to get back to Naples as quickly as possible – It doesn't sound too good. When you have returned the car you fly back from Heathrow and join me in Naples as soon as you can. Here's $2,000 – that should cover your expenses.'

CHAPTER 52

Lorenzo kissed Sylvia farewell in the suite at the Ritz Hotel before hurrying down to the lobby, where the taxi driver was waiting to take him to Charles de Gaulle Airport at Roissy to the north east of Paris.

But it was noticeably a fleeting peck on the cheek considering how raunchy their relationship had been over the previous three days.

'Will I see you again soon darling?' she asked, anxious not to lose touch with her gangster sugar daddy.

Lorenzo, his mind preoccupied with concern about Tara, almost brusquely, shrugged the query aside and said: 'Yeah, yeah – I'll be in touch some time. Just give Tomas your phone number in London so that we can reach you.'

In just over an hour he was in his first class seat as Air France Flight 98 headed south towards Rome where he would change to a connecting domestic flight, to carry him on to Naples.

*   *   *

The sickly-sweet smell of ether, that pervades hospitals the world over, stung his nostrils as he strode purposefully towards the ufficio of Dottore Nino Bottelini, the medical officer in charge of Tara's case.

Lorenzo knew Doctor Bottelini well for he was a brilliant surgeon who had performed undercover operations for Unione Siciliano, clandestinely removing bullets and stitching knife wounds in mobsters who had been involved in gang wars or shootouts with the Caribieneri.

'How is Tara?' Lorenzo asked urgently.

The medic, stroking his beard thoughtfully, replied slowly and sadly: 'The prognosis is not good. In fact Tara is terminally il.! She has cancer of the oesophagus! She left it too late to come to us and the disease is in an advanced stage. She has not got long to live. Perhaps hours, a day or so – a week at the most.'

It was not the kind of news that Lorenzo had wanted to hear about the woman who had taken a motherly interest in him since he left the orphanage as a lad of 14 years of age.

'Is there nothing that can be done for her?' Lorenzo queried desperately. 'I am prepared to pay for the best treatment in the world if it will do any good.

The medical man could only shake his head sadly.

'All that can be done by anyone is to make her departure as easy as possible. This I give you my solemn promise I will do, Signore Berni.'

Lorenzo wept, for the first time since he had left the Orphanage, as the nurse led him towards the private room where Tara lay.

*   *   *

Her face was pallid, almost skeletal, there was a tube running through her nostril and saline drip in her left arm. She could only communicate in a hoarse whisper after refusing to have her vocal chord removed surgically which, theoretically, might have slightly extended her ebbing life by a week or so, or a few days – no one could give any guarantee.

Tara was dozing, but seemed to sense Lorenzo's arrival as he sat down at the bedside.

'Lorenzo darling,' she said weakly. 'I was praying that you would come in time. I have a lot to tell you. But hold my hand while I get my strength back in a few minutes.'

He held her outstretched left hand and stroked it gently as she fell into a morphine-induced sleep.

She awakened after half an hour, smiled as felt his hand still gripping hers, and said in almost a whisper: 'I am not frightened now that you are here. I know I am dying but I will go, happily knowing that you have been almost like my own son. That is why I have left everything to you. My avvocato will see that you will inherit the money I have accumulated over the years I have been in charge of Charley Luciano's bordello – it amounts to more than $750,000 US – my jewellery I have left to your lovely wife Sophia.

'But before I go-and I know that will not be long now-I want you to know the truth about your mother Gina.'

*   *   *

In between frequent laps of unconsciousness Tara began to relate the horrific circumstances of Lorenzo's birth. She told him how Lucky Luciano had seduced his mother, made her pregnant, paid her father to arrange an abortion and after the mysterious death of her father placed her in Tara's brothel and had her forcibly

265

transformed into a prostitute and a heroin addict – effectively inflicting a premature and agonising death.

Lorenzo was furious, his Sicilian blood, inherited from the father who never wanted him, prompting him to murder Lucky Luciano. Just like the mobster *capo* had ordered the gory slaying of so many of his enemies over the years.

Tara slipped peacefully away that night holding the hand of the orphan she had befriended since he had started work for her at the *bordello* two decades earlier. Her passing emphasised the strange phenomenon that even a hard-bitten harlot is capable of affectionate maternal feelings

Lorenzo Berni, one time brothel porter, vicious murderer, bank robber, smuggler, evil drug runner and gang chief, sobbed unashamedly as the woman who had been so kind to him died holding his hand.

Beyond Lorenzo's grief white-hot anger lurked. The seeds of vendetta had been sown – Sicillian style vendetta passed down in the sperm from the father who had tried to have him aborted while still in his abused mother's womb.

CHAPTER 53

It was as if the heavens had opened up to weep for the demise of Elizabetta Maria Tara as 200 mourners, raincoats dripping from the heavy rain that had fell in torrents since overnight, crowded in to the chiesa di San Filippo de Girolami.

They were gathered to pay tribute to the woman who, known as Lisa Tara, had risen from street corner prostitution in the red light districts of Paris and Rome, to become Tara, Madam of the most notorious, luxurious and raunchiest bordello in the teeming sea port of Naples. A servant of the brothel-owning Unione Siciliano capo di tutti capos, Lucky Luciano, for more than a decade yet, despite her seamy role in life, had retained a warm and generous spirit.

Lorenzo was there elegant, immaculate, in his black silk suit, snowy shirt and black tie. His heart was sad yet, conversely, seething with hate for the biological father, Luciano, who stood beside him as the priest intoned the Requiem Mass.

'Soon you'll get what's fucking coming – you pig.' was the silent promise made with a glance at the loathsome Luciano, standing alongside him again in the rain, as they each tossed a handful of earth on to the coffin in the pit below. 'Just how I'll fix you, I ain't worked out yet,' Lorenzo continued to muse as the manovales di cimitero swung their palas and filled in the chasm of infinity.

*　　*　　*

Lucky Luciano, always a believer in putting on the style, saw Tara his long-serving brothel Madam off in true gangster-funeral style.

He completely took over the plush Trattoria di Vesuvio, near Napoli's waterfront for a reception where, at his expense, more than 200 guests sipped champagne, vino and acquavite by the litre and consumed an impressive buffet of Mediterranean seafood by the kilo! Even Napoli's Chief of Police was there! Why not? He was one of Tara's most important clients.

The still brooding Lorenzo departed for Sicily after the reception to see his wife Sophia who had been unable to attend the funeral because she was pregnant.

Lorenzo planned to spend some time relaxing after successfully completing the task of disposing of $5 million worth of stolen bearer bonds for Unione Siciliano, which had prompted Lucky Luciano to hand him a $50,000 bonus while they were talking during the reception after Tara's funeral.

That handsome handout, however, did not deter Lorenzo's determination to inflict a terrible punishment on Luciano for the merciless and malevolent way he had treated his mother three decades earlier.

*   *   *

Despite Sophia's condition they made passionate love that night in their luxury apartment above the restaurant in the town of Corleone.

There was not even a thought of remorse on Lorenzo's part about his recent escapade in Paris with the ridiculously named English actress, Sylvia Stardust, as he lustily seduced his wife. However over the next few days Sophia noticed that Lorenzo frequently lapsed into brooding silences. She tried hard to get him to share his problem with her, to no avail. He knew he could never tell her of what evil plan he intended to assuage the unappeasable rage he felt towards Lucky Luciano.

268

He had never confided in the lovely Sophia that Luciano was indeed his father and he certainly was not going to recount the awful disclosures that Tara, on her deathbed, had made about his mother.

On the third morning after he arrived in Corleone, for the reunion with Sophia, the thoughtful Lorenzo took leave of his wife and said he would not be back until evening as he was going to visit his old friend Aldo Caramusa, the local bandit chief and Unione Siciliano Don.

It took Lorenzo 45 minutes along a winding dirt road to get to Caramusa's headquarters in the mountains where he received a warm welcome from Caramusa and his men.

Over a pot of strong caffé Nero, accompanied with large snifter-glasses of acquavite, something Caramusa said set Lorenzo's pulse racing.

'There has been a team of USA Drug Enforcement Agency cops again on the island for several weeks now,' Caramusa disclosed. 'We captured one of them when he became a bit too curious, for my liking, about one of our warehouses on the waterfront at Siracusa. We brought him back here and with a bit of persuasion and prodding with a stiletto from one of my men he told us what the Drug Enforcement team was looking for. He fuckin' won't be talking anymore because the prick is laying, with his throat cut, in several sondares of sea water, in a giacca of cemento off the Golfo di Catánia!

'But he told us before he croaked that they were looking for hard evidence to prove that Charley Luciano is the Capo of the drug running racket between Italy and the USA. Apparently when the New York State Parole Board ordered Luciano to be exiled to Italy in 1945, after serving only ten of his 30 to 50 year prison sentence, there was a clause that if he was ever found to be involved in running drugs to the USA that he could be extradited back from

269

Italy and made to serve out the rest of his sentence in the States. 'Charley knows they are looking for him because I phoned tell him what we had learned from the mother-fuckin' agent we had chilled!'

The Sicillian bandit chief's news gave Lorenzo food for thought and an idea how he could wreak revenge on the father who had so malevolently mistreated his mother!

On the road back to Corleone from Aldo Caramusa's hideaway in the mountains Lorenzo pondered about what would be the best modus operandi he could use to give Lucky Luciano his comeuppance. The Sicillian blood that coursed through his veins, inherited from the very man he hated, urged him to inflict an awful and painful end for Luciano.

However the unwritten but strict rules of Unione Siciliano insisted that no 'made-up' man could kill a brother-member without getting the nod from the organisation's Dons. Permission to terminate the life of the mob's capo di tutti capos was unlikely to be sanctioned. It would mean his own death sentence for breaking the oath when he was indoctrinated into the sinister global crime cartel.

Aldo Caramusa's information about the USA Drug Enforcement Agency currently based in Sicily, however, gave Lorenzo an idea how, carefully organised, he could devise a terrible punishment for Luciano.

If he could lead the D.E.A agents to the evidence that clearly fingered Lucky Luciano as the arch-architect of the supply line of raw heroin from Europe to the USA the notorious gangster-chief would be extradited and spend the rest of his life in prison across the Atlantic.

There was risk, deadly risks, in such a ploy. If caught he would face the usual gory extermination inflicted on squealers by the mob. Such a plot would have to be very carefully planned. The Drug Enforcement Agency would have to promise his anonymity in exchange for providing them with the prize of cornering the infamous Lucky Luciano.

Some devious scheming would be required if vengeance against his vile father was to succeed.

CHAPTER 54

Lorenzo Berni had amassed, over the years, an enormous amount of data about the modus operandi used by Lucky Luciano in his vile trade as an international drug runner.

Lorenzo formulated a devious plan to shop Luciano to the USA Drug Enforcement Agency who were earnestly seeking information that would put the evil capo di tutti capos of the sinister Unione Siciliano behind bars for the rest of his life.

He knew he would have to very careful and extremely astute if he were to be the instigator of entrapment against the depraved father who had tried to destroy him in his tragic mother's womb.

In the seething pangs of his anger against his noxious parent it mattered nothing to Lorenzo that in recent years Luciano had sponsored his acceptance as a 'made-up' man in the iniquitous Unione Siciliano.

He would have no qualms about providing the USA Drug Enforcement agents with the concrete evidence that would enable the Italian judiciary to extradite one of their citizens to the USA where he would certainly be returned to the New York State Prison at Dannemora for the rest of his life.

Thousands of tonnes of heroin, most of it in its raw state to be skilfully cut by expert chemists in illegal laboratories on the other side of the Atlantic, had been shipped to the USA under the auspices of Lucky Luciano since he was paroled and exiled to Italy in 1947.

Yet not one gram of the rancorous resin had ever been traced back to Luciano. He had always distanced himself from the nefarious traffic in narcotics through a chain of three, four or even more accomplices who had never even met him.

Lorenzo mulled every detail he could remember, over the years, about the way Luciano operated his rackets. Finally it became clear that the only chink in Luciano's armour was the visit he made every three months or so to the Freeport of Trieste to buy raw heroin. Eventually this by-product of the opium poppy would be shipped across the Atlantic by Luciano's organisation where it would cause the death of thousands of young addicts in the back streets of New York, San Francisco, Chicago and even Washington.

*   *   *

Lucky Luciano always made his 'buying' trips to Trieste in his stretch limousine, with his bodyguard Bernardo Provenzano, Lorenzo's brother-in-law, at the wheel.

The other passenger was usually Luigi Bertusconi, a highly qualified chemist and an expert in assessing the quality of the raw opium, which was presented as a chestnut coloured globular mass.

The trunk of the huge Buick was crammed with folding American money. Dealing in opium was strictly a cash transaction.

In the private back room of a luxurious bordello, situated in the outskirts of Trieste and owned by Luciano, the Unione Siciliano big-shot met with Sulaman Sharif a Turkish born middleman raw opium supplier.

At these clandestine meetings Sharif always arranged that several tons of raw opium would be waiting for Luciano's and farmacista Bertusconi's approval in one of three warehouses on the Trieste waterfront that he owned.

274

Impoverished farmers in isolated rural areas of Turkey, Afghanistan and India eked out a living by growing fields of poppies. Sharif paid them by weight, in their own currency, for the drying resin of unripened capsules of the special opium poppy known in the pharmaceutical world by the Latin title of Papaver Somniferum.

Sharif then multiplied the money he paid those struggling farmers for their illegal crops two hundred fold when he collected a heavy satchel of $1,000, USA, bills after Luciano's chemist accomplice approved the quality of the opium.

When Luciano had shipped the opium across the Atlantic it was worth millions of dollars on the streets where it was sold as a powder or a dark brown solid mass to the unfortunate addicts hooked on the deadly stuff.! Drug Enforcement Agency men estimated that Lucky Luciano's global drug peddling caused the deaths of more young Americans than GI's killed in World War II.

Although Lorenzo had no such noble intention, if he did succeed in getting Luciano put away for life, he would be performing a great public service for the Washington government. But Lorenzo's only motive was savage revenge against the father who had so cruelly abused his mother.

It is estimated that the annual global demand by the medical profession for the potent poppies as a powerful opiate analgesic is about 700 tonnes, which is processed into painkilling alkaloid morphine. Several times that amount of heroin was sold in the underworld, with Lucky Luciano's Unione Siciliano handling most of it.

Lorenzo was aware that if Unione Siciliano discovered that he had squealed to the Drug Enforcement cops against Lucky Luciano that his own end would be gory and horrifically painful.

CHAPTER 55

Lorenzo knew that he would have to strike a hard deal with the USA Drug Enforcement agents if his vendetta against his father was to succeed.

That was his dominant thought when he telephoned Hank Wayne, head of the Drug Enforcement Agency team currently based in Palermo. Wayne readily agreed to a meeting for, as a top DEA man and a former FBI agent, he knew that Lorenzo Berni was a 'wise guy' - a very important member of Unione Siciliano and the widespread Crime International.

There was something else buzzing around Hank Wayne's brain. Something, that he had once heard about the 26-year-old Italian mobster, which now escaped his memory - at least, temporarily.

*   *   *

They talked aboard the four-berth cabin cruiser that the DEA men had chartered for their investigation into Lucky Luciano's drug running activities. Lorenzo had crept aboard wearing a peaked cap, blue sweater, dungarees and a reefer coat - the kind of working garb a Sicilian stevedore would wear

It was a perfect disguise for such a clandestine meeting. The hinged shutters were pulled across the three portholes in the main cabin as Lorenzo and Hank huddled over the table to share a bottle of wine and to talk.

'I can hand you Charley Luciano on a plate,' said Lorenzo. 'On a fuckin' plate red-handed with the cast iron evidence for your Agency to get an extradition order from the Italian Government to take Charley back to the USA to spend the rest of his life in jail.'

Hank Wayne felt his pulse race as he considered the enormity of the statement this Italian hoodlum had just made.

'Yeah, yeah--I don't mind admitting that's the purpose of the USA Drug Enforcement Agency's mission here in Sicily,' said Wayne, recalling with a jolt that the young gangster who sat across the table from him was rumoured to be the bastard son of the notorious Unione Siciliano capo di tutti capis, Lucky Luciano.
'What's your angle, Mr Berni? What is the price you are asking to betray your father? Oh, yeah I have heard Lucky is your father. Whatever your reason any arrangement between us can only succeed if we can trust each other.'

Lorenzo knew that this was the point of no return. He would have to believe this high-ranking narcotics cop if he was to avenge his dead mother.

'You know the score Signore Wayne,' replied Lorenzo. 'You were once an FBI agent - a fuckin' G-man - and know I am putting my life on the line even just talking to you now. If I give you what you want you will have to protect me. Only you and I must know about this even your own men must not know that you got your information from me. There must be top secrecy. I know you cannot speak for the Guardia de Finanze, Italy's Secret Police, but I want to be guaranteed immunity from prosecution
as far as the American cops are concerned.
'My life would not be worth a centesimo if the Unione Sicilliano assassinos discover I have squealed on Charley Luciano. Just why I am fingering the rat is a personal matter and I am certainly not going to fuckin' tell you. I'd like to fuckin' kill the bastard but that would be too good for him. Getting him put away in prison for life will give me more satisfaction.'

Lorenzo said that there was one chance only of Lucky Luciano, the acknowledged master of the cover-up and false alibi, of being caught red-handed in the despicable business of drug trafficking. He described that Luciano periodically travelled to Trieste to meet the supplier from whom he would purchase tons of the raw opium that would end up in the streets of the USA as the deadly narcotic heroin - known in the underworld as 'H'. There was a short window of opportunity during these narcotic buying trips to Trieste when Luciano could be captured alongside tons of the lethal raw opium during its assessment by the Unione Siciliano chemist.

Lorenzo's most difficult problem would be to pin-point the date and time that the USA Drug Enforcement Agency men could move in and catch Luciano in the act of buying a large quantity of narcotics to ship across the Atlantic. With concrete evidence like that against him the Unione Siciliano's numero uno would be booked to spend the rest of his life in New York's tough State Penitentary at Dannemora.

'I'll be in touch with the information you need as soon as I get it,' promised Lorenzo saucily doffing his cap as he climbed ashore from the cabin cruiser. 'Just make sure your men are in fuckin' place in Trieste and ready to move quickly when I give you the word.
'Remember our deal about secrecy or I'll be a dead man.'

CHAPTER 56

Hank Wayne surreptitiously moved his team of heavily armed narcotics agents into place in the bustling port of Trieste as he waited patiently for word from Lorenzo when to spring the trap on the most powerful chief of organized crime the world had ever known.

Four of Wayne's men stayed aboard the chartered cabin cruiser, which they had sailed around the foot of Italy to Trieste the week after the Drug Enforcement Agency leader had first met Lorenzo Berni. Three of their colleagues were billeted in an inconspicuous ten-bedroom rural locanda six miles from the outskirts of Trieste

Wayne and Lorenzo had met again at a little tavern in Venice, only accessible by gondola, two weeks after their first tryst.

'I understand that Luciano will be going to Trieste to buy several tonnes of raw heroin in two weeks time,' said Lorenzo. 'He will travel there in his stretch limousine driven by his bodyguard Bernardo and a farmacista called Luigi Bertusconi who will test the heroin for quality before Luciano hands the payment in cash to the Turkish drug supplier, Sulaman Sharif.

'Luciano's itinerary is always the same on these buying trips. His party of three arrive in the early evening at the Trieste bordello he owns called the Casa di Bombola – a inglese, House of Dolls-which he owns! All four men will stay in private rooms at the bordello overnight
'The following morning all four men travel in the limousine to one of the warehouses owned by Sharif where the raw opium will be stashed. That is when your men should move in quickly if they are going to catch Luciano red handed.

Hank Wayne took a long pull at the aquavite they were drinking as he considered Lorenzo's vital dissertation.

'Your information as regarding date and time must be dead accurate,' he reminded the young Italian mobster. 'If you fuck up, my ass will be in a sling.'

Lorenzo gave a wry smile and said: 'Well I guess I just wont have to fuck up. I hate that prick Luciano and I have been waiting for this chance to shit on him. You should be hearing from me within a week when I will phone you with the exact information you want.

'This is the last time you will see me – I take a 'ell of a risk every fuckin' time I meet you. Remember you promised me top secrecy if you fuck with me I'll come fuckin' lookin' for you even though you are a G-man.

CHAPTER 57

Lorenzo Berni had promised Hank Wayne that he would hear within a week the information that would lead to the most important arrest he had ever made in his 20-year law enforcement career with the New York Police Department, the FBI and, latterly, the US Drug Enforcement Agency.

But it was nearly three weeks before the narcotics' cop received the magic word from the young Italian mobster that would, hopefully, put the world's biggest drug pusher, Lucky Luciano, back behind bars for the rest of his life in Clinton Prison at Dannemora, New York. It could summarily end the criminal saga of the evil Sicilian-born Salvatore Lucania the only American gang leader to survive a 'one-way ride' when in 1929 he was abducted by four hoodlums in a sedan car and taken to a beach on Staten Island beach, beaten up, repeatedly stabbed with an ice-pick and had his throat cut from ear to ear. Soon after that frightful experience he changed his name to Luciano – the nickname 'Lucky' was appended by the underworld amazed at such a dumfounding decampment from death.

Although the wait for that vital tip-off of treachery from Lorenzo Berni against the father that he hated took 19 agonising days to arrive, the impatient Wayne used the time to prepare his team of narcotics' agents.

'Any of you guys think this scam is going to be easy-you're fuckin' nuts,' Wayne briefed his men when they met in a country tavern a few miles outside Trieste. 'We are going after the biggest and most sinister crook in the world. Lucky Luciano is acknowledged by the underworld as the capo di tutti capis – boss of bosses – a man who has ordered hundreds of killings and responsible for the deaths of tens of thousand young American drug addicts.

283

'New York special prosecutor Thomas E Dewey got Luciano put away in 1935 for a 30-to-50-year term after painstakingly gathering evidence about his brothel and call-girl empire and his related violent extortion methods. The influential Luciano still ruled and issued orders to the underworld from his cell. During World War II he helped US Navy Intelligence to tighten waterfront security after Hitler's secret agents blew up the French luxury liner, Normandie, in New York harbour. One word from Luciano sufficed to end all sabotage on the docks because of his muscle and control of the longshoremen's union. His sentence was commuted, after he had only served nine years, and he was deported to Italy in 1946.

'But under the terms of his deportation if Luciano is caught smuggling narcotics to America the USA has the power to demand that the Italian government extradite him back to the States to serve the remaining 40 years of his sentence-which would virtually mean spending the rest of his life between bars.

'But throughout all his evil life of crime no law enforcement officer has been able to pin a narcotics rap against the infamous Lucky Luciano.

'He is noted as a master of the cover-up and almost always distances himself from the criminal coups he plots immaculately. The perpetrators of the robberies, hijacks, burglaries, extortion, violence and murders he has ordered have never met him personally. They receive their instructions at second hand or even third hand from a chain of criminal command that Luciano ensures could never lead back to him. He always prepares a cast-iron alibi, with influential witnesses, when hoods are doing his dirty work.

'Because global drug running involves the handing over of such large amounts of cash – no cheques in that business – the only time that Luciano can ever be caught near even a microgramme of opium or cocaine is when he is buying a bulk consignment of the raw drug to ship to the USA.

'This is how we hope to catch him red-handed. I cannot give you the name of the informant. That is only known to me, the head of our organisation in New York, and the head of Italy's secret police – the Guardia de Finanze – who will back us up on this operation and pave the way for Luciano's quick extradition back to the USA.

'This high security is necessary because this is the condition laid down by our informant for his cooperation. Furthermore if there is leakage of information that gets back to Luciano, via the extensive network of his evil Unione Siciliano, and the scam fails then my neck will be on the block.'

Hank Wayne told his men exactly what each of them would have to do when they pounced on the warehouse where they expected to catch Luciano.

'The Italian cops will actually make the arrest,' said the Drug Enforcement Agency chief. 'That way will make it easier for the Italian High Court to issue an extradition order and hand Lucky Luciano over to our jurisdiction. I have ordered a US government chartered jet to be fuelled and ready at Rome's Leonardo da Vinci Airport to fly Luciano, and escorts, back to New York at a moment's notice.

'Good luck gentlemen.

'If this operation succeeds you will have done a service for your country as important as any soldier, sailor or flier ever performed in the two world wars.'

CHAPTER 58

Lorenzo Berni was just as impatient to get the treacherous information, to secure his depraved parent behind bars for life, into the hands of Drug Enforcement Agency captain Hank Wayne.

It was important to Lorenzo that he did not draw suspicion on himself by being too curious, so he decided that his best route to the information he needed was via his brother-in-law Bernardo Provenzano who was Lucky Luciano's chauffeur and bodyguard.

Lorenzo was getting increasingly anxious for his wife Sophia, back at their home in Corleone, Sicily, was nearing her time and he dearly wanted to be with her when she gave birth to their first child.

He had called at the villa in Naples at Luciano's request one morning to discuss problems concerning one of Lucky's most lucrative rackets of smuggling illegal immigrants from all parts of Europe into the USA. These unfortunate people, from the most deprived countries in Europe, had borrowed from money lenders to pay $2,000 a head to be shipped across the Atlantic and then smuggled into the USA via the vulnerable Mexican and Canadian borders.

It was a racket that coined Unione Siciliano several million dollars a year with the unfortunate 'illegals' crammed into the rat-infested holds of rusty cargo ships. Nor did the extortion against these luckless 'illegals' end there. Unione Siciliano would find these people work with unscrupulous farmers and fruit growers and take a slice of the cut rate of pay these unfortunates were paid. They had no immigration papers, work permits or Social Security documents and, unable to complain to government welfare officials, were virtually enslaved by the ruthless enforcers of Unione Siciliano.

* * *

Lorenzo found it difficult during the talk about the next shipment of illegal immigrants not to show his hatred for his malevolent father.

As he left the villa he made a point of stopping to talk to his wife's brother, Bernardo Provenzano, who was diligently polishing the new green armour-plated Cadillac that Lucky Luciano had recently shipped over from the USA.

'You'll rub all the paint away if you polish that any more Bernardo, pal,' said Lorenzo. Provenzano, checked in his task for a moment and said: 'Yeah, yeah 'Renzo, I've always said bullshit baffles brains. But I am driving the boss on a trip to Tr....., waal, lets say somewhere tomorrow.

'You know how he likes arrangements to be perfect when he travels! I spoke to my mother in Corleone on the phone last night and she said that my sister Sophia is near her time. I expect you will be going over to Sicily soon? Geez, I'm really looking forward to becoming an uncle for the first time.'

* * *

Lorenzo, sure that he now had the information that would sell Luciano down the river, returned to his tiny apartment in Naples and rang the contact number in Trieste that the narcotics cop Hank Wayne had given him.

'The fuck-pig Luciano travels to Trieste tomorrow,' rapped Lorenzo over the line. 'He will be accompanied by his driver bodyguard Bernardo Provenzano who is not in the picture about the business – he just drives the car.

288

Travelling with them will be a guy called Luigi Bertusconi. He's a highly qualified farmacista who will assess the quality of the shipment of raw opium they are going to buy.

'They usually travel in a stretch Buick but this time they will be using a green armour-plated Cadillac, which Luciano has had specially delivered from Detroit in the past month. They will stay overnight in a private apartment at Luciano's bordello in Trieste. There they will meet up with a Turkish prick called Sulaman Sharif who is a dealer in raw opium.

'The following morning the four men will travel in the Cadillac to one of three warehouses owned by Sharif where the raw opium will be stashed – so it is important you guys don't lose them, or go to the wrong warehouse. If Bertusconi gives the nod about the quality of the raw opium, the payment in US dollars will be transferred from the trunk of Luciano's Cadillac to a Ford van owned by Sharif.

'Your men will have to move in at exactly the right time to secure the evidence you need. That's it Hank! You wont hear from me again.

'Don't forget our deal to keep my name out of it-or else I'm a dead duck.'

CHAPTER 59

The trap was set for the most evil drug runner in the globe to be caught red-handed, with indisputable evidence that he had, once again, procured a staggering amount of raw heroin and was shipping it across the Atlantic to be refined, cut and cut again, sealed into tiny plastic bags and sold on the streets of New York, Chicago, San Francisco and Washington to the alarmingly growing army of young narcotic addicts.

The plan to ensnare the sinister Lucky Luciano had been ongoing for years and now, with the help of his bastard son, a mobster in is own right, the trap would be sprung. Hopefully, at last, a circle of steel would be clasped around Luciano to return him to a grim cell in the tough Clinton Prison at Dannemora, New York, to rot for the rest of his life.

Captain Caeasare Parelli, the commander of the Italian Police squad that would cooperate in the raid, was present as Hank Wayne, the Drug Enforcement Agency commander, briefed the combined party of Italian cops and American narcotics agents on the eve of the important 'sting' to net the notorious Lucky Luciano.

'Captain Parelli and his men will make the actual arrest,' said Wayne. 'Let's be clear about that. This will ease the way for the Italian government to issue an extradition order quickly - for they want Luciano out of their country just as badly as we want to put him back behind bars in the USA.

'Our part will be to shadow Luciano from the time he arrives at his brothel where he will stay overnight with his bodyguard and driver Bernardo Provenzano, a farmacista

291

by the name of Luigi Bertusconi and a Turkish supplier of raw opium called Sulaman Sharif.

'My informant tells me that the following morning at ten o'clock all four men, with Provenzano at the wheel of Luciano's Cadiilac, will drive to one of several warehouses owned by Sharif.

'There the narcotics will be stashed ready for the farmacista Bertusconi to take random samples from the parcels of raw opium and test them for quality before Luciano orders the $500,000, in large denomination US bills, be transferred from the trunk of the Cadillac to a large Ford van belonging to Sharif which will be driven by his son Yasser. On the streets of the USA that raw opium, when cut and recut with talcum powder or milk powder, will be worth $10 million to the mob.

'My men, waiting in two cars, some distance away from the brothel so as not to arouse suspicion, will trail the Cadillac. Our first car will travel in front of the Cadillac, with the agents inside keeping a sharp eye out through the mirrors and back window to where it turns. Our second car will follow the Cadillac trying to keep other cars in between without losing sight of the target.

'Captain Parelli and his men will already be posted in two armoured police trucks on the waterfront area and will move in to join us when I contact him on the radio phone to inform him which warehouse Sulaman Sharif has taken Luciano and his men to.'

Hank Wayne them warned that Luciano and his body guard would be armed.

'I would also think that the Turk, a known villain, and his son, who acts as his bodyguard, will be carrying weapons. What I am not sure about is whether Sulaman Sharif will have more of his men in the Ford van to protect the cash that he will be collecting from Luciano.

'If any shooting opens up inside the warehouse Captain Parelli and his policemen will return the fire. As for my agents, and me we will not use our guns unless Captain Parelli calls for our assistance. That way the US government will not become embroiled in a controversy with the Italian authorities. The Italian government have arranged for a judge to be waiting in Rome to issue an immediate extradition order once Luciano is in custody. Three of my men, with myself in charge, will escort Lucky Luciano to the USA aboard the chartered aircraft our government has ordered to be standing by at Rome's Leonardo da Vinci airport.'

Hank Wayne thanked everyone for listening and asked for any questions.

'Signore Wayne,' asked Captain Parelli. 'If this turns out to be a shooting match will your government be content if we take the notorious Lucky Luciano dead or alive?'

'Captain Parelli to use a well worn phrase in your country-que sera, sera,' replied the Drug Enforcement Agency squad commander. 'Whatever will be, will be. Italy and the USA will both benefit if the sinister Lucky Luciano is permanently put out of action! Let all of us have a drink now to the success of our combined mission.'

CHAPTER 60

Hank Wayne's planning of the most important 'Sting' ever in the global fight against hard drugs, which were already accountable for the deaths of more American youngsters than World War II, seemed to work smoothly.

At 9pm that evening he was sat patiently, with four of his men, in an inconspicuous black Fiat saloon, watching the front of the notorious Trieste bawdy house which, it was well known, owned by the sadistic capo di tutti capis of the sinister Unione Siciliano.

They had been there, on alert, for more than two hours whiling away the time with endless paper cups of cappucino and formagio sandwiches from a nearby cafe_. At ten minutes after 9 o'clock their vigil was rewarded when an impressive green stretch Cadillac rolled smoothly up and eased slowly to a halt outside the bordello.

Wayne saw the driver, who he recognised as Bernardo Provenzano, climb from the front and hold open the rear door of the car for his boss, Lucky Luciano, to alight. A third man, who Wayne figured was the chemist, also got out of the car and all three men climbed the four flights of elegant marble steps that were the feature of the brothel entrance.

The Drug Enforcement Agency chief picked up the radio phone installed in the Fiat and spoke to Captain Caeasare Parelli, the commander of the Italian police squad who were cooperating in the 'Sting'.

Using the code name they had agreed on he said: 'Operation Poppyhead is under way. Our target has arrived at the bordello with his driver-bodyguard and another man who I assume is the farmacista they have brought to test the quality of the raw heroin. We'll maintain a watch here all night and be in touch with you again in the morning.'

Just before midnight they observed another man arrive at the brothel by taxi. He was certainly not an ordinary client of the bawdyhouse who was always admitted through a side door. But this man was kept waiting at the front entrance until Bernardo Provenzano appeared, shook his hand and guided him into the building.

This man, Hank Wayne assumed, could be Sulaman Sharif the Turk who was supplying the raw opium, which the following morning would be bought by Lucky Luciano on behalf of the mob for $ ½ million, and destined to be loaded aboard a USA bound ship in the Trieste docks.

*   *   *

Hank Wayne, and the three men who had been on alert with him throughout the evening, were relieved by four other members of his squad and went off to their hotel for a few hours sleep before what they anticipated would be an eventful morning.

By 8.30am the following morning Wayne was back at his post with three of his men in a second car parked 100 metres from the bordello. They would use the old police trick of 'shadowing' Lucky Luciano's green Cadillac by travelling in front while a second car carrying Drug Enforcement agents would follow at a discreet distance behind the target.

The bell on a nearby medieval church tower was tolling 10am when the Cadillac carrying Lucky Luciano, his bodyguard Bernardo Provenzano and the two other men, rolled smoothly away from the bordello in the direction of Trieste's bustling port.

There was little chance of Hank Wayne's squad, with a shadow car in front and behind, losing touch with the distinctive armour-plated Cadillac as it sped towards the docks, where it slowed down and braked in front of a massive warehouse.

'Close in, close in quickly,' rapped Wayne over the radiophone to Captain Parelli, the commander of the Italian police squad. 'They are using warehouse number 12, and the four men are entering the building. Get into position, set your watches at zero -one, two, three, four, five - NOW. Be ready to move in and attack in exactly ten minutes.'

The plan was for the Italian police squad to burst into the warehouse through the warehouse loading bay entrance while Wayne and his men would storm through the only other entrance at the rear.

After nine and half minutes both groups of raiders were in position and talked with each other over the radio telephone.

'I'll begin the countdown in a few moments - good luck everyone,' yelled Hank Wayne through his 'phone. 'Ten - nine - eight - seven - six - five - four - three - two - one - go -go -go.'

*   *   *

Captain Parelli's policemen quickly smashed through the loading bay entrance with the three heavy fire axes they were carrying, while Hank Wayne's narcotics agents only needed several thumps with a heavy pair of shoulders to breach the side entrance.

'Put your fuckin' hands in the air,' Wayne yelled at Lucky Luciano and his three companions! 'We have you surrounded and covered by automatic weapons. Twitch an eyelid and we'll blow your fuckin' eyelids off.'

Lucky Luciano, appearing amazingly cool under the pressure of the moment, replied audaciously: 'Who the fuckin' 'ell are you shit-arses - the fuckin' Seventh Cavalry?'

The police commander now took over the dialogue and said: 'I am Captain Parelli of the National Police and I have orders to arrest you and your party for suspected trafficking in and exporting out of Italy, heroin and other illegal drugs.

'The squad behind you are USA narcotics agents under the command of Signore Hank Wayne. We have all been instructed to shoot if you resist arrest - you are so outnumbered if would be very foolish of you to do that.
'You will lean with your arms against the sidewall while my men will search all of you for weapons. We will then conduct a thorough search of the warehouse before we question you.'

Two of Captain Parelli's police officers broke from the ranks and frisked the four men who were now leaning face forward to the wall.

'They are not armed, Sir,' was the surprising information from one of the police officers, directing his comment at Captain Parelli. 'They are not carrying any weapons, not even a pocket knife, Sir.'

Parelli then ordered the two policemen who had completed their frisking to keep Luciano and the other three men covered with their automatic machine guns while the warehouse was searched.

The search party, comprised of Captain Parelli and three policemen, combined with Hank Wayne and three of

298

his most experienced narcotics agents, were primarily very interested in a sizeable quantity of blocks of hard resin-like material stacked several feet high on several lines of wooden pallets.

Wayne estimated there must be two tons of the stuff. He felt it, smelled it and even tasted it. It was a substance that he had never come across during his long experience as a Drug Enforcement Agency officer.

Wayne called up one of his men, Randolph Welsh, who was a qualified chemist and asked: 'Randy, what the fuck is this - its something I have never seen before.'

Welsh produced a leather wallet containing analytical equipment and took more than half a dozen random samples from various pallets of the strange rock-like, resin type material before giving his expert opinion.

'It is meerschaum boss,' he opined with a puzzled look at Wayne.

The narcotics squad commander was equally perplexed and asked: 'Fuckin' meerschaum? What the 'ell is that doing here?'

Agent Randolph Welsh, drawing on his degree in chemistry at Harvard, said: 'It is a mineral used for making pipes, Sir....'

Hank Wayne, growing more frustrated and angry by the minute, rejoined sharply: 'Pipes?'

Agent Welsh responded quickly: 'Yeah, Sir, special pipes for smoking tobacco. Meerschaum pipes are most prized by smokers. They are white and gradually tone into a beautiful amber colour from the nicotine as they age. This shipment of meerschaum probably comes from Turkey, where most of this mineral is found.'

An icy feeling of foreboding rose from the pit of Hank Wayne's stomach and he had to choke back the bile as he muttered to himself: 'This is beginning to look like a complete fuck-up.'

Wayne's professionalism quelled his nausea for a moment and, pointing to a mountainous pile of jute covered bales rapped out an order to his men: ' What's in those fuckin' bundles over there?'

When one of the narcotic agents jumped to obey the instruction, split one of the bales with a huge Bowie knife, and replied: 'They contain carpets, Sir. Bundles of Turkish carpets, Sir,' - the stunned Hank Wayne feared that his well-planned 'Sting' had turned into a disastrous fiasco.

Slicing open several more of the huge bales produced the same calamitous result - there were just more and more high quality Turkish carpets.

In a final throw of the dice Wayne instructed his men to prise open some drums stacked in another corner of the warehouse.

Once again the answer from the agents who rummaged into those mysterious drums was a devastating disappointment.

'It's tea, Sir,' explained one of the men. 'Dry tea leaves.'

Agent Randolph Welsh, who seemed the fount of all knowledge, chipped in: 'Tea is a speciality crop in Turkey and much appreciated in Boston and other traditional English style tea-houses in the USA.'

It was then that Hank Wayne arrived at the horrific realisation that this was one 'Sting' in which the 'stingers' had been stung themselves. In his rage at the humiliating failure of his mission he strode over to Lucky Luciano and asked: 'What the fuck is all this crap, Meerschaum, carpets and fuckin' tea?'

One of Luciano's companions took a step forward and said: 'Perhaps I can answer that question Signore Wayne....'

The irate narcotics squad boss brusquely interrupted: '...and who the fuck might you be asshole?'

The reply was yet another blow to Hank Wayne's ego.

'My name is Dino Tollini,' came the surprising answer. 'I am Signore Luciano's attorney. This "crap", as you so crudely put it, is a consignment of goods being sent to the USA aboard the Spanish cargo ship Don Carlos II, currently docked in Trieste and due to set sail for New York in four days time. This gentleman with me here is Signore Ibrahim
Assad, of Istanbul, whose lorries have brought these goods from Turkey which are being shipped to the USA by Signore Luciano in his capacity as an exporter and importer.
'Furthermore Signore Wayne I warn you that I will be making a representation of complaint to the Italian government about the embarrassment you have caused Signore Luciano and the damage you have done to his property in this warehouse today.' Hank Wayne could only agonise about what had gone wrong.

That night, after a protest from the Italian authorities at the way they had been embroiled in such an internationally disconcerting affair, Hank Wayne was recalled to Washington to explain the breakdown of the 'Sting' he had orchestrated.

'I'll cut that Lorenzo Berni's balls off,' was the mental threat he made as the very aircraft chartered to transport the discreditable Lucky Luciano back to a life of incarceration in New York's Dannemora Prison hurtled himself to official disgrace across the Atlantic.

It was a threat that could never come to fruition. Three months later Hank Wayne was forced into early retirement by the Drug Enforcement Agency with a much reduced pension.

With the colossal collapse of 'Operation Poppyhead' the devilish master of the cover-up had once again wriggled free from the long arm of the law.

CHAPTER 61

Despite his knowledge as a 'made man' about the secretive and sinister methods of the organisation Lorenzo Berni felt sure there was no way the influential Dons of the Unione Siciliano could ever discover that he would inform against his father, the mob's capo di tutti capis, Lucky Luciano.

Lorenzo figured that the only way his treachery could possibly be revealed was via Hank Wayne, the Drug Enforcement Agency captain, currently in Italy on a mission to gather evidence to get Luciano returned to prison in New York for the remainder of his life. But it was very much in Wayne's interest to respect the secrecy Lorenzo demanded for his part in the artful plot to trap the elusive Luciano.

Little did Lorenzo Berni know that his fate was already sealed a few days before the disastrous failure of 'Operation Poppyhead' when he was called to Luciano's villa in Naples.

'Renzo, I know you are going to Sicily tomorrow to see your wife Sophia who is about to give birth to your first child,' said Luciano. 'I need you to do a job for the organisation while you are in Sicily. We are scheduled to send out a shipload of illegal immigrants, Afghans, Iraqis, Russians, Czechs and few Polish people. At $500 a head, most of which the "wet backs" have borrowed from the mob's "shylocks" the organisation could make a million bucks out of the trip.

' But our man in Sicily, who you know well, Don Aldo Caramusa, is having a little trouble with the owner of the ship who is trying to go back on his word and asking for more than the $50,000 we agreed for the passage of the "wet backs" to the USA.

'The ship owner's name is Reuben Applebaum.   I want you to join up with Aldo Caramusa and give Signore Applebaum a reminder that it is in own interest to stick to the deal we have agreed.'

Lorenzo had no option. An order from the capo di tutti capis had to be obeyed.

*   *   *

Earlier that morning Luciano had summoned his chauffeur-bodyguard, Bernardo Provenzano, and instructed him: 'When your brother-in-law, Lorenzo, arrives to see me, make sure you let slip the information that we will be driving to Trieste in the Cadillac tomorrow.'

Although that request puzzled Bernardo everyone in the mob knew that no one, for the good of their health, questioned an instruction from the boss.

*   *   *

The global network of corruption in high places originally set up by the old Mafia and then extended and improved by its successor, Unione Siciliano, until it was popularly called in the media 'Crime International', swept into action the following day when Lucky Luciano received two phone calls.

The first, over a crackling trans-Atlantic line, came from the powerful underworld Don, Frank Costello, reputedly second in Unione Siciliano's complicated chain of command to the capo di tutti capis himself.

'Charley,' said Costello, aware from their days as teenaged hoodlums in New York alongside Meyer Lansky, and others, that Luciano hated the pseudonym Lucky. 'The

304

narcotics cops under that cocksucking Hank Wayne are planning to ambush you when you go to Trieste to collect our next shipment of "H". Their shit-ass squealer is none other than that lump of excreta Lorenzo Berni.

'Look Charley, Meyer Lansky and the other guys here have known for some time that Berni is your illegitimate son. We appreciate that it is a family job and hard for you. But that mother-fuckin' Berni has to be dealt with and we'll arrange it from our end - if that's what you want! Don't forget that the bastardo Berni is a made man and under mob rules only another made man, with permission from the Dons, can be allowed to chill the fuckin' pig.' Luciano indignantly turned down his old buddy Costello's offer!

'This is my fuckin' contract Frank, so keep out of it' Lucky roared down the phone, his hoarse voice at a decibel level that it might have been heard at Coney Island. 'It is not a family matter any more it's strictly business. I arranged for that fuckin' crum Berni to be a made man - now I'll undo him. By the time I've finished with the asshole he'll wish he had never been born to the dirty fuckin' hooker who spawned him...I fuckin' paid her well to get rid of him before he was born and she double crossed me...I have never really been sure he is my son anyway. Yet I used my influence to get him into the organisation as a "made man"...look how he's repaid me. Leave it with me Frank the cow son will be with his pox-ridden mother in 'ell inside 24 hours.'

It was an amazing, and almost incoherent, tirade from the capo di tutti capis, who the underworld had always admired for his coolness since the day in October 1929 when he became one of the very few gangsters to survive a "one-way-ride". He had been abducted by four hoodlums in a car, beaten, stabbed 20 times with an ice pick, had his throat sliced from ear to ear, and left for dead on a beach at Staten Island. Although he lived to become the most

305

powerful gangster in the world he never named the four men who had so nearly murdered him.

*   *   *

The second phone call that morning came from a very high ranking police officer in Rome who had been on Lucky Luciano's payroll as a tip-off man for several years.

'They have sent a squad of specially armed police to join up with the American narcotic cops in Trieste,' said Chief Inspector Salvatore Masseria. 'They are hoping to catch you in possession of a large quantity of heroin. I hear that their informant is someone inside your organisation.'

Luciano smiled in the knowledge that he already knew who that "someone" was and chuckled down the line: 'Thank you Salvatore. You are now $10,000 richer for that information. I'll see that the money is delivered to you personally in the next few days! Keep in touch.'

*   *   *

Lucky Luciano then spent the next hour on the telephone. He spoke to Sulaman Sharif and told him to alter his plans and bring the consignment of opium, which was already enroute to Trieste, to a factory premises he owned in Naples. He made plans for a cargo of legitimate goods to be switched to the warehouse in Trieste.

Luciano then contacted an ex-US Army helicopter pilot and ordered him to standby with his machine to fly him to Sicily and back to Italy the following day. He then instructed his chauffeur Bernardo Provenzano to collect his attorney, Dino Tollini, the next morning and to drive to a tiny airfield near Trieste where he would fly in by helicopter to meet them that evening.

All his arrangements finalised Lucky then told Bernardo what time to drive him to Napoli airport, early the next day, where the helicopter would already be warmed up and waiting for his arrival before taking to the sky.

*   *   *

'Fly me to Sicily,' Luciano told the helicopter pilot naming a former US Airforce flying field near the coast. 'I have some business to conduct there which will take about three to four hours. Then I will need you to fly me to a little airfield near Trieste.'

As always, Lucky Luciano had woven an intricate cover-up that would confuse anyone trying to trace his tracks.

CHAPTER 62

Lorenzo had sailed for Sicily on the car ferry from Naples, with his Mercedes roadster secured below decks, a few hours after his meeting at Lucky Luciano's villa.

He had telephoned his wife, Sophia, at their apartment above the restaurant in Corleone and she told him that it was arranged for her to be admitted to the local clinic in readiness for the birth of their baby the following day.

'Don't worry honey I am on the way,' Lorenzo assured her. 'I just have a little job to do for Lucky in Catania after the ferry docks. But it won't take long and I will be there for the birth.'

*   *   *

Luciano had told Lorenzo he was to meet local bandit chief Aldo Caramusa and the errant ship owner, Reuben Applebaum, who was to be taught a sharp lesson that it was unwise to try and squirm out of a deal made with the mob, at the ruins of the ancient Roman aqueducts on the edge of town.

The time set was 8 pm - dusk. A strange and isolated meeting place and, at that time of the night, almost certain to be deserted.

But an ideal site if the mother-fuckin' Applebaum needed a little roughing up. It should not prove too difficult a job. He parked the Mercedes roadster as near to the ruins of the ancient Roman baths and aqueducts as possible.

He walked slowly the remaining 150 metres, and as he drew near to the old aqueducts a shadowy figure appeared from the dark. A broad-brimmed fedora slanted over the face and the upturned collar of a black trench coat made it impossible for him to identify who the person was. 'Aldo? Aldo Caramusa - is that you?' queried Lorenzo, for that is who he was expecting to meet.

The voice that came back in stentorian-American-accented Italian was immediately familiar: 'No I am not Signore Caramusa - my name is Salvatore Lucania, I am also known as Charley Luciano......'

In a desperate motley of blind hatred, cold fear and overwhelming panic Lorenzo could only stutter: 'What the shit are you doing here, you filthy fucker?' There was no doubt now about the situation between the young hoodlum and the ageing Don - war had been declared. Only one of them would be left standing when the conflict was settled. Trapped like a rat in a cage, cunning eyes searching every cranny for an escape route, Lorenzo, trying to hijack the element of surprise from Luciano, surreptitiously slid his right hand beneath his mohair jacket towards the former Waffen-SS issue Luger pistol that was holstered under his left arm-pit.

It was a fatal mistake although it was doubtful that anyone could have advised him differently against such a malevolent enemy.

Lucky Luciano spotted Lorenzo's move and from the voluminous depths of his black trench coat quickly slid out the menacing spout of an old friend from his prohibition days. A ten-second burst from the tommy gun showed why the British Army had chosen it as their World War II short range sub-machine gun.

Lorenzo was in no position to give that fact any thought as the agony raged from the dozen 11.4 mm bullets that had left his right arm hanging helplessly and the shoulder above it a gory mess of raw meat.

'I could have put a fuckin' contract out on you with anyone of the top ten hit-men in the world,' growled Luciano. 'But I wanted to save this particular pleasure for myself! Does that fuckin' shoulder hurt then? Well see how you like the next item on the agenda....'

Another ten second stutter from the sinister snout of the Tommy gun left Lorenzo Berni's left knee cap obliterated and leg below it dangling like a boy's kite caught on an overhead telephone cable. Lorenzo was in a terrible state. Blood oozing from the ghastly gunshot wounds in his right arm and left leg, his eyes misted with agony, his usual cockiness spilled into the cool Sicillian night.

'Father, father have pity on me,' he pleaded pathetically using that form of address for the first and only time to the man he believed had sired him.

Lucky Luciano roared with rage at Lorenzo's plea.

'Don't call me father,' he stormed. 'My sperm would never spawn a fuckin' filthy cucaracha like you. Your mother was a poxed up, drug addicted, whore and your father could have been one of a hundred of the scum that haunt the Napoli waterfront. I befriended you, sponsored you in the mob and had you become a "made man" - look how you have betrayed me and what is worse the organisation.
'You have broken the solemn oath of Unione Siciliano that one blood brother never squeals on another. You have contravened the code of "omerta" handed down from the Mafia more than 100 years ago. The sacred vow of silence in front of the cops and observed throughout Sicily and Italy ever since and wherever the mob operates.
'There is no pity available after what you have done. You will die like the cockroach that you are and you'll be

full of fuckin' shit when I squash you! You have not even got the balls to die with courage like a man of honour.

'Tomorrow your head will be sent to Frank Costello in New York to mark the mistake I made in sponsoring you and that the strict rules about informers, squealers and dirty fuckin' cop lovers have been fullfilled.

'Rot in fuckin' 'ell - shit house!

With an expert sweep of his venomous tommy gun Luciano stitched a salvo that left a symbolic gory double cross pattern across Lorenzo's midriff. It took him ten minutes to die, ten minutes of unspeakable pain during which the man who had disowned him just sat and savagely watched.

It was the first time in more than 30 years that Lucky Luciano, a man reputedly responsible for a thousand gang killings, had pulled the trigger himself.

Ten days later a parcel was delivered to Frank Costello in New York. Wiping the surplus butter off his fingers from his breakfast bagel, the old gangster chief opened it, smiled at the gory contents and muttered: 'Well done Lucky. The Dons will be well fuckin' pleased with that.'

CHAPTER 63

Fate took a new twist to send Unione Siciliano into further confusion only six weeks after the threat to their heroin pipe-line from Rome to New York had been averted with the savage gang killing of the traitorous Lorenzo Berni.

The mob's most respected and feared capo di tutti capis, Lucky Luciano, was struck down and died after a heart attack at Capodicino Airport, Naples on 26 January 1962.
He was waiting for the Unione's courier to deliver his personal cut of £2 million from the organisation in New York in lieu of the last shipment of heroin he had sent to the USA.

But the tradition of Unione Siciliano, which had followed on from the Mafia, was that the 'King is Dead, God Save the King.'   As second in command Frank Costello called a Board meeting of the Unione's top Dons to decide who would take over the crown from Luciano.

Surprisingly Costello ruled himself out of the new job when he told the meeting: 'Look I am 71 years of age and I have been in the rackets since I ran the streets of NewYork with Lucky Luciano sixty years ago. I have just done a five-year stretch in prison for tax evasion - I don't want no more.   It's time for me to take out the fishing pole and finda nice riverbank - time for me to smell the roses.'

It was a crossroads for Unione Siciliano but as the proverb from the old country said: Cometh the hour; cometh the man.   That man was Joseph Bonanno, a notorious gangster who ran one of the most powerful Mafia families in New York.   It was said, many years later, that he was the inspiration for Marlon Brando's character of Vito Corleone in the Godfather films.

He hated the name Joe Bananas hung on him by the New York media and public. He was only 57, having been born in Castellammare del Golfo, Sicily in 1905. Working in the liquor industry during prohibition he fought his way to the top of the criminal world as head of one of the five New York Mafia families.

Having been inducted as capo di tutti capis in the usual way after taking the oath and mixing his blood by making a small knife incision in Frank Costello's and his thumbs and pressing them together, he swore to serve the Unione Siciliano loyally.

His first edict on induction was: 'We'll fly Charley Luciano's body back to New York and give him the biggest send-off the Big Apple has ever seen. I don't give a fuck what the State Department think about that - I've got enough suckers in Washington who I hold markers on to clear that.'

*   *   *

That was how it came to pass that the legendary Lucky Luciano was given the biggest gangland funeral New York had ever seen.

It was estimated that crowds of more 5,000 people lined the streets outside New York's St John's Cathedral to see the hearse drawn by four plumed and prancing black horses. The coffin was draped in Luciano's racing silks a reminder of the days when he lorded it up at Santa Anita and every other racetrack in the country.

All five of New York's crime families heard the Archbishop read Mass and paradoxically how generous

Charley Luciano had been to the poor people of the East Side of the city.

*   *   *

Back in Sicily, only eight hours after her husband's "disappearance" Sophia Berni's boy-child was stillborn. The combined shock of the loss of her baby and her beloved Lorenzo sent the lovely Sophia into a deep depression from which she never recovered. Finally she was admitted into a Palermo mental institution where she died some years later at the age of only 36.

EPILOGUE

There were many visitors to the ornate grave the Unione Sicilione Dons had funded in St John's Cathedral Cemetery, Queens, New York, to honour the mob's legendary capo di tutti capis.   His successor Joseph "Bananas" Bonanno rolled up in his stretch limo accompanied by four bodyguards, a few days after Lucky Luciano's interment and spotted a uniformed bank guard standing by the grave.

'..ain't you Hank Wayne, the former narcotics cop?' growled Joe Bananas. 'Come down in the world a bit ain't ya? What a sucker you were thinkin' you could fuckin' put one over on the great Charley Luciano. Now fuck off! If I see , or hear of, you hanging around this grave again I'll let my boys chop you up for mincemeat.'

Another visitor was Luciano's mistress, former show girl Igea Lissoni. He had seduced, betrayed, abused and beaten her up. But she had just heard from Lucky's New York attorney that he had bequeathed her $5 million plus his villa in Naples.

'He loved me,' sobbed Igea. 'That great big hairy gorilla Charlie, really loved me!'

His bodyguard, Bernardo Provenzano, was left $100,000 and a similar amount each year as long as he worked for Igea Lissoni as her chauffeur and man servant at the villa.   'He was always a good boss,' mused Bernardo, knowing that he would be a dead man if he ever let slip even a whisper of the dreadful fate that overcame his brother-in-law. He was sorry for his sister - but business is business.

There were more than 100 bequests in Lucky Luciano's multi-million dollar will. Amongst the most humourous was the gift of his collection of 5,000 Havana cigars in a

317

gigantic gold, cedar-wood lined, humidor to his old buddy Frank Costello with the warning that: 'Smoking is no good for your health!' One of the most generous bequests was the gift of $500,000 towards the restoration fund for the local church at Lercara Friddi, the town in Sicily where he was born in 1896.

Luciano, the world's most sadistic mobster, it seemed had a streak of generosity and charity inside his hard-nosed character.

Only Lorenzo Berni, the son he had spurned from birth, was forgotten.

A rotting oil barrel, filled with cement to weight his bullet-riddled torso to the bottom of the ocean and a cardboard box, that used to contain margarine, carrying his severed head around New York's gangland as a warning, was a legacy fit only for a crum.

ENDS

ISBN 141202080-8

9 781412 020800